THE ARMOR OF LIGHT

THE ROAD
—— TO ——
WAR

THOMAS SUMMERLIN

Trilogy Christian Publishers
A Wholly Owned Subsidiary of Trinity Broadcasting Network
2442 Michelle Drive
Tustin, CA 92780
Copyright © 2024 by Thomas Summerlin
All rights reserved, including the right to reproduce this book or portions thereof in any form whatsoever.
For information, address Trilogy Christian Publishing
Rights Department, 2442 Michelle Drive, Tustin, Ca 92780.
Trilogy Christian Publishing/ TBN and colophon are trademarks of Trinity Broadcasting Network.
For information about special discounts for bulk purchases, please contact Trilogy Christian Publishing.

Trilogy Disclaimer: The views and content expressed in this book are those of the author and may not necessarily reflect the views and doctrine of Trilogy Christian Publishing or the Trinity Broadcasting Network.

10 9 8 7 6 5 4 3 2 1
Library of Congress Cataloging-in-Publication Data is available.
ISBN 979-8-89333-509-5
ISBN 979-8-89333-510-1 (ebook)

Dedication

I dedicate this third book to my children: Arwen, Tristan, and Griffin. Thank you for reminding me daily about the need for adventure in our lives. I can't give you the world, but I can at least create a new one for you. As you hold this book in your hands, remember you can do all things through Christ, who gives you strength.

I again would like to thank my friends and family for supporting my writing and for being an endless source of encouragement. I love you all.

Table of Contents

Chapter 1 1
Chapter 2 8
Chapter 3 14
Chapter 4 22
Chapter 5 27
Chapter 6 33
Chapter 7 42
Chapter 8 49
Chapter 9 56
Chapter 10 62
Chapter 11 67
Chapter 12 73
Chapter 13 78
Chapter 14 84
Chapter 15 90
Chapter 16 93
Chapter 17 99
Chapter 18 104
Chapter 19 113
Chapter 20 122
Chapter 21 130
Chapter 22 141
Chapter 23 146
Chapter 24 155
Chapter 25 162
Chapter 26 170
Chapter 27 176
Chapter 28 186
Chapter 29 193
Chapter 30 198

Chapter 1

The *Sea Sprite* crept silently through the dense fog. The only sounds disturbing the quiet were familiar creeks emanating from the wooden ship and oars slipping slowly into and out of the water. Fog swirled like smoke around the ship's hull as it cut through the haze. The sea was unnaturally still, its water reflecting the ship like a mirror through tiny breaks in the fog. Adhira looked at his rippling reflection, wondering what was hidden behind the tan-skinned, dark-haired copy of himself.

Every now and then, the wreckage of another vessel could be seen just beneath the surface. Remains of their once proud masts broke the surface like petrified hands reaching from their watery graves. What had sent so many vessels to the ocean floor? The waters were shallow, but there was no evidence of what had downed so many ships.

Adhira manned the bow of the *Sea Sprite*, sitting as far forward as he could on the forward railing. He wasn't completely focused on the present but instead was using his gift, an ability given to him by the mysterious Re'u, to split focus between the now and the immediate future. He didn't need to turn around to know all eyes were on him. There was an enemy out there, but they didn't know exactly where it was. Unfortunately, since coming to that strange world, enemies were seldom human and never weak. There was a sound, a guttural attempt at a whistle. Adhira used his gift to look ahead.

He suddenly staggered backward when an arrow pierced his chest. The arrow was made out of some sort of bone, and the fire spreading through his lungs told him it was poisoned. Despite the searing pain, he looked around to gather any information he could. A moment after the arrow struck him, the fog around him exploded with projectiles. He fell to his knees and turned to see spears and arrows striking down his friends and crew as grappling hooks appeared over the railings.

"Now!" Adhira yelled in the present. They only had a few seconds before the vision came to be. Fifteen seconds, to be exact—the limit of his gift. The sails hung bereft of wind. Victoria, who was gifted with the ability to control the world around them, raised her right hand in the air, and a tempestuous wind washed over the ship and swelled the sails. Oars were retracted as the ship suddenly lurched forward.

The enemy still sprang their trap, though less organized. Spears fell short of the fleeing ship, while only a few arrows managed to make it aboard.

One arrow struck a sailor in the back while he tightened a rope on the lower part of the mast.

Adhira sprinted down the deck toward the sailor, pushing him out of the way just as the arrow thudded into the pole he was working near.

"Thanks, lad!" the man breathed before returning to his task.

The ship shuddered as the hull struck a sunken vessel. They listed heavily to the starboard side, sending supplies and several crewmen over the side.

Adhira ran to the back of the ship where Captain Carrick was manning the wheel. When he saw Adhira coming, he didn't need to ask but stepped aside. The Indian grabbed the wheel and turned hard to starboard. Everyone not holding onto something fell to the deck as the large vessel leaned so far it threatened to tip over. Using his gift, Adhira knew the ship would stay upright.

With Adhira at the helm, they distanced themselves from the enemy ambush. Their greatest remaining danger was the debris beneath the water. After two more quick maneuvers from Adhira, they broke free of the fog into the open ocean. The wind picked back up on its own, and Victoria was able to take a break. The Indian remained at the helm until the new first mate, a stocky man with a permanent inquisitive expression on his face, relieved him. Captain Carrick motioned for him and a few others to join him in his quarters.

"Well, that went as well as expected," Adhira said as he entered the room and shut the hatch behind him.

Asa laughed, but everyone else looked deathly serious.

"We need to go back," Neviah said sternly.

Captain Carrick's eyes opened slightly wider, which, for him, was a tremendous display of surprise. "Have ye been asleep this whole time? We barely escaped with our lives just now."

"I thought the fog would protect us," Neviah admitted. "But it just provided concealment for our enemies."

"I told ye before. No one returns from Shipwreck Bay. The fish people sink any vessel *foolish* enough to traverse those waters." The emphasis was obviously directed at the teens.

Adhira sat quietly through the conversation. His gift to see into the future meant he had to re-listen to the conversation patiently again in real time.

"What is the best way to avoid the fish people?" Asa asked, his brows drown in thought.

"Ye can't," the captain stated simply.

"Well, then, what's the best way to defeat them?"

"Ye can't do that either," Carrick said with poorly concealed frustration. "I've told ye before. They live under the sea. No man can get to them. They surface to kill and plunder and disappear beneath the waves again."

"Under the Sea," Adhira sang in his best Sebastian impression from The Little Mermaid. *No one laughed.*

He decided to try a different joke.

"Well, we have a wo-man who can get to them." Asa chuckled, and Victoria shifted around nervously.

He decided to skip the joke altogether. "Look. Couldn't Victoria make a protective wall of fire around the boat or something," Adhira said instead. Everyone looked at Victoria.

Asa sat up straighter and said, "Um, or she could turn the water near the island to ice." Adhira thought his own idea was much cooler.

"Asa, bro, question: why don't you want to use my idea?"

Asa was the most in tune with the Indian's ability. They had come up with a code for Adhira to let Asa know when he was asking something no one else would actually hear. They termed it the "bro question."

"Victoria doesn't always have complete control over her gift, and I wouldn't want her to accidentally set the ship on fire."

Victoria stared at Asa in shock.

It was a good thing he never actually said it.

"Yeah, that would work too," Adhira conceded. "A good layer of ice would keep the fish people at bay."

Captain Carrick gave a short "Ha," which was the closest he ever came to laughing. The man did find the oddest stuff funny. "Good one."

Adhira had no clue what he was talking about.

Despite the laugh, the captain was shaking his head. "Ye nearly got everyone on this ship killed with ye fog idea. I can't ask my crew to risk their lives again. We are just simple merchants."

"We have to," Neviah insisted. "Every life in the world is at risk."

"Ye don't have to tell me the importance of that island. I'm the one who told ye where the shadow gate might be."

The shadow gate was a portal to another world, the Abyss, a barren land void of sunlight and filled with horrible creatures called Shayatin, monsters with a thirst for destruction. The four teens were the only ones standing in the way of the dragon, Iblis, opening the largest of the shadow gates and releasing an unstoppable beast upon the world.

"My men are sailors, not warriors. What ye need is a hardy group of fighters."

"Where are we going to find a group of men who will risk their lives against the fish people?"

"There are two ways I know to recruit men to do a fool's errand. One is ye get them to fully believe in what ye need them to do. Two, and this is much more likely to work, ye pay them, and I mean ye pay them well."

There was silence for a moment while everyone considered his words. They had no money at all and didn't know how they would convince anyone to help them destroy the shadow gate. Adhira doubted they could even convince anyone it existed.

"Where would we even go to recruit fighters?" Asa asked.

"It depends."

"Depends on what?" Asa asked.

"Whether ye be wanting men who fight with honor or men who fight to win."

"Men who fight with honor," Neviah was quick to reply.

"Ye be out of luck. There be no such place."

"Then why did you give it as an option?" Neviah asked angrily.

"To prove a point. Ye kids have heart, but war is nothing like what you've read in tales. There is no honor when folks are killing each other. Hire them big and tough, and the more scars, the better." Adhira nearly pointed out they'd fought in a war already, but Carrick already knew that.

"Don't scars mean they stink at fighting?" Asa said with a raised eyebrow.

"It may, but it also means they don't run from a fight, even when they should. That be the type ye need." Asa nodded, seeming satisfied with the advice.

"Well, where can we find these men?" Neviah asked.

"South Bay be as good a start as any."

"Why South Bay?" Asa asked.

"Because that is where my cargo should have been a month ago," the

The Road to War

captain said, sure to scowl at each of them in turn.

✶✶✶

It was two more weeks at sea before they drew close to South Bay. Captain Carrick leaned over a map of the city, giving them the lay of the place, when the cabin door suddenly sprang open.

"Captain!" exclaimed a shirtless man with shoulders as broad as the door. "There be heavy smoke to the west."

The cabin emptied as everyone rushed onto the deck. On the horizon, smoke drifted above a shore stretching as far as they could see from south to north.

"Something be burning at South Bay," stated the captain as calmly as if he'd said the sky was blue.

"Could Tanas have made it here already?" Asa asked.

"He's a dragon," Adhira pointed out.

"With dragon friends," Neviah added.

"What's that?" Asa asked, pointing at the shore. A bright light could be seen blinking off and on.

"That be a mirror," Captain Carrick said. He stared at it for a moment before turning to his first mate. "Gunther, set a course for Mallus." He continued to watch the signal as his order was carried out. The ship turned so the shore was to the port side.

"What does it say?" Asa asked at length.

"Death here. Go north."

"That's it?" Asa questioned, but the captain ignored him and walked back to the cabin. Asa looked at the signal again.

"They couldn't exactly detail how to make grandma's homemade chicken casserole with a mirror," Adhira pointed out, watching as the flashes faded from view.

As the ship continued a path parallel to the coastline, the smoke slowly disappeared in the distance. Adhira overheard a few of the sailors muttering about having to spend another week away from port.

The days were uneventful as they followed the never-ending coastline around the giant island of Tarsis. It was like a vacation for the four teens. Since coming to that world from Earth years before, it had been one chaotic adventure after another. The captain had tried to awe them with his talk of war, but the truth was, they'd already fought in one. Though they were barely approaching eighteen years of age, they'd already traveled much of the world, fighting dragons and other shadow creatures, legions of the undead, and engaged in aerial combat with Shedim hundreds of feet above the ground. It felt like they were always fighting.

In the early morning on the sixth day out from South Bay, they made anchor in an overcrowded bay in Mallus. Before anyone could disembark, a rowboat made its way out to them. After climbing up the port ladder, a balding man with a rather rotund belly stood before them in a dull yellow uniform with large copper buttons down the front.

"What is or was your cargo's destination?" the man asked in an official-sounding voice.

"That be South Bay," said Captain Carrick.

"You will unload at dock four and collect your payment at the corresponding station." He nodded his head to the captain and made to leave.

"What be happening in the other port?" the captain asked.

"That," said the man in yellow, turning back to face the captain. "It is a most unfortunate affair. The Finn Folk attacked the ships anchored there, sinking many before the rest could escape."

"The fish people?" one of the sailors asked in surprise. "They never leave Shipwreck Bay."

"Tell that to the hundreds of men lying at the bottom of South Bay," the yellow-dressed man said with a little heat in his voice. "They sunk ships and set fire to the piers."

"Did they come on land?" Captain Carrick asked.

"Only in the initial assault. They quickly retreated when our soldiers showed, but the whole city is on edge, what with having to get all their supplies by land and not being able to fish at all for fear of getting a bone arrow in the gut."

"What does King Darious plan to do about the situation?" Captain Carrick asked. He said the word king with more than a hint of disdain.

The man in yellow smiled and said, "Nothing." He looked around at the questioning looks passing between the surrounding sailors. Captain Carrick was the only one who seemed unfazed by the simple statement. The man in yellow raised an eyebrow as he looked around, waiting for something. It was obvious to Adhira that the man enjoyed the attention.

"Why nothing?" the captain asked, his tone bored.

"Because," the man said with a smile, "the king taxes all shipments coming into the country. He also taxes all trade between cities."

The Road to War

"And now he gets to double tax everything bound for the Southern City," Asa said absently. The man in yellow grimaced, having been robbed of his clever conclusion.

"Well, yes," he said. "Anyway, dock four is open for you now." The man in yellow left the ship the way he came.

"What are ye all standing around daydreaming for?" Captain Carrick yelled to the men crowding the deck. "Ye be wasting daylight! Get to the oars, pull anchor, and get my ship moving!"

"Will the king of this island really do nothing?" Neviah asked amid the flurry of activity.

"That be the king I remember," Captain Carrick said as the ship slowly moved forward, the first mate at the helm relaying orders to the oarsmen.

"I thought you said there were soldiers here that would help us," she said. "If getting rid of the fish people will hurt the king's bottom line, how are we to convince anyone to join us?"

"First," Captain Carrick said, holding up a gnarled finger in front of her face. "I never said 'soldier,' I said 'fighter.' Second, I told ye there were two ways to convince men to join your suicide mission. Since persuasion is out of the question, ye'll just have to hire someone."

"Who?" Neviah snipped, obviously annoyed at the lecture.

"There," the captain said, nodding behind the teens. They looked over their shoulders to see an enormous vessel anchored in the center of the bay. "That's Captain Gold. Some call him the Merchant King and it is him ye want to join yer cause. He has more power than King Darious cares to admit and more men than the king dare know."

"And how do we convince him to join us?" Neviah asked.

"Why do ye think we call him Captain Gold?"

Chapter 2

"What do you mean we can't see him?" Neviah asked the group of guards standing on the floating pier in front of them. The men laughed uproariously, staring down at the teens in the small rowboat they'd borrowed from Captain Carrick.

The four teens glared at the three men barring their access to Captain Gold's ship. The ship was completely surrounded by a floating pier where half a dozen smaller trade vessels were parked. Three of Gold's guards stood on the pier looking down at them.

"Why is that…?" Asa could not finish his question because the soldiers started laughing louder, leaning on each other for support.

"They…" one of the guards began but began to wheeze. "They want… they want to see the Merchant King!" Another burst of laughter.

Neviah pulled her black book from her backpack with a mischievous look in her eyes. Adhira frowned in disappointment when Asa put a hand on her shoulder and shook his head. The book could turn into the most powerful sword in the world. Adhira would have loved to see how that would've played out. At length, the laughing subsided.

"What do you mean we can't see him?" Neviah repeated, though with the strain of barely repressed rage evident in her voice.

"Are ye royalty in disguise?" one of the men mocked.

"Are ye hiding the Jewel of Sea in yer purse?" another quipped. "If so, right this way."

"Surely ye wouldn't really believe the captain would see just anyone." When the men saw the serious looks on their faces, they began laughing again.

Adhira tried to see how it looked from the soldiers' points of view. From the moment the teens entered that world, they'd constantly held company with lords and kings. It was just donning on them the privilege they'd taken for granted. In all appearances, the four of them were nobodies.

"We have news concerning the fish people and the wars to the north," Neviah said.

"And we already know everything we need to know about both matters," one of the men said. "Besides, information alone will not gain ye an audience with the Merchant King."

"What will?" Neviah asked.

"Ye are persistent," the man said almost approvingly, though his voice took on an edge that said he was growing tired of the exchange. "Only people of Captain Gold's station are permitted to speak with him. Go amass ye-selves some wealth and come back in a few years, and we can have this talk again." He turned to leave.

Adhira stood, grabbed the man's shoulder to turn him around, then punched him in the face as hard as he could.

Adhira used his gift again, more constructively, to ask a series of questions until he found the one that caught the soldier's attention again. "What do you consider to be wealthy enough to see the captain?"

The soldier paused and spoke over his shoulder, "If ye come back with a gold piece each, ye would stand a good chance." There was a pause before the soldiers started to laugh again as they dispersed, leaving one smirking soldier to watch the teens push away from the pier.

"A gold piece each!" Asa breathed as he started to row their little boat. "That's a fortune!" Though gold was rare back on Earth, that world contained even less. A single gold piece was enough money to support a person for their entire life.

They rowed back to the *Sea Sprite* in silence. Upon arrival, Asa, Victoria, and Neviah went below deck while Adhira paced along the rail. Most would think his balance upon the rail precarious, but his gift protected him from falling.

Asa was the thinker of the group. At least, everyone knew him as the thinker. What they didn't know was that Adhira was smart, too, and this was his chance to finally show the others. He paced for a while, watching the mast's shadow shift, then lengthen as the warm day turned into a cool afternoon. The Indian watched as two sailors came back to the ship to relieve the men who were on watch.

"It's about time," one of the sailors said as he was relieved of duty and made to climb down the cargo net to reach the rowboat quicker.

"Sorry, but I couldn't lose! I won nearly half a silver!"

Gambling. The thought reverberated through Adhira's mind like a struck bell. He quickly climbed down the netting to the rowboat before the two liberated sailors shoved off. As the larger one rowed, Adhira asked the other for a tin piece, one of the smaller denominations. The man flipped him a coin, which he deftly caught without looking and put it in a small pocket hidden under his shirt. His book of prophecies, an identical copy to Neviah's, which could also turn into a sword, was in a small satchel he kept strapped around his waist like a belt. He kept his shirt pulled down over it so no one could see it, mostly because he thought it looked like a fanny pack.

The ride to the dock only took a few minutes, and Adhira spent the entire time wondering about the morality of his plan. Was it wrong to use his gift to gamble? It was kind of cheating, wasn't it? Cheating used to be his specialty back on Earth. Why did it matter now? He smiled when he realized a moral loophole. What if he only gambled with other cheaters and crooks? That would make it more fun anyway.

When they made it to dock, he thanked the sailors for the ride and set off into the city with a purpose. At first, he wondered if he should have asked one of the sailors where a good place to gamble was, but it didn't take long for him to stumble upon a few guys crowding around a table on a street corner.

There was a crowd on one side of the table and a man wearing a red leather tunic on the other. The red tunic guy was playing a very familiar-looking game. He was moving three cups around on a table with practiced speed and dexterity.

"Place your bets, gentlemen," the guy said as he stopped moving the cups. The cups were identical, except one had a small glass ball under it. Adhira knew which one, since he already used his gift to look. Coins were quickly placed on the table in front of each of the cups. Adhira was about to make his bet, but a hunch told him to watch again with his gift.

When the bets stopped flowing, Red Tunic lifted the cups one by one. Adhira smiled when he noticed the ball had moved.

In real time, he was able to place his tin piece on the table just before the red ball was revealed. Adhira wasn't sure how the guy kept up with all the bets, but two tin pieces were placed in his hand before the game started again. After looking ahead again, he placed his bet and soon had four tin pieces. His streak continued for several minutes before others started to notice he hadn't lost yet.

The problem came when quite a few guys began to copy his bet. Since it was obvious to him that Red Tunic Guy was moving the ball to whichever cup had the fewest bets, Adhira finally had to walk away, though he didn't have to go far to find more people gambling. If something could be bet on, the city had it. Looking through one tavern door, he saw guys sitting around two bird cages, each with a bird in it, betting large sums of money on one or the other. When asked, a woman told Adhira they were betting on which bird would sing the longest.

He stepped into an ally to cut across to another main street when his gift showed him a hooded man waiting with a crossbow. Adhira smiled to himself, immediately wondering if he could catch a bolt with his bare hands. He stepped into the alley and greeted the robber before the man had a chance to speak.

"It's a good day for a mugging if I do say so myself," Adhira said with a smile.

The eyes stared out of the hood for a moment before the man cleared his throat. "Umm. Give me all yer coin," Hoodie said awkwardly.

"I'd rather not," the Indian said, hoping to provoke the man to shoot. The crossbow looked so weathered it was a wonder the thing didn't go off by accident.

"I mean it," the man said, obviously taken aback by the glib attitude he was receiving.

Before the man could react, Adhira snatched the hood off his head. The robber was revealed to be a middle-aged man with short blond hair. Blondie just stared in disbelief. The boy sighed. Even without his gift, Adhira knew the man wasn't going to shoot. Sweat glistened on the man's arms despite the cool afternoon weather.

"Is this your first mugging?" Adhira asked loud enough to make the man look around nervously. "Well, I'm honored. No, really. Word of advice for your next mugging: you have to really sell it. Sneer a little next time and maybe furrow your brow more, though I guess that would be hard to show if you insist on wearing this hood. You might want to swear a little, too; nothing covers the jitters like a few swear bombs, though that might be offensive to some of your victims." Adhira turned to go but paused to say over his shoulder, "Oh, and you never actually threatened me. Rehearse more next time."

The alley led him to another street full of gamblers. He was really intrigued by a game where spinning tops would bump into each other until one was the victor, but the process took too long for his gift to give him an edge in betting. There were races with every kind of animal imaginable, but nothing he wanted to bet on. It wasn't long before he found one of the more popular games.

The game looked fun and, more importantly, quick. It consisted of a large bowl of water with a small leather ball floating on top. The man running the contraption pulled a plug out of the bottom, and the water began spiraling out. At last, the ball came to rest in one of the three compartments at the bottom of the bowl. They were painted blue, yellow, and red.

"How do you play?" Adhira asked a bystander as soon as he walked up.

"You can bet on blue or yellow," the man said. "The Keeper will pay whoever chooses right. If the ball lands on red, the Keeper keeps all the money.

The water drained, and the ball landed on yellow.

Adhira snatched up the ball and shook it, startling the crowd. The ball seemed legit. The man running the show reached for his ball back. Adhira grabbed the man's arms and reached up his sleeves. There were several balls hidden there. Adhira didn't know what the trick was, but the man running the game was definitely cheating somehow.

In real time, Adhira put his money on yellow. He received sour looks from those around him. The majority of the crowd seemed to be betting on blue and took offense at him betting differently.

"They don't like you betting against them," someone warned him.

Adhira ignored them. He wasn't there to make friends. The ball landed on yellow, and he gladly received his money. In the next round, he refrained from betting, and the ball landed on red. Everyone booed, and the Keeper raked in all the money. Adhira stood at that game for what felt like hours. He varied his bets and purposely lost a few times so no one would catch on to him, but as with the ball and cup game, people began copying his bet.

He reluctantly walked away, but with considerably more money than he started with. After changing up to bigger coins, the small gaming houses began refusing his bets, saying he was over the house limit. After gambling at several higher-stakes games with better-dressed patrons, it was evening before he felt he had enough money to buy their interview with Captain Gold.

He made his way to the docks whistling, bouncing a fat purse on his palm. When he turned a corner and saw the skeletal remains of a ship floating in the harbor, he nearly dropped his money. It looked like a ghost ship from a horror movie.

There were no sails, and the main mast was broken off. The boards of the hull were so sparse and rotted that there was no way it could be treading water. And yet it was. What's more, it was floating next to the *Sea Sprite*.

The spectacle had drawn several wary onlookers to the docks, but Adhira was eventually able to make his way to the front and hire a rower to take him to the *Sea Sprite*. He found his friends waiting.

"Guess what?" Asa said excitedly when Adhira climbed aboard. "We found a way to gain an audience with Captain Gold, and we don't need any money at all. Isn't that great!"

Chapter 3

Adhira lounged in the crow's nest with one leg hanging through the railing, wondering aloud, "How many times have I had an idea just to have Asa come up with a better one?" Balancing a coin on the back of his fingers, he moved it back and forth as he thought back.

"When we were in the changing maze, I had the idea to climb the gate and walk across the tops of the walls but didn't say anything." He was glad they hadn't tried that since the punishment for breaking the rules was the appearance of a giant rock monster who would have simply plucked them off the wall. Asa was the one who figured out how to get into the giant building at the maze's center and solved the puzzles within.

"We were low on drinking water on our first boat trip, and I was like, 'Everyone should save their pee.' It was gross, but it would have kept us all alive until the next port." Asa's sea water purification contraption was much better. "I'm just glad I never voiced that particular idea." Now that he thought about it, it was at that moment he became more hesitant to voice his ideas. He was afraid of looking dumb when someone came up with a better solution.

Adhira had ideas for killing dragons, getting through the Finn Folk, and how to find the other pieces of the Armor of Light. He wasn't shy, exactly. Far from it. If only his friends could see he was smart, too. Just once, when a problem arose, it would be nice if Neviah would look at him instead of Asa.

"Hey, Adhira," he heard Neviah yell up. *"Is that your leg I see swinging up there?"*

Before she said anything, he went ahead and swung over the side, grabbed the thick netting, and started his climb down. He'd tried jumping into the sails to slide down, but that never worked out as well as it did in the movies. Neviah was coming up the ladder from below deck just as he reached the deck.

The Road to War

"Perfect," she said as she walked past him. "Let's go."

"She found it then?" Adhira asked with gritted teeth. She wouldn't answer for fifteen seconds, the limit of his gift. It was her way of forcing him to ask questions in real time.

After waiting, she said, "Yes. She and Asa should have already had a rowboat lowered." They climbed over the side to the waiting rowboat.

"Do you want to see it?" Asa asked, already holding out the treasure they'd been hoping for.

Adhira took the bracelet as he stepped into the small boat. It looked in remarkable shape for something trapped at the bottom of the bay for a hundred years.

"We didn't even have to clean it much," Asa said. "It was sealed in wax inside a wall safe."

The Queens Circlet, also known as the Jewel of Sea, was a beautiful gold bracelet with evenly spaced rubies and diamonds inset all around it. It had been lost to the bottom of the bay when the *Leaping Cricket* was sunk by a sailor revolt a century before. Adhira twirled it on a finger, pretended to drop it over the water, and then handed it to a scowling Neviah. She was always more beautiful when she scowled.

While Adhira was off gambling, the other three had talked to a local loremaster, whatever that was, and learned about the fabled ship. Asa had convinced Victoria to use her gift to find it in the middle of the harbor and raise it to the surface. The ship now lay beached on the shore where Asa and Victoria searched through it all morning.

Asa rowed them through the harbor. It may have been faster to walk the pier to shore and over to Captain Gold's private pier, but they all enjoyed rowing around in the boat. The entire bay, as far as they could see, was crowded with large ships and small boats moving about. Half an hour later, they found themselves pulling up to a landing with three guards watching them approach.

"Ye four again," said one of the guards they talked to on the previous day. "I told ye not to come back unless…"

"Unless we had gold or the Jewel of Sea," Adhira interrupted. He held up the bracelet. "Well, here is the Jewel of Sea, the Queen's Bracelet." The shock on the soldiers' faces was priceless. "We would like to see Captain Gold now."

At length, the man found his voice again. "How do I know that's really the…the Jewel of Sea," he finished with reverence.

"Because it is," Adhira said simply.

"Can I hold it?"

"No."

The man scowled for a moment but finally motioned for them to follow him. He spoke over his shoulder as the teens wobbled behind him on the floating pier. "The captain is meeting with the Merchants Trade Commission but may have time to see ye after. The rest of the afternoon is booked, however, so if he can't see ye today, it will have to be tomorrow."

The ship they approached was magnificent. It was several stories tall and made out of giant redwood beams and shiplap. Dozens of large windows looked out over the bay. There were wide stairs running up the port side of the ship, and it looked like they were permanently attached to the pier.

The ship felt as solid as land after walking on the bobbing pier. They were led through two large ornate doors into a red-carpeted room with a receptionist at a table near the door. The guard talked to him for a moment. The only part of the conversation Adhira caught was when the guard said, "Well, it looks pretty real to me."

At length, he walked back over to the doors where the teens waited. "The captain will be free after his meeting. Have a seat, and he will see you when he can."

The waiting room had several plush couches and chairs and tables with fruits, bread, and cheeses on them. Adhira plopped down on one of the couches and lounged the long way, sinking pleasantly into the cushions. Asa walked over to a bookshelf, Victoria in tow. They rarely went anywhere without the other. Neviah sat, admiring the bracelet she now wore.

"You should put that on the other wrist," he said closing his eyes, suddenly ready for a nap. "If the Forest Shield expanded while you were wearing that thing, it would be destroyed." He smiled when he heard her quick rustling as she removed it.

Something hit him in the face. He opened his eyes to see Neviah had thrown a strawberry-like fruit at him.

Without opening his eyes, Adhira caught the fruit before it hit him and began eating it.

He looked up to see the look on her face. It was perfectly annoyed.

He hadn't realized he'd fallen asleep until Neviah's complaining woke him up. When he sat up, he saw her talking to the receptionist.

"His meeting is very important," the man said calmly. "I assure you he takes all his meetings very seriously, which you will appreciate when it is your turn. If you would like, I can place you on the schedule for a different day."

"No, we will wait," Neviah grumbled as she came over and sat on the couch next to Adhira. "Wow, no wonder you fell asleep on this thing," she said as the cushions partially swallowed her.

"How long was I out?" he asked Asa.

"About an hour," he said, not looking up from the book he was reading. Victoria had fallen asleep over the one she was reading.

Adhira stood and stretched. He walked over to a set of closed doors. The receptionist looked at him but didn't say anything.

Adhira threw open the double doors and walked into the lantern-lit room. There were four men and two women sitting around a table, playing a card game and smoking pipes. The smell of sweet tobacco permeated the air. In front of each person sat a considerable stack of coins.

"Well, hello to ye, too," a portly man in a red and gold coat said when Adhira barged in. The man's hair was black as night and was pulled back in a ponytail. He had a fierce intelligence in his eyes, which were framed by thin gold glasses. "I think our stakes may be a little rich for ye lad," he said with a laugh.

Adhira walked back over to his friends. To Neviah, he said, "You have to promise not to get mad."

"Have you met me?" she said, turning her head to look at him sideways. "If it has something to do with you, then nope. I will not promise and will most likely be furious. What is it?"

"Captain Gold's meeting is nothing more than a card game. They are sitting around smoking and having a good ol' time."

"What?" Neviah said loudly as she stood and took a step toward the receptionist. Adhira caught her arm.

"I think this may be the best thing for us," he said. "I might be able to get into their game. I just need the Jewel of the Sea."

"You what!" she said even louder. "You are not going to gamble away our only leverage."

"You should give it to him," Asa said, finally looking up from his book. "It's Adhira. It won't be gambling for him. Not really. He can get to know the captain a little before we ask to borrow a bunch of his fighting men to attack the most dangerous island in the world."

"The most dangerous so far," Adhira added with a smile. "Who knows what we will face next."

Neviah scowled between the two boys for a moment. At an almost imperceptible nod from Victoria, who'd awakened at the other girl's near yelling, Neviah finally gave in and handed the bracelet to Adhira. Like before, but for real this time, Adhira threw open the door and walked into the lantern-lit room.

"Well, hello to ye, too," the man in red and gold said when Adhira barged in. "I think our stakes may be a little rich for ye lad," he said with a laugh.

The receptionist rushed through the door behind Adhira. "I'm so sorry for the intrusion. He is your next appointment and was told to wait."

The man reached for Adhira's arm, but the Indian easily sidestepped him and took three long strides to the table. Tossing the bracelet on the center pile of money, he took one of the two remaining seats directly across from the man in red.

The eyes of everyone at the table bulged appropriately when they fell on the bracelet. One of the women timidly reached out a hand to touch it, but the man in red deftly plucked it from the pile. He seemed to be the only one who'd fully recovered from the initial shock of seeing the treasure.

Waving away the receptionist, he held the bracelet over his shoulder. A skinny man in a thin leather apron, who Adhira hadn't seen on his first trip into the room, took the bracelet and left the room.

"We indeed have business, Mr.…" the man in red said, pausing for Adhira's name. He gave it. "Well, Adhira, I am Captain Golt. Not Captain Gold. Golt. I despise that nickname." One of the men smirked and looked sideways at the captain. Golt probably loved the nickname. "My goldsmith will run the required tests while ye wait, but I'm afraid this is a private game."

Adhira smiled. The real game was finally at hand. To everyone at the table, it would look like Adhira was quiet for a moment, but in reality, he was following several conversation paths.

"Private," Adhira said. "Who's allowed to play?"
"Only the leaders of the respected trade guilds have a vote."
"What are you voting on?"
"That is need to know and I think it's time for ye to wait outside."
That was a dead end. It was time to take a different path.
"So, what are you guys voting on?" Adhira asked.
"How do ye know that?" Captain Golt asked, though everyone else just looked at Adhira with mild surprise.
"I'm a good guesser," Adhira said.
One of the women, a golden-haired beauty in a blue satin dress,

spoke for the first time. "I told you it was time for us to find another way to break ties when the vote is split."

So, gambling was how they broke ties when they couldn't agree among themselves. Adhira started over again.

"What's the harm if an outsider plays? If I win, then the runner-up gets to break the tie."

"For an outsider, ye seem to already know a bit about our politics," Golt said. He looked around the table. Everyone was either noncommittal or nodded.

"Fine. Fine," one of the older gentlemen said after Adhira repeated the conversation in real time. "Let's just be on with it. You've already interrupted my streak."

"I wouldn't call two wins a streak," one of the other men said with a laugh.

"He will need some actual coin," the red-haired beauty said.

At this, a short, classically handsome man with just a bit of gray at the temples perked up. "Well, I would be happy to spot the boy half a silver's worth of coin. Of course, it would be collateralized by the bracelet with only the smallest of interest…"

"That is quite all right," Adhira said as he pulled his bag of money from his satchel. It was good to know it was handy after all. After spreading his coins out in even stacks before him, he found that his considerable wealth was dwarfed by the smallest stack at the table.

"If your intention was intrigue," said an older lady whose hair was completely white. "Then you have succeeded. You have the swagger of a seasoned soldier. You're dressed like a sailor. Yet you show up with our kingdom's most desired heirloom and enough money to buy a halfway decent ship. Who are you exactly?"

"They call me 'The Gambler,'" he said with a raised eyebrow, trying to give as smoldering a look as possible. Everyone looked at him like he was an idiot.

After trying a few more one-liners that bombed, he settled on, "You wouldn't want to ruin the mystery, now, would you?" This followed with a wink.

He used his gift to ask how to play the game, though, in real time, he made it look like he knew the game well. There were sixty cards in all, sequentially numbered. The object of the game was to bluff and trade cards until the betting was over. Then, the person with the highest combined numbered hand shared the pot with the person with the lowest numbered hand. When the game came down to two players, the last person to lose had to continue playing without betting until there was a victor.

Adhira felt a little bad using his gift to cheat but told himself this money was inconsequential to the other players. He figured he'd give it all to the poor or something. Robin Hood was seen as a hero when he robbed the rich to give to the poor. Besides, the whole purpose was to find out if he and his friends could convince Captain Golt to help with the Finn Folk.

On the first hand, without looking at his cards in real time, Adhira pushed all his money into the middle. Only then did he pick up his cards. He could have played without actually looking at his cards but figured they would peg him for a cheat if he won without knowing what his cards were. Two others, Captain Golt and Gray Temples, matched his bet, also without looking at their cards initially. This told a lot about them, but most importantly, they believed they could win strategically, whatever their starting cards were.

Everyone else looked at their cards, and all but one matched Adhira's initial bet. Then, the real fun began. Everyone started negotiating with each other for cards. There was a lot of bluffing going on, though sometimes the best bluff was telling the truth. Adhira had already used his gift to look at all his opponents' cards. He knew exactly what he needed to have the lowest possible hand. He won half the pot, more than tripling his money.

He immediately pushed it into the center again. Beauty made a smoke ring as she studied Adhira, then her cards. She folded her hand. The others soon did the same.

"It's hard to bet strategically when you put all your money on the opening bet," Gray Temples said.

Adhira realized he would have to ease up and win their money slowly and steadily. Which he did. He was sure to lose a hand every now and then so they wouldn't get suspicious, but within two hours, he had a huge stack of money in front of him.

"Well played," said the lady who found him intriguing. She was the runner-up in the card game. Standing up, she said, "You know my vote. Is there any further business to discuss?"

"No, ma'am," Captain Golt said. "I will see ye all at the next meeting."

After exchanging pleasantries with Adhira, the merchants all left, leaving Adhira alone with Golt. No one seemed at all worried about the money they'd lost.

When everyone else had left, Golt turned his attention to Adhira. "Ye lad are a cheater," he said, pointing at Adhira with the stem of his pipe. He stood to lean forward across the table and scowled down at Adhira. "And there is only one thing I do with cheats."

Chapter 4

"I hire them!" Golt said, suddenly letting out a guffaw of a laugh. Adhira laughed with him.

"I cheated," Adhira admitted.

Captain Golt laughed again. "Well, of course ye did. We all did. Ye were just the best at it. Ye would have a mighty fine career in politics if ye ever wanted one. Ye may bring in yer friends now," the captain said, still laughing.

Adhira went to the door and motioned for his friends to come in. When he walked back into the room, the captain had taken a seat at a desk across the room. The goldsmith had magically appeared again and was whispering in Golt's ear.

Neviah practically marched up to the desk, Asa and Victoria in tow. Asa was still reading a book while he walked. Neviah put both fists on the table and leaned toward the captain, but Adhira tugged hard on her sleeve. She scowled at him but took her seat, one of several high-backed chairs in front of the large wooden desk.

As soon as the goldsmith was done speaking quietly with the captain, he left through a small door behind the desk. Captain Golt was holding the bracelet.

"Name your price," he said, skipping introductions and looking over each of them in turn.

Asa finally shut his book. He was the one who spoke, stopping whatever Neviah was about to say, which was probably for the best. She still scowled at the captain. "We need to buy a seaworthy ship and rent another."

"Done and done," the captain said quickly with a smile.

"And we need to hire about a thousand fighting men."

Golt's eyes widened as he stared at each of them again. "And what would ye be needing an army for?"

"We need to get to Shipwreck Bay."

"And why do ye want to doom a thousand men to their deaths?" Golt asked, completely serious.

"We have personal business on the island, but we plan to defeat the sea people, too."

Captain Golt's eyes looked at nothing as if he were doing great calculations in his head. He slid the bracelet across the table. "No deal. The bracelet is one of the most valuable pieces lost to the sea, but it cannot pay for what ye ask." He made a motion like he was going to stand. From one hustler to another, Adhira recognized the man's move as a negotiation tactic.

Neviah's pot finally boiled over. "Sit back down," she said angrily. "First, you keep us waiting for hours while you play games, and now you dismiss us without hearing what we are offering!"

Captain Golt sat back down and leaned forward, a different glint in his eye. He showed no outward sign that Neviah's outburst bothered him in the least. "There's more?" he asked, almost eager. Adhira loved his friends, but they were horrible negotiators.

He was about to step in when Neviah gave him a wink. Asa added a slight nod.

In real time, he nodded at them, letting them know he would follow their lead. Apparently, while he was playing cards, his friends had come up with a plan.

"I told the others we should have gone straight to the king," Neviah said, picking up the bracelet and standing. "I'm sure he can spare the men for a short expedition."

Golt leaned back in his chair, fiercely calculating again. Then he smiled and said, "Very well, then. Good luck."

Now, the real game was afoot. The rest of them stood and slowly made their way toward the exit. With his back to Golt, Asa showed Adhira crossed fingers as if to say, "I hope this works."

Before they got halfway across the room, Adhira smiled when he saw who would win the bluff.

"Enough of this," Captain Golt said, waving them back. "Tell me the offer, the whole offer and I will tell ye what I can do."

When the teens returned to their seats, Asa walked over to a porthole cover and opened it so they could see the beach in the distance. The ship Victoria salvaged remained there, drying in the sun.

"We can do that," Neviah said, laying the bracelet back on the desk, all pretense at being angry over. "Name a ship, any ship, and we have a method of bringing it to the surface."

"Counteroffer," Golt said, leaning back in his chair, almost caressing the bracelet as he spoke. "Teach me the salvage method instead."

"We can't," Asa said. He looked at Adhira for support.

"He's going to find out how we do it eventually," Adhira said. "You might as well tell him."

"It is a power given to us by Re'u," Asa said. "It can't be taught."

"How do ye plan on dealing with the fish people?" Golt asked. "They live at the bottom of the ocean."

"We can get to them the same way we can get to sunken ships. We can move the water out of the way and walk to the enemy on dry land."

"Bishop!" the captain yelled, making everyone but Adhira jump. The receptionist quickly poked his head into the room. "Bishop, prepare my dinghy for a trip."

The man disappeared behind the door as quickly as he appeared.

"Do ye need to retrieve any tools or laborers before we leave?"

"Leave where?" Asa asked, squinting warily.

"Ye say ye can divide the waves so a man can walk upon the ocean floor as on dry land. I am ready to entertain those terms, but only after a demonstration."

Everyone looked at Victoria while trying not to look at her. She gave the slightest of nods, staring at her hands in her lap.

"We can give you a demonstration," Neviah said. "We do not need anything and can go now."

The captain's "dinghy" was as large as most of the ships in the bay. It rode high on the water, allowing them to glide swiftly through the sea. The mainland was on their left as they zipped toward a group of smaller islands. They slowed to navigate between them before dropping anchor beside the smallest one. It looked to be all sandy beach with no vegetation at all.

Captain Gold had a boat lowered and had the teens row him to shore. He walked around the island, looking at the sun and the other islands. Adhira had already used his gift to learn that the man was trying to position himself so he was facing the right way for something. After several minutes, Golt stopped and pointed.

"There," he said, pointing at the water. "I want to walk there."

Victoria concentrated on the spot for a moment before the water began to move back, almost as if a giant fan were blowing the water out of the way. Thousands of gallons of water were soon held back, and the girl didn't even break a sweat.

The Road to War

The captain looked at Adhira and nodded his head toward the hollow spot where the water had been. "After ye," the man said with a smile. Adhira was amazed at how easily the captain accepted what he was seeing.

The Indian walked down the now-dry ramp of sand to what had been part of the ocean floor. Golt followed, though his confidence was finally cracked a little. His eyes kept shifting between the giant walls of water being held back around him.

As they reached the bottom of the hollow, the captain transferred his attention to the sand and reefs around them. He paused his search when his eyes came to rest on the remnants of a small boat. After digging through the sand, which had mostly claimed the small vessel, he found something. Standing, he held up a lump of metal covered in small barnacles.

"What's that?" Neviah asked, walking up to it.

"This," the captain said, awe playing at the edges of his voice. "It be my grandfather's music box. He gave it to me when I was still a lad and I lost it to the sea when my fishing boat sunk when I was about yer age."

"I'm sorry it was ruined by the sea," Asa said sympathetically.

"Nonsense," the captain said, tucking the music box into a small satchel he carried on his hip. "My goldsmith is a master at restoring items once claimed by the sea. I bet he can have this looking good as new in no time at all."

They walked back toward the beach, and Victoria slowly let the water refill the hole she'd made in the sea. If Adhira had her power, he would have snapped his fingers and let the water crash back with flair.

"We best get back to the ship," Golt said. "With this stagnant wind, the return trip will be a bit slower."

"No, it won't," Asa said, smiling at Victoria.

The trip back was far quicker with Victoria filling the sails with wind. It wasn't long before they found themselves standing on Captain Golt's dock.

"When the fish people are dealt with, there are several ships near their island I would like to raise," the captain said.

"We can find three ships for you," Neviah said, all business again.

"I require ten," Golt said firmly.

"Ten!" Asa said. "And the bracelet? That's a bit much, don't you think?"

"Well, the reward for the bracelet will barely pay for the men ye require. I need fair compensation for my time."

"Reward?" Neviah asked. "What reward?"

Captain Golt's smile split his face. "That's the best part," he said, clapping his hands in excitement. "There is a standing reward for the bracelet if it were to ever be fished from the bottom of the bay. And of all the people in the kingdom, it will be given to the king by me!" He laughed out loud. "He will have to hold a feast in my honor and give a speech praising me. That will likely be the best day of my life!" He dabbed a kerchief at the corners of his eyes.

"We are so happy for you," Neviah said, rolling her eyes so only Adhira could see. "We can raise five ships."

"Ten."

"Six."

"Ten."

She scowled at the captain. "Eight," she said, then quickly held up a finger to cut him off. "And you don't want to say ten."

Captain Golt was all smiles, though. "Oh, I like ye. Deal. I can have yer two ships for ye within the week, though it will take the better part of a month to gather the men."

Asa nodded. "I figured as much. We need time to prepare anyway."

"And I changed my mind on which ships I want. I would like ye to raise the eight ships before ye set sail for Shipwreck Bay. I wouldn't want yer eminent deaths to cheat me out of our deal."

"Deal," Neviah said.

"Excellent," Golt said. "I will have a map in yer hands before morning with several shipwrecks marked. I will send a message to the *Sea Sprite* when the ships are ready."

The teens looked at the captain, surprised. He smiled a knowing smile before he walked away. How did he know what ship they were from?

Step one was done. Now, they just needed a way to destroy the shadow gate.

Chapter 5

"This is it," Adhira said a couple of days after their negotiations with Captain Golt, walking up to the charred remains of a building.

"And you were told it exploded?" Asa asked Neviah, picking through the rubble. He picked up and examined several rocks and crystals. "How does a rock store explode?"

A man approached them from a building across the street. "Can I help you with something?" the man asked in a way that really meant, "What are you doing with my stuff?"

"Yes," Neviah said with a smile. "We were curious how this happened."

"So am I," the man said with a sigh. "It took more than a little effort to convince the city guard I wasn't a witch."

"What was over here?" Asa called from "inside" the building. He was standing on a mostly bare section of stone near what appeared to be the center of the explosion.

"That is where we kept the farming powders and creams."

"We?" Asa asked. "Was there someone here during the explosion?"

"Just the store clerk."

"I'm sorry," Asa said sincerely.

"It's okay," the man said without a hint of remorse. "Nobody liked him anyway."

"What is farming powder?" Neviah asked, shaking her head.

"It is made from ground-up salt crystals. Farmers and gardeners mix it with manure, and it's great for growing stronger crops."

"What about the creams?" Neviah asked. "I didn't know you could make creams from rocks."

The man smiled. "You would be amazed what you can do with the right minerals. I once had a crystal smith make the most beautiful lantern by combining emeralds and crystals in layers to magnify the light."

"The creams," Adhira said to get the fellow back on track. The man would have kept talking about the lantern otherwise.

"Oh yes," the man said. "The most popular was the fungal cream."

"What kind of rock is that made from?" Asa asked.

"Its primary component is sulfur."

"What did you burn in the fireplace?" Asa asked, turning to inspect the remains of the fireplace. "Wood or charcoal?"

"Charcoal," the man said.

"I think that's one of the key ingredients," Neviah said.

"And I know for sure sulfur is one," Asa said, walking through the building to stand with his friends. There was soot smeared across his forehead where he'd moved his long hair out of his face.

"Ingredients to what?" the man asked, obviously intrigued.

"Black powder," Asa said absently.

"And what is black powder?"

"It's what I think did this," Asa said, waving his hand at the building.

The man looked at Asa, obviously expecting more of an explanation.

"Do you think the salt crystal was a component?" Neviah asked.

"Maybe," Asa said, scratching his chin while he thought, depositing more soot on his face. "There could also be other factors. I think we have enough to start experimenting."

Neviah turned her attention back to the store owner. "Do you have another store like this one?"

"Several," the man said. "I am also part owner of several mines, where I get most of my stock."

"We are in need of a lot of supplies," Neviah said. She bounced a bag of coins on her palm, part of Adhira's winnings from the card game with Captain Golt.

The man looked hungrily at the bulging purse. "Right this way, miss." Neviah and Asa were already exchanging ideas about how they wanted to proceed.

"It looks like you two have everything covered on the nerd front," Adhira said. "I was thinking I could recruit some sailors for the ship we bought."

"Good idea," Neviah said, pausing long enough to nod toward Victoria. "Why don't you take her with you? It's going to be pretty boring for both of you while we try to reinvent black powder."

"Deal," Adhira said. "But you will have to let me blow something up when you figure it out." Neviah rolled her eyes and walked away, leaving Adhira alone with Victoria.

If staring at the ground was a sport, she would be the number one athlete in the world.

"This way," he said, walking down the street.

She walked beside him, quiet as usual.

"Who would have guessed it?" he started, fighting a grin.

She looked up at him but didn't voice the question in her eyes.

"Asa and Neviah, of course. I think I see wedding bells in their future."

Victoria grabbed his arm with a grip that was surprisingly strong, stopping them. She had the most horrified look on her face, but when she saw the grin he was fighting, she gave him a good shove and continued walking.

"The look on your face was priceless," he said, catching back up to her.

The streets were packed with people and carts, the city thriving on the increased trade coming through its harbor.

"Wait, you're counting under your breath!" Adhira said accusingly. Neviah had taught her the trick of waiting before reacting to him so he wouldn't see it coming right away.

He saw what was coming, but she had secretly wrapped him in air so he couldn't move! Suddenly, she donned the most mischievous look he'd ever seen.

Then, he was flying straight up in the air, the wind stinging his face as he rocketed higher. He was easily a hundred feet off the ground before he slowed. The city looked amazing from that angle. There was no pattern to the buildings; the architectural designs were likely influenced by every culture in the world. The bay was filled with ships, the giant piers reaching toward the ocean like a giant hand. He thought he could make out the *Sea Sprite*.

"I can see my house from here!" he yelled as he started to fall back down. His clothes whipped around as he hurtled toward the ground. His freefall quickly slowed until he was placed gently on the ground beside a smiling Victoria. Adhira was sure he looked as disheveled as he felt.

"Right," he said as they pushed through the gawking onlookers. Every person in the square was stopped and staring at them. "Remind me to never mess with the girl with superpowers."

It took a few blocks before they could blend into the crowd again. Adhira led them down an alley and took a few turns, staying in the alleyway. Looking ahead, he smiled.

A hooded figure jumped out, yelling obscenities, leveling an old crossbow at Adhira. Victoria quickly crouched, summoning a fireball in one hand and a ball of lightning, which looked awesome, in the other hand.

"Down, girl," Adhira said, stepping between Victoria and the wide-eyed would-be robber.

"Oh, it be ye again," the man said, lowering the crossbow.

"You need to watch your language in front of the lady," Adhira said, turning back to face the man.

"What!" the man said incredulously. "You are the one who told me to cuss!"

"And I told you it would be offensive to some people. Well, I'm offended."

The man just stared with his mouth open. Adhira used his gift to ask a few questions until he got what he was looking for.

"Look, Brone, I didn't come here to give you tips on thieving again," Adhira said. The man looked horrified that Adhira knew his name. "Let's face it, you are really, really bad at it."

Brone pulled back his hood and sat down on a crate with a sigh. Victoria had let her lightning and fire disappear and leaned against the far alley wall with her arms crossed. She didn't look at the ground like she usually did but instead watched Brone warily.

"I know I'm bad at it. Dozens of people have walked through this alley, and I've only had the nerve to jump out twice. And both of those times, it was ye!" he finished accusingly.

"Well, today is your lucky day, Brone. I'm here to offer you a job." The man stared at him with eyes wide and mouth open.

"And why in the world would ye want to hire a thief?" the man asked slowly. "Especially someone who is bad at it."

"Because you are bad at it. You can't even rightly call yourself a thief anyway; you haven't stolen anything. I can tell you are a good person and a hard worker, and that is what I need." The man still looked confused.

"How in the world could ye know something like that? Ye don't know anything about me."

"The crossbow's trigger mechanism is obviously disabled," Adhira said. "Which means you don't want to hurt anyone, even by accident. You move around in those boots as if you've never worn them before, which tells me you are one of those barefoot sailors. Your hands are heavily calloused which means you are used to hard work. Your accent seems different than the other people here, so my guess is you are from the city that was attacked by the fish people."

"Yes," the man said in awe. "My ship was sunk while docked. I came here looking for work, but alas, there are more sailors than there are ships."

"Well, you are in luck. I have a boat in need of a crew. Or, at least, I will have a boat in a few days. I need you to find me another thirty or so men to crew it."

"I don't know what to say," the man said, his voice thick.

"If you cry on me, the deals off," Adhira said, causing Brone to smile. "Now, I want you to meet me with potential new hires near dock four in a couple of hours. I'll try to rent a booth or table or something to do my interviews."

"Yes, Captain," Brone said, taking the coins Adhira held out and holding them tight. He all but ran down the alley.

"Captain. I like the sound of that," Adhira said, then walked with Victoria out of the alley. As they strolled, he caught Victoria studying him out of the corner of his eye.

"You might not be a blue, but you are one of the purest whites I've seen," she said with an absent nod of her head.

Adhira remembered that when she looked at people, they had colors or some such around them, which allowed her to immediately tell what type of person they were.

"What color did you see when you looked at Brone?" he asked. She annoyed him by waiting fifteen seconds before answering. Neviah had definitely ruined her.

"He's yellow. He's overall a good person."

"So, white is really good, yellow is pretty good, red is bad, and blue is…?"

"It's more of a spectrum, but basically, yes," she said, not telling him what blue stood for.

"And Brone is a yellow. Is that why you didn't smash him in a fireball and lightning sandwich?" he asked. She laughed but nodded. "When we go to the docks, I have something I want you to do for me," he said as an idea came to him.

After listening to his plan, she rolled her eyes, another hand-me-down from Neviah, but she agreed to help.

✶✶✶

A group of nearly forty sailors waited at the ramp leading to dock four. Suddenly, there was a scream followed by surprised shouts and excited voices. Everyone froze what they were doing and stared as Adhira flew through the air. He did a circle around the docks once before coming to float in the air above the water in front of the gathered sailors.

"Good morning," he said, lounging in the air on Victoria's invisible bonds. "Before I interview you, I would like you to know what you are signing up for." The men still looked so shocked by his "flying" that he wasn't sure if they even knew what he was saying. "I want to start off by saying my sailors will be paid ten times the going rate." He had no clue what that rate was, but he still had a ridiculous amount of money left from his card game with Golt.

The men suddenly perked up, one man actually licking his lips at the offer.

"Unfortunately, I will only need you for one voyage."

This didn't seem to bother them, but he knew, even without looking into the near future, that his next statement would get a big reaction.

"The voyage is to Shipwreck Bay." A collective groan went up, mixed with a few obscenities. Six men immediately turned and walked away. Several more looked to be thinking about it. "Oh, no, the fish people!" Adhira said in a mocking, high-pitched voice. "We'll be slaughtered!" Then, in his normal voice, he said, "The fish people will not be a problem." He pointed to the water below him, and on cue, the gently rolling waves turned into a sheet of ice all around him.

The murmurs from the men soon turned to excited and awestruck exclamations. One man made some kind of weird hand sign and ran away. After a moment, Adhira counted the men left. It was about right.

"Who here has served on a ship before?" he asked.

They each raised a hand.

"You're all hired," he said. "The ship will be available in a week or so. Brone there is my chief mate. He will notify you when you are needed. See him for job assignments and pay and such. Brone, meet me here around this time tomorrow and we'll talk specifics."

He looked up in the sky, and Victoria took the cue. She flew him around the bay before she set him down on the *Sea Sprite* beside her.

"Worked like a charm," he said. The men on the ship gawked at him.

They knew about Victoria's abilities but hadn't made the connection yet. She smiled. Adhira knew she was more than happy to make him the center of attention instead of herself.

"Now, we just have to wait for Asa and Neviah to introduce this world to black powder."

A couple of weeks later, they heard their first boom.

Chapter 6

Over a month after receiving their ship, Adhira stood on the deck, running his hand over the varnished railings, some type of redwood that shone in the morning sun. The cabin at the aft of the ship was painted white and was large enough to have two bedrooms, a sitting room, and a dining room. It was a beautiful ship. When the shadow gate was destroyed, he hoped to become a captain for real and sail the seas as an explorer.

"Good morning, Sky Captain," one of the sailors said as he rolled a barrel up the gangplank and past him. The men he'd hired were filling the cargo hold with several hundred barrels of the black powder Neviah and Asa had made.

"You never did tell me why they call you that," Asa said, leaning on the rail beside him. "Some of them look at you like they see a spotted unicorn that grants wishes."

"Weird, huh," Adhira said, thoroughly impressed Victoria hadn't spoiled his fun.

Asa was about to say something else but was cut off when they saw Captain Golt walking down the pier toward their ship with a handful of his guards in tow.

"Is the *Wooden Boar* to yer liking?" he asked, walking up the ramp to stand in front of them. They hadn't seen him since that first meeting, the merchant king preferring to communicate through messengers.

"I guess it's all right," Adhira said with a smile, making a mental note to change the name of the ship when they returned.

"And now, to complete my end of the bargain," he said, waving grandly over their shoulders. He was indicating three large ships that were arriving at the mouth of the bay. "I was able to secure ye nearly 1,200 soldiers."

"That's amazing," Adhira said. "You went above and beyond the agreement." The Indian was genuinely surprised. Hiring 200 more men than agreed upon wouldn't have been cheap.

As the ships drew closer, Asa asked, "Aren't those the king's flags they're flying?"

"Yes, they are," Golt said with a huge grin. He looked like a man who had just won a game of cards by a landslide.

"I don't understand," Asa said.

"First of all," Golt began, "the look on the king's face when I gave him the bracelet was the best experience of my life. He couldn't say a word for five minutes!" The captain laughed uproariously.

"And the soldiers?" Asa prompted.

"That was me doing what I do best."

"Which is?"

"Negotiating."

"For the bracelet?"

"No, I turned down the reward for the bracelet."

"What?" Asa asked in shock. Adhira wondered if his friend was truly intrigued or if he was hitting the conversational cues on purpose. Either way, it gave Golt the attention he desired for his story.

"I turned down the reward," Golt repeated. "And I did it in front of everyone, of course."

"I bet the king didn't like that."

"No, but it set me up perfectly for the hook. It was as easy as catching a blind sloth fish in a bucket. During the feast, the one he held in my honor, I let slip in conversation that I had a way to eliminate the fish people. Well, by the end of the night, the king was insisting I take his soldiers for the fight."

"Why would he do that?" Asa asked.

"He couldn't very well let me be known as the one who rid the kingdom of the fish people, now could he?"

"He would trust you with the lives of his soldiers? I thought you hated each other."

"Oh, we do, lad. But that is precisely why he gave me those men. If ye succeed in killing all the Finn Folk, it will be with the king's men. If ye fail and ye all die, it will be because I was wrong."

"He would bet the lives of 1,200 men just to see you proven wrong?" Asa asked, incredulous.

"That's right, I keep forgetting ye are new here," Golt said, patting Asa on the shoulder and laughing.

"Well," Adhira said, "the important part is we have the men we need."

"Wait a minute," Asa said. "So, we found the bracelet, the king provided the men, and you got the treasure we dredged up without so much as lifting a finger?"

"There's a reason they call me Captain Gold," he said with a laugh.

✯✯✯

"Shipwreck Bay is in sight, Captain," Brone announced as he approached Adhira two weeks out from port. There was a nervous energy permeating the ship. Adhira could almost taste the fear, and for good reason. No one in recent history had set foot on the island. Set foot and lived, that is.

Before, when they had been on the *Sea Sprite*, they'd tried sneaking to the island under the cover of fog. Now, they were coming in force, making a straight line toward the large sandy landmass in broad daylight. He glanced up at Victoria in the crow's nest. She was staring at the water, waiting for Adhira's cue.

Thanking Brone, Adhira moved into his position at the front of his ship. The other three ships traveled close behind theirs. He could always see fifteen seconds into the future, but he focused on it now. With an enemy that struck so fast and so decisively, they needed every second.

The ships plowed through the water, each heavy with cargo and men. He suddenly felt a sting on his neck. He quickly pulled out a poison barb made of bone as fire spread through his veins. His vision swam as projectiles leaped from the water, followed by grappling hooks.

"Now!" Adhira yelled up to Victoria. In an instant, the water began to crystallize around the ships. The ice hardened, leaving a channel the ships could freely move through.

The Finn Folk never sprang their trap. Victoria filled the sails with wind, bringing them to the island within minutes of the foiled ambush. After getting as close as they dared to the shallow waters, they dropped anchor. Victoria brought the ice in all around the ships, only leaving enough room for the ships to bob safely where they sat.

She then looked at Adhira, and he nodded. Picking him up, she lifted him through the air and out over the island. Of course, to everyone else, it looked as if he was flying. She sent him to the center of the island. Then she flew him in a slow circle that spiraled out from the center.

He noticed a weathered rock formation to the east. At the top of the rocks was a black smooth platform that looked untouched by the weather. The island itself was relatively flat, covered mostly in sand, with a few rock protrusions scattered about. Where was the shadow gate? His immediate mission was to locate the Finn Folk, though finding the gate was vital.

The spiral carried him out over the crystal-clear water, where an enormous barrier reef several feet below the surface curved out away from the island.

"That would be a good place to live if I was an underwater dweller," he said, though there was no sign of life. After a couple more passes, he was close enough to the reef for a better look.

Suddenly, he was free-falling through the air, hurtling toward the water. The wind grabbed him again, stopping his descent so abruptly that he felt like his insides were all squeezed tight. Then, he slipped again, but this time, the wind returned immediately and pulled him away from the underwater reef. What in the world was Victoria doing?

He continued to spiral out, though she pulled him away from the reef anytime he came near. His spiral passes were beginning to take him close to the ships. When he was on the far side of the island again, he caught a glimpse of something protruding from the smooth sand, which had continued underwater everywhere except where the reef was. It looked like a white rock the size of a large house and was quickly gone from view as he spiraled away. After one final pass, Victoria brought him to hover in the air next to her in the crow's nest.

"What was the deal with dropping me earlier?" he asked in real time so she would remember the conversation. More and more, he decided it was best for him to let others know he'd asked them something. Her cheeks reddened considerably at the comment.

"I'm sorry," she squeaked. "Anytime you approached that area of the water, it was like the wind no longer obeyed me. It felt like I was trying to hold onto a wet bar of soap."

"Well, we can scout that area with a ship later if we have to," he said.

"Did you find anything?" she asked.

"Maybe. Can you swing me back over there?" he asked, pointing. "Push me out a little further if you can." She nodded, and he flew away toward his target.

When hovering in the air above the large house-shaped rock again, he realized it looked more like an upside-down ship than a house. As he moved further out, Victoria moving him around randomly, he noticed more and more of the strange rocks. Then he saw one that wasn't quite as fossilized as the others.

It was a ship, a ship graveyard with hulls covered in some type of white sea coral. Then, he saw the fish people, hundreds of them. They had somehow converted the old vessels into underwater buildings. The water was shallow enough for him to see a weapon in the hands of each and every one of them, even the smallest ones. He wondered if he was looking at a war camp or homes.

He hoped they'd be facing fighters only. In battle, sometimes innocents were hurt, and he would do anything to avoid that. Maybe they really were pure evil, like the Shayatin and the Shedim. He'd learned that when the Finn Folk attacked South Bay, many women and children were killed. That couldn't be allowed to continue.

Then, it occurred to him. He'd always fought to protect himself and those around him. This was the first time he and his friends had set out looking for a fight. Even their attack on Ba'altose was in defense of the northern kingdoms.

A few poison quills shot from the water at him. He easily deflected them with his shield, which sprang up on his wrist at a thought. Victoria immediately brought him back to the crow's nest. This time, Asa and Neviah were there, too.

"Welcome back, Sky Captain," Asa said with a laugh, happy to know where Adhira had gotten the title.

"Thanks for getting me out of there," Adhira said, holding up his hand for a high five. He got the gentlest high five he'd ever received.

"What did you learn?" Neviah asked.

"Well, I didn't see the shadow gate," he said, earning three looks of disappointment. "I did see a suspect-looking black pedestal. It could have something to do with the gate."

They nodded. That would have to be enough for now.

"I found a Finn Folk fort, I think. I don't know if it's all of them, but they're the only ones I saw. It looks like they repurposed sunken ships and turned them into underwater buildings."

"How many are there?" Neviah asked.

"I saw a few hundred, but there were enough buildings to hold more than a thousand."

"Have you seen anything, Neviah?" Asa asked. Her ability to see the future was sporadic, even cryptic sometimes.

She was slow to answer. "I wasn't going to say anything." Uncertainty was completely out of character for her. She was always so confident all the time.

"Shyness doesn't suit you at all," Adhira said, turning to lounge casually in the air. The statement earned him a scowl.

"It doesn't even make much sense anyway. We win today." She took a deep breath. "And we lose." Everyone stared at her, weighing her words. "Hey, I told you it doesn't make sense."

"Maybe we win the fight, but don't find the gate," Asa said.

"Or maybe we destroy the gate, and the fish people get away," Adhira said.

"Should we withdraw and come back?" Asa asked. "Regroup?"

Neviah shook her head. "That shadow gate has to be destroyed. It would be nice if we could rid Tarsis of these Finn Folk, but I don't care if they all get away if it means we successfully blow up the gate."

"Well, let's get 'er done while the day is young," Adhira said.

Victoria set Adhira on the deck of the ship before climbing down with the others. Adhira had one of his sailors signal the other ships using flags, a chalkboard, and binoculars.

So they wouldn't have to risk using rowboats, Victoria made ice ramps from each of the ships to the island. It was awesome watching soldiers in full armor slide to the island on their shields. Adhira slid down on his shield, though it was awkward since it was attached to his wrist. When his feet were on the beach, he gathered the officers together to explain what he'd seen and where they should form up.

Adhira accompanied them to detect any enemy surprises as they moved into position. When everyone was assembled, one of the captains stood with Adhira and Neviah out in front of the shield wall the men were holding expertly in place. The shields had a structural design Adhira had never seen before. Each shield had an eye bolt and a hook on each side, allowing them all to interlock together. That way, if one man fell, the shield would remain in place long enough for another to take his place.

Adhira could see hundreds of fish people gathering beneath the waves, holding an assortment of wicked-looking bone weapons. He didn't see any armor or shields, however. The enemy was used to surprise attacks and having the terrain advantage. That was all about to change.

Neviah nodded to the captain, and he began to speak, "Too long we have tip-toed through this area of the sea. These creatures have attacked us. Killed us without reason. We have dreamed of the day when we could hit back, but the enemy always hides beneath the waves. Well, today, the sea will not save them."

The men cheered, beating armored fists against their breastplates in a steady rhythm. Adhira wondered if he could get them to beat the rhythm to "We Will Rock You."

As they'd rehearsed before leaving Tarsis, they began to march forward. They were an impenetrable wall as the second row of men brought up another row of shields they held above those in front.

The enemy was a bunched-up frothing mess beneath the waves, confused as to what was happening. Adhira nodded to Victoria, who stood back on the sandy beach, surrounded by a few soldiers for protection. Before the front line of soldiers could step into the water, the sea, for hundreds of feet, suddenly erupted into mist, then turned quickly to steam. The soldiers were ready for this and continued to march forward.

When the steam cleared, the entire landscape before them had been changed. The beach now extended all the way past the Finn Folk structures, the sea held back by an invisible barrier. It was as if they were inside a giant aquarium but with the water on the outside. Not for the first time, Adhira stared in awe at what Victoria could do. She likely could kill all the fish people at the snap of her fingers, but none of them could ask her to do so.

The fish people were in a heap on the ground, where they'd been dumped when all the water evaporated around them. The soldiers slowly advanced, filling the width of the gap.

As the fish people righted themselves, they tried fleeing into the walls of water around them but bounced off. The sea would no longer accept them. They moved like snakes, propelling themselves across the sand on their long tails. Adhira couldn't tell how they were communicating, but they all retreated and organized themselves somewhat, though it was obvious they were not used to any conventional formations.

One of the fish people stood out in front of the others, pointing with his jagged spear. A leader, perhaps. Adhira pulled out his book of prophecies and let it turn into a magnificent silver bow. From the high ground, it was easy to shoot over the soldiers' heads. He shot the arrow, which streaked silver across the battlefield, and took the leader in the chest. From beside him, Neviah and Asa began shooting arrows also.

The fish people rushed forward, leading with a volley of the poison darts from their tails before crashing against the wall of shields. The soldiers stabbed out from their protected position with long spears and continued to push deeper into the valley. Asa put away his bow and rushed to the back of the soldiers as they began to pass back their wounded.

Asa used his gift, the ability to mend any wound with a touch, to heal the soldiers, allowing them to immediately rejoin the battle. Could it be called a battle? The fish people were being slaughtered. They were inevitably pushed back among the structures.

The fight waged fiercely for several minutes as the soldiers had to break around the buildings and push inside of some. The fish people took a final stand when they were pushed against the water barrier. They threw themselves against the shield wall, but in moments, it was over.

Adhira walked down to where Asa was swiftly moving among the bodies, healing where he could. Adhira helped bring his friend's attention to the most critical, dragging a few soldiers out of the buildings where the fighting had been the most intense.

There was a sudden commotion in one of the sunken ships. Soldiers yelled in surprise, and then two men emerged, dragging one of the smaller fish people out.

They stumbled when the creature spit acid into the face of one of them. The man screamed as the acid sizzled and acrid smoke rose from the man's skin. Asa was there in a heartbeat and healed the soldier. After taking a few more shocked breaths, the man kicked the creature in the face.

Before the creature could actually spit the acid, Adhira ran forward and forced the fish creature's mouth shut.

"They can spit acid," he said. Both soldiers looked at each other, horrified.

He called for rope and cloth and soon had the creature bound with a spit guard fashioned around its mouth.

"What's your name," Neviah asked, walking up beside Adhira.

The creature didn't respond. Its eyes darted around as it pulled against its bond. It shied away from Neviah when she spoke.

"Can you speak?" she asked.

"I didn't see them speaking during the fight at all," Adhira said. "Maybe they can't."

"What should we do with it?" Neviah said. "Should we kill it?"

"It looks way smaller than the rest," Adhira said slowly. Killing in combat he understood but didn't like the idea of an execution. "It could be a child."

"Well, we can't let it go," one of the soldiers said.

"We don't have to make a decision right away," Neviah said, looking sideways at Adhira. What was that look for? "Let's bind it a little better for now and post a guard."

The soldiers nodded and dragged the fish person away, its tail leaving a trail through the sand. It didn't have any poison barbs. Had it used them all, or was it not old enough to have them? What were they going to do with it?

Chapter 7

"Does any of this look familiar?" Asa asked, running a hand over the smooth stone, if it was stone. They stood upon the dais at the center of the island.

"The one I fell through didn't have a keyhole," Neviah said. "Not that I saw anyway. But the color is right, and it looks like the same type of material."

"But where is the gate?" Asa asked.

"We don't need the gate," Adhira said. "We can just blow this up. They can't use the key if there's no lock." The others slowly nodded.

"Can I get a lift?" he asked Victoria.

She flew him straight to their ship, which had the explosives. The three ships carrying the king's men remained nearby, all the soldiers having boarded. Adhira picked up one of the smaller barrels and waived back to Victoria, who hoisted him back. He set the barrel beside the keyhole and backed up to where the others stood several yards away.

"Go ahead," he said to Victoria.

She made the tiniest of flames on the tip of her finger and sent it forward to light the short fuse. The explosion was loud and sent a satisfactory fireball into the air. When the smoke cleared, the dais was blackened with soot but completely unharmed.

"It doesn't work," he said in real time. "There wasn't even a scratch on it."

"We have a ship full of this stuff," Asa said. "Do you think more will help?"

Adhira shook his head. "I already tried the Sword of Re'u on it," he said. "And that is supposed to be able to cut through anything."

"Do you think we can blow the ground out from under it?" Asa asked, indicating the weathered rock the dais was sitting on.

The Road to War

"I don't think burying it under a bunch of sand will slow Tanas down much," Neviah said. "Victoria, can you rip it from the ground with your gift?"

Victoria stared at it for a moment, lifting her hand like she did sometimes. Shaking her head, she lowered her hand and said, "I can't get a grip on it. Any energy I use slips around it."

At further requests from Asa and Neviah, she also used lighting, fire, and even water to try to destroy it. It remained unmoved and looked pristine again after the pressure washing.

"Any more ideas?" Neviah asked.

"Several," Asa said. "Where did Victoria almost drop you?"

Adhira pointed.

"We should take the ships over," Asa said. "I don't know what that area is doing to Victoria's abilities, but we don't want to try flying out there like you did."

"What about the fish creature?" Neviah asked, almost absently. She seemed distracted by something unseen. "I don't trust its guards not to kill it while we're gone."

Adhira sighed in agreement. Already, many of the men had lost their feeling of awe around him. Some had even looked at him with open disdain. The truth was, he didn't even completely understand why he'd spared the thing's life. Either way, it was his responsibility now.

"I'll stay behind and guard it," he said reluctantly.

The other two walked away, but Neviah hesitated. Walking slowly toward Adhira, she wrapped her arms around his shoulders and hugged him tight. She had always been a hugger, but never like this.

"Never give up," she whispered in his ear. "Promise me."

"Neviah, what…" he was cut off when he felt her trembling. He wrapped his arms around her. "I promise, okay. What's wrong?"

"There will be a moment, Adhira. *The* moment. You will have to let go. Choose to let go." She pulled away and quickly turned. Over her shoulder, she said, "I'll see you when I get back." She jogged to catch up to the others. What was that all about?

Adhira watched as they walked to the water's edge, and Victoria lifted them all up and flew them toward their ship. It looked just as cool as he'd expected. After the remaining few soldiers took a rowboat back to their waiting vessel, three Tarsis ships followed the *Wild Boar* as his friends navigated around the island to where the giant reef was.

The creature he guarded sat on the ground beside him, blindfolded, gagged, and tied up with a sack tied around the tail in case the poison barbs grew back. It looked rather pitiful.

"Are you really evil, or are you something else?" he asked, more to himself. Man had the capacity for great evil and great good. Was the fish creature any different?

As his friends approached the area with the reef, he watched them with a pocket telescope. Suddenly, the wind went out of the sails, though he could see Victoria was pointing at them. The reef, or something there, really was affecting her ability somehow.

Oars were extended on their ship, and they slowly made their way around the area with the reef.

Asa held up a chalkboard that said, "Reef is gate."

So much for their plan to blow up the gate. If Victoria couldn't use her gift to move the water out of the way, the explosives were useless. They might as well stack everything they'd made against the dais with the keyhole. It might not do anything, but at least that way, they'd get to see a really big explosion.

Suddenly, there was a ground-shaking thud behind him. He turned to see the Imprisoned One straightening from where he'd landed.

The creature's name was Siarl, and he'd been imprisoned at the center of Alya before it was destroyed by dragons months before. Adhira's mentor, Mordeth, had been one of the best swordsmen in the world before Siarl killed him in a duel.

Adhira spun and searched the sky. A couple of Shedim could be seen ducking away among the clouds. Hurtling through the sky toward the ground was the Imprisoned One.

Adhira quickly raised the Sword of Re'u, letting the sword turn into a bow before sending several arrows toward Siarl as he fell.

With lightning-fast reflexes, the creature used his own blade of power to knock the arrows from the air. How could anyone be that fast?

Despite Adhira's best efforts, the Imprisoned One reached the ground unscathed. He landed with a spray of sand. A fall from that height would have turned a normal person into a pancake. Siarl straightened to his full height, well over six feet tall. His body was that of a gray-furred humanoid, and his face looked distinctly canine, like a dog with a short snout but a mouth that was very human.

"A worthy adversary," Siarl said, though there was a strong hint of question in his voice. He raised his sword before him with a slight bow before moving toward Adhira, who found it odd that such an evil creature would show any semblance of respect.

Adhira fought the sudden flood of adrenaline that urged him to rush at his opponent. This was the one who killed Mordeth, his teacher, his friend. He wanted to strike at his foe but needed to remember his training. Every move he made needed to be on purpose. A swordsman needed to practice to the point where the blade flowed by instinct and muscle memory. This allowed the brain the freedom to plan. Adhira glided sideways to the more compact sand to give him slightly better footing than his opponent for first contact.

Siarl led with a thrust that was so fast that Adhira barely got his shield up to deflect it. He struck out with the Sword of Re'u and hit nothing. Siarl brought down his own blade, slicing open Adhira's bicep.

Adhira went through the same motions but feigned a strike instead.

When Siarl struck down at his bicep, Adhira pulled his arm barely out of reach and thrust forward as fast as he could. There was a shower of sparks as the two blades met for the first time.

Siarl parried Adhira's blow and stabbed him through the shoulder. Adhira ignored the pain and stabbed at his opponent's legs but was not nearly quick enough.

Adhira went through the entire encounter for real but blocked the stab to his shoulder.

The exchange continued, and despite being able to see the future, Adhira was unable to land a single blow. Every sword strike Siarl made was like a viper. It was like a dozen vipers. Each strike was met with a follow-up, never slowing and always adapting to anything Adhira did. Every sword stroke Adhira blocked jarred him with its power.

Adhira's breaths were coming in great gulps. He was slowing. Finally, a blow came that there was no way for him to avoid. Moving away, he managed to take the slash as little more than a scratch, but the alarm bells were sounding in his mind. His opponent was too fast!

To catch his breath, he let the Forest Shield grow until it covered him completely, making a large half-circle that touched the ground all around. Suddenly, hands showed up around the bottom edge as Siarl lifted the edge of the shield and twisted. Adhira's arm snapped, breaking below the elbow.

There was no way to hide or rest. He needed to think, but keeping the enemy blade away from him was taking all of his concentration. Taking another cut, this one deeper, across his shield arm, he became aware of the blood dotting the sand around him, his blood. The enemy was so fast that the shield could barely expand in time with Adhira's thoughts.

Blood continued dripping to the sand, growing with each cut he received. Siarl wasn't even breathing hard. If his friends came, they might be able to slay this creature together. If Victoria saw what was happening, she could fry Siarl with a lightning bolt. Using his gift, he spared a glance for the ships.

Any hope of salvation from his friends was lost. There was a swarm of Shedim attacking all three ships. Silver arrows dropped many, but there were no lightning bolts or other elemental attacks. They needed to get away from the shadow gate so Victoria could use her abilities again.

Adhira stopped trying to strike back at his opponent but instead focused on lasting as long as possible. His muscles were burning from exertion, screaming at him to take a break. A cut to his leg caused him to stumble backward. It had been the only choice that didn't end with a more serious wound. Siarl's blade sliced across his back several times before Adhira could turn to block again. Siarl should have been able to end it there. The zigzagged cuts across his back burned fiercely, but they could have been death blows. Siarl was trying to capture him alive!

Another exchange and Adhira received several more cuts to his chest and arms. His vision swam, earning him a cut to the side of his neck. It felt like his limbs were moving in slow motion while Siarl was as fast as ever. Another cut to his upper thigh and one on his shin caused him to stumble forward to land on his knees. Adhira tried to stand, but a sudden wave of dizziness forced him back to his knees. His entire body hurt from the strain and from the myriad cuts. Siarl paused with his blade at Adhira's throat.

"You must be one of the four Dragon Slayers," Siarl said. He looked out over the water to where the battle was continuing on the ships. "Iblis wants you alive, I believe." He looked over to the captive fish creature, who'd somehow slipped out of his bonds during the duel. "Tie him," Siarl said, and the Finn Folk moved to do as told. So they *could* understand speech.

Siarl picked up the book of prophecies. Adhira didn't remember dropping it.

"Be sure to bind his arms behind him at the forearms so he cannot summon his shield."

His cuts protested at the rough bindings, but the pain was almost dim as he fought to remain conscious.

Siarl stood to the side where Adhira could barely see him. He bore no marks or signs at all that he'd just been in a life-or-death struggle. He stood with arms crossed as he watched the fighting going on at sea.

Somehow, the ships had come together, forming a tight circle. Arrows flew from many bows, though a lot of the fighting was on the decks of the ships. After a moment, he found his friends. They were on their ship, Neviah holding off the Shedim trying to come at them from above while Asa and Victoria cut down any bold enough to land near them. The humans were winning.

Adhira smiled as the Shedim broke combat, some falling to arrows as they tried to fly away. The last clang of steel on steel echoed across the water, and then all was quiet. The sail of his friends' ship was in tatters. The other ships looked a little battered but remained seaworthy.

"You may have beat me," Adhira said. His voice sounded foreign, his words slightly slurred. "But my friends are coming."

"Are they better at dueling than you are?" Siarl asked. His eyes looked eager. "Will they honor the code?"

Adhira didn't know what the Imprisoned One was talking about. He didn't think he could summon the strength to speak again. Siarl looked thoughtful for a moment.

"No, they won't, will they? They will attack me all together." He sighed. "They will likely deploy their archers," he said, almost spitting the last word.

Across the water, everyone was abandoning the ship with the gunpowder. A rope was tied to it and to one of the other ships so they could haul it behind. Adhira desperately needed someone to look his way. Even without binoculars they should be able to see something was wrong.

The ships began to sail away from the reef, one towing the dilapidated ship. The only one left aboard that Adhira could see was Neviah. She stood at the back, steering the vessel. Adhira would have smiled if he could. His friends were coming. Then he saw with his gift what was coming and screamed as loud as he could manage. It would do no good, even if his friends could hear him.

Siarl had mounted the pedestal and removed a key from around his neck. Quickly, he inserted it in the keyhole and turned it. The water where his friends were turned black as the gate opened beneath the sea. Water began to rush toward it, swirling as if it were a giant drain.

Two of the ships quickly moved away from the whirlpool, but the other two weren't making any progress. Neviah's ship was dead in the water. The towing ship's sails were full of wind, but it wasn't enough to break free from the force of the water rushing away from them. There was some kind of commotion on the seaworthy vessel. He thought he saw Victoria and Asa standing between a group of soldiers and the rope tied to Neviah's ship.

The soldiers wanted to cut Neviah's ship free! As they argued, both ships began to drift backward. The gate was swallowing all the water around them. It wouldn't be long before they were at the point of no return.

The soldier ship suddenly lurched forward. Neviah stood at the front of her vessel, sword in hand and the severed rope before her. The soldiers' ship slowly pulled away from the whirlpool, but Neviah's ship was soon caught in the spiral as the water rushed down toward the gate.

Before the ship sank from sight, Adhira saw Neviah turn toward him and wave before rushing below deck.

Adhira was forced to watch the scene over again in real time. The ship plummeted into the Abyss.

"Not her," he whispered, closing his eyes. His eyes snapped back open as a roar like nothing he'd ever heard before thundered from the shadow gate.

Chapter 8

The roar sounded like that of a lion, only louder than an avalanche. A claw like a bear's, but ten times larger than a ship, reached through the shadow gate, crashing into the ocean. The wave it generated nearly capsized the ship carrying Asa and Victoria, spinning it around like a toy. The other ships fled as fast as the wind would take them.

A second claw reached forth and slammed into the ocean on the other side of the ship carrying his friends. This time, the ship capsized, turned over and over by the waves before sinking from view.

"No!" Had they gotten far enough away from the shadow gate? Maybe they were still alive. Adhira pulled against his bonds and tried to stand, but he felt so weak, drenched in his own blood. What was going on? It had all happened so fast. How had they failed?

A head like a lion, though it was black as ink, emerged from the shadow gate. It pulled the rest of its feline bulk from the Abyss, crushing debris from his friends' ship. It walked through the ocean as if strolling through a puddle. It was a behemoth, large enough to crush cities into nothing. And the only ones who could do anything about it were now gone.

Adhira felt blackness creeping in at the edge of his vision. Looking over, he watched Siarl turn the key back before stepping down off the dais, though he left the key where it was. The Imprisoned One walked over to stand before Adhira, who glared as best he could as if through a fog.

"Chemosh is free," Siarl said. "I don't have time to escort you to Iblis, but we can't have you getting away." Siarl spoke too mater-of-fact like. "Prepare the prisoner for transport, take his vision, and then bind his wounds so he doesn't die." He said more, but Adhira didn't catch it all. Siarl walked away, and Adhira thought he could hear heavy footfalls landing behind him.

The young Finn Folk grabbed Adhira's face in his hands. He saw what was coming but was helpless to do anything about it.

"I saved you!" Adhira yelled, and though he knew it was hopeless, he tried to struggle. The last thing he saw was the face of the sea creature spitting acid into his eyes.

Everything turned black as he screamed, trying to thrash around, but his body was too weak. He fell on his side as the searing pain continued. He didn't know how long he screamed but grew hoarse by the time someone started wrapping bandages around his wounds. All he wanted was for them to let him die or at least pass out, but the release never came.

Rough hands lifted him from the ground and placed him on a stretcher. They carried him downhill before the stretcher leveled out, continuing for several minutes. At length, he was let down where he could feel the soft bobbing only a rowboat could produce. He thought about throwing himself into the water, but his arms were still tied behind his back, and his legs wouldn't obey him. Oars could be heard dipping into the water as large waves pushed the boat high into the air before crashing back down. There was no talking, no sound from a person, not even a cough.

The boat bobbed on the waves for some time before it bumped into something solid. The rocking stopped as the rowboat was hoisted into the air. After being carried down some stairs, he was dumped onto what felt like a bed. There was a scraping sound followed by a click, the sound of a cage being shut. After the footfalls faded, he was left in silence. Pain and darkness. He couldn't stop the scenes of his friends dying as they played over and over in his mind. He would never see again, and the worst moment of his life was seared into his mind.

The pain of the cuts began to fade, growing numb, but the burning from the acid was nearly as intense as it had initially felt. Dizziness hinted that he might pass out, but it didn't actually happen. He just wanted it all to be over, but somehow, he lingered still.

Adhira could still see into the future, though "see" was likely not the right word anymore. Sounds and smells came to his attention before they happened. It was torture, only reinforcing the fact that he would remain conscious for another fifteen seconds. He couldn't even cry because of his ruined eyes, though he felt too emotionally numb for tears anyway.

Somehow, after what seemed like forever, he fell asleep.

The Road to War

✦✦✦

He was startled awake at the sound of something dropping to the cell floor and the door slamming shut, then footsteps moving away. Of course, with his gift, this all happened to him twice, costing him fifteen seconds of precious sleep. The burning in his eyes immediately returned, only slightly less painful than the day before. Or had it only been a few hours, minutes even?

Nearly every inch of him throbbed. The slightest movements made his skin feel stretched thin and prickly. Scabs crisscrossed his body all over.

Setting his jaw against the pain, he sat up. Blood could be felt leaking from the wounds. The cuts and bruises protested his movements, but though they were many, none were particularly bad on their own. Though his sight was gone, his nose told him there was food in the cage with him.

He thought about lying back down, even with his stomach growling audibly. It's not the way he would choose to go, but if he didn't eat, he could end this.

"Promise me," Neviah's voice echoed in his head. Had she known she would die? He'd promised to keep fighting. Moving slowly so as not to aggravate his wounds unnecessarily, he knelt on the floor.

With his hands trapped behind his back, he was forced to hunt along the ground with his chin until he bumped into the tray of food, getting food all over his face. It tasted like some type of vegetable stew. There was also a helping of beans and an apple. Fishing around with his chin more, he knocked over a mug of water.

Using his gift, he was able to find his food without making a mess and ate it as best he could. Grabbing the mug with his teeth, he avoided spilling any as he awkwardly gulped at it. When he was done eating, he stood.

Pacing his cell, he was able to get the general layout. His head brushed the ceiling, and he could take three small steps in each direction. Turning his back to the bars, he felt around until he found a jagged piece of metal. With difficulty, he found an angle that allowed him to begin sawing at his bindings.

"What are you doing?" a deep voice said from outside the bars. A key rattled in the lock, and the door was opened. Rough hands grabbed him.

After Adhira stood from his meal in real time, he sat down on his cot and turned his head toward where the voice had come from. Asa wasn't around to think of a way out of this situation, so it was left to him. He needed to get information.

"What is your name, sailor?"

There was a quick creak. Did the man jump?

"Uh, Harmon, but I am no sailor."

"You are a soldier, then." There was no response.

He started over.

"Harmon, how long have you been a soldier?"

A chair scraped across the wooden floor.

"How did you know my name?"

"You haven't undergone the change yet," Adhira said, hoping the soldier knew what Tanas was doing.

There was a process many of Tanas' soldiers had undergone which changed them into something else. Neviah had seen one of the Shayatin transforming ordinary soldiers into things that looked more Shayatin than human. Afterward the soldiers seemed to lose any semblance of what they had been before. They had become the Soulless.

"I will never give up my soul," the man said heatedly.

Adhira ran up against his fifteen seconds and decided how he wanted to start the actual conversation.

"I can sense you still have your soul, Harmon. This is good." The chair scraped again, this time crashing to the floor as it fell over. "The time is rapidly approaching when Tanas will require all to undergo the change."

"How do you know these things?" Harmon asked, breathless.

"It is one of the reasons for my capture," Adhira said. "Tanas doesn't want the world to know what I know." The chair scraped as it was brought closer to the cage.

"Please, tell me of these things," Harmon said eagerly.

Adhira started his story with how his friends and he defeated Ba'altose and his army of undead. Tanas was really the king of the dragons, Iblis, and had united many of the northern kingdoms under the guise of fighting Ba'altose. Most saw Tanas as a savior after Ba'altose's defeat, but many were trapped in an alliance they didn't know a way out of.

In the name of unity, Tanas was conquering the remaining kingdoms in the north. Any who did not join him willingly were fed to a shadow gate, allowing Shayatin to take their place.

Now, the monster from the Abyss, Chemosh, had been loosed

upon the world. When Tanas was done conquering, he planned to wipe out mankind completely. He was a monster himself and would hold dominion over a world full of monsters.

"What can be done?" the soldier asked, nearly pleading. Then, in a whisper, "I could set you free."

"No," Adhira said as he began to see something far bigger than escape coming to life right in front of him. "There is a trade route that links the southern kingdoms and the northern kingdoms."

"The Via Maris," the soldier said. "What about it?"

"At the southern end of the route is a place called Esdraelon. That is where the last stand for mankind will happen. You have seen enough with your own eyes to know something very wrong is happening."

"I have," the man said quietly.

"For every person who blindly follows Iblis, there is one like you who is wise enough to question what he sees."

"If I free you, you can explain these things to others."

Adhira shook his head. "If you free me, we will both likely be killed. I need you to tell others the truth as I have told you. But be wary. Even those you would see as friends could already be beyond reach."

"What is your name?" the soldier asked.

Adhira almost said his real name, but after hesitating a moment, he said, "I am called Sky." He didn't know why it mattered, but he didn't feel like the same person he was the day before. Or was it two? He'd enjoyed being called Sky Captain, but he couldn't be a captain without a ship.

Thinking of the lost ship caused his thoughts to circle back to his friends. He didn't want to talk anymore. Laying down slowly on his cot, he faced away from the soldier.

Sleep brought troubling dreams, but nothing he remembered when he woke. He heard a tray set down on the floor again, this time much gentler. He sat up before kneeling on the floor to eat as he'd done before. There seemed to be more food. Once he was seated back on his bed, he spoke.

"Hello, Harmon. Thank you for the meal."

"Sky, this is my friend Tryg. Can you tell him the story you told me?"

Adhira started over.

"Hello, Harmon, and hello, Tryg," Adhira said.

"You told him my name," another voice, Tryg, said angrily.

"No, I didn't," Harmon said. "Like I told you, Sky knows things."

Using his gift, Adhira learned about the man and used the information in the real conversation.

"You are here because of your brother, Tage. He underwent the change, becoming more Shayatin than human. I am sorry, but your brother, your real brother, is dead."

"You lie!" Tryg said, heat in his voice, though he had the presence of mind to keep his voice down. "My brother is still in there somewhere."

"When he speaks to you, it is as if he doesn't know you. It is almost as if he hates you. Hates all who have not undergone the change. Your brother's spirit is no longer with that body. It has been replaced by that of a Shayatin. He is one of the Soulless now."

"There has to be something I can do," Tryg all but begged.

"There is plenty you can do for your other three brothers and for the brothers of others."

Then, Adhira told them the story he'd told Harmon. This time, he slowed at the process where the Shayatin turned the humans into monsters. He gave the men as much detail as he remembered from Neviah's account. She was the only one who'd seen it firsthand.

"You were right, Harmon," Tryg said when Adhira was done speaking.

"We can desert," Harmon said. "We can travel south to Esdraelon and join with the people there."

"Not until I've talked to my brothers and gathered the rest of my family," Tryg said.

"Of course," Harmon said. "There are others who've been questioning our orders. We should tell them, too."

"We can free you when we make port," Tryg said.

"No," Adhira said. "I will free myself when the time is right, but I want to make sure it can't be linked to you two in any way. Now, if you don't mind, tell me what is happening in the world. I have been at sea for several months."

The soldiers were not well informed, but from rumors and their orders, Adhira was able to piece together the basics of what was happening. Tanas had conquered nearly all of the northern kingdoms. Most had submitted, but some, like Moriah, had been utterly destroyed. Dragons were no longer present during the fighting, not since Moriah.

Adhira didn't know how many dragons were left, but he and his friends had killed about a dozen of them. Maybe they didn't want to risk any more of their kind, fearing a silver arrow could come from anywhere.

The two soldiers seemed almost excited. They had been shown a path and were convinced and committed. Adhira couldn't help but wonder why he bothered. These men might be free from Tanas' schemes, and they might reach many more, even hundreds, but in the end, when the final battles came, there was no one left who could kill a dragon. Adhira was the last wielder of the Sword of Re'u, and he was blind. And Siarl had taken his sword.

Chapter 9

In his permanent state of night, Adhira didn't have much concept of the passage of time. He tried to mark the passage with meals, assuming two meals a day, which felt right. He soon lost track and decided it didn't matter. It felt like he was stuck in purgatory; the only breaks he got were when Harmon was on shift, though that was considered the easiest job, so the rotation would have him at other duties for a day or so. Sometimes, Adhira wouldn't hear from him for several days.

After the ship had been unusually still in the water for the better part of a day, his cage door creaked open one morning; at least, he assumed it was morning. It smelled like morning. But instead of giving him food, as he'd grown accustomed to, someone entered his cell. His gift told him there were actually two someones, men in hardened leather armor. They each carried a short sword on one hip and a thin metal-covered club on the other. These weren't soldiers but professional jailors.

Without a word, they grabbed him, one on each arm, and yanked him roughly from his cage. Thankfully, his cuts had long since healed. After stumbling a moment, he walked on his own, his stiff legs thankful for the chance to be used again. Loud thuds, scraping, and wood banging on wood could be heard amidst the commotion of feet and conversations.

One of the guards moved ahead of him and after prodding from the other, Adhira climbed a steep set of stairs to the main deck, which was difficult with his arms bound behind his back. The feeling of the sun on his skin felt refreshing, the warm breeze giving him his first taste of fresh air in what seemed like months.

Adhira couldn't pause to enjoy it, however. The guards pushed him along. One of them kicked him forward, telling him to move faster, though he was already moving as fast as he could. His gift was the only reason he didn't stumble when he moved down the gangplank to the dock. There they paused for a moment, one of them yanking hard on his shirt collar, nearly choking him.

"Your orders," a man said sternly, "are to keep this one alive and secure at all costs. He is the most dangerous prisoner you will ever carry."

"But I was told he's blind," one of the guards said from behind Adhira.

"He is. Don't underestimate him. And under no circumstances are you to remove the bindings from his arms. I repeat." Dirt crunched as the man stepped closer. "Do not untie his arms. Do not let him untie or cut them. If you do, if he doesn't kill you, you will be executed. This came from Siarl himself. And deliver this package with the prisoner. Don't open it."

The men acknowledged with a quick "Yes, sir" before pushing Adhira along.

"Who is this guy?" one of them said, voice raspy like someone who'd smoked his whole life.

"They wouldn't say, but they executed all the other prisoners we were guarding," this guard's voice sounded very young, like someone not quite out of their teens yet.

"What?" raspy voice said. "We were transporting ten men."

"They said there was no room for them here, and they wanted all our attention on this one."

"Six guards for one man? Who is this guy?" he repeated.

Adhira walked where he was guided. A moment of sorrow came over him for the murdered prisoners, but there seemed to be a lot of that going on in the world. Hopefully, they were bad guys. He felt the uneven cobblestone beneath his bare feet and heard horses and carriages travel past.

"Where are we?" Adhira asked.

"Prisoners don't talk," the young guard said, striking him in the back with the metal studded club. Adhira was sure it cracked a rib.

They were in a port city. He wished he knew where but supposed it didn't matter. Even if he escaped, where would he go? There was no mission, no destination for him. What could a blind man do to help save the world from what was coming? They'd failed to stop the beast from being released from the Abyss. The world was doomed.

The cobblestone streets soon gave way to hardpacked gravel that dug into the bottom of his bootless feet. Adhira was pulled roughly to a stop. He could smell hay and manure and could hear horses shuffling nearby.

"Get in," Young Voice said. Of course, Adhira had no clue which way to move, which would have earned him a strike from the club, but using his gift, he found a cart with a cage upon it. He felt the cudgel across his back anyway, which he realized was going to happen no matter how fast he moved. It sent him stumbling into a metal bar, which he hit heavily on his shoulder. After fumbling with a step leading into the cart, not being able to use his hands, he fell face-first into straw.

The cage door slammed shut. His guards could be heard talking to a group of men, but Adhira wasn't close enough to hear anything of importance. In a few minutes, the cart he was on began moving. Hoofbeats could be heard following.

"What's your story?" one of the horsemen asked. This voice was different from the two who'd brought him to the cage. This man spoke with the confidence that was borne of authority.

"I was fishing without a license," Adhira said.

The man laughed. "Tell me," the officer said, "how is it a blind man is reported to be the most dangerous prisoner I've ever transported? They made it sound like I was guarding a starved Se'irim."

Adhira shrugged. He didn't want to get to know this guy. Now that he had it set in his mind to escape somehow, he didn't know if he'd have to kill these men to do so. How would he even escape when he couldn't see?

"I guess," the man continued, "the real question is, who did you kill?"

"It's who I didn't kill," Adhira said.

"Ah," the man said. "I heard it was Siarl himself who captured you. You should count yourself lucky."

Adhira turned his face up in the direction the voice was coming from so the man could see his bandaged eyes. "I don't," he said with a grimace.

"Well, that turned dark really fast," the man said with another laugh. He didn't seem like the type who was affected by much. A horse could be heard galloping up from behind.

"Good afternoon, sir," the newcomer said as he slowed his horse behind the cart.

"Good afternoon," the officer said. "What is this about?"

"I wanted to make sure you were aware there would be two, um, augmented soldiers waiting for you at the gate. They will be accompanying you to Chaldea." There was a collective groan from the other guards.

The officer cursed. "I should have known this would happen."

"Is there a problem, sir?"

"No. It's just that the soldiers who have been transformed kind of creep the rest of us out. Don't get me wrong, they are handy to have in a fight, but they aren't any good at campfire stories."

"Sir?"

The Road to War

"Nothing. Thanks for letting me know. You are dismissed."

When the horse galloped away, another guard said, "We aren't really going to spend two months on the road with a couple of them, are we?"

"It doesn't look like we have much choice," the officer said. Adhira smiled. It looked like something was finally affecting the officer's mood.

The cart moved between stone and dirt several times as they slowly moved through the city. Grilled fish and woodsmoke permeated the air, the salty breeze from the ocean diminishing the further they traveled. A few people threw general curses Adhira's way, but most people seemed to ignore him and his entourage. He heard only bits of conversation, mundane things about fashion and the weather. Then, as if someone had flipped a switch, quiet descended. There were no more civilians walking about, or if there were, they were being quiet.

The cart slowed, and at least two horses could be heard approaching from the side. The faint smell of sulfur came to him from that direction.

"You two," the officer said to the newcomers. "Take positions at the front of the column. We will form up once we are outside the city."

"We will stay where we can see the prisoner," came an unnaturally deep voice.

"What was that, soldier?" There was heat in the officer's voice for the first time. "I know I did not just hear you disobey an order."

Adhira heard a sound, a low rumbling that sounded almost like a growl. There was silence, except for the slow clap of hooves on the cobblestone. The trip just got interesting. Without another word, the horses of the two Soulless moved ahead of the cart.

"And what are you smiling at?" the officer asked, jovial again but with an underlying strain that wasn't there before.

"I was just thinking," Adhira said, "you would have enjoyed being on my side of the war. Then you would get to kill the Soulless."

One of the soldiers beat on the cage with his small cudgel. "That will be enough out of the prisoner!" That sounded like the guy who'd cracked his rib earlier. Well, he didn't actually do it. So, it was the one who'd not hit him earlier. Adhira thought about it for a moment. Was there a correct tense for something that happened but at the same time didn't happen? Asa would know.

"That's enough, Roan," the officer said. "The man has fallen on hard times recently and is likely a couple of months away from being hanged."

"Yes, sir," Roan said. To Adhira, he said, "You're lucky Daddy's here to save you." His horse moved away, and the rest of the trip out of the city was devoid of conversation.

Soon, the sharp clap of horses' hooves on stone and gravel was permanently replaced by the dull thud of hard-packed dirt. The weather was warm with a gentle breeze stirring his hair. He usually kept it short, but it was starting to feel unruly. It prickled his skin on his shoulders. When was the last time he had anything resembling a bath? All he could smell anymore was sweat.

He stuck his feet out of the bars so they could dangle freely. They'd let him keep his socks, but his boots were a distant memory. It looked like he wouldn't do much walking anyway.

"You didn't react," the officer said, coming to ride beside the cage. "When I mentioned you'd be hanged soon."

"Do you really think death would be worse than this?" Adhira asked. They rode in silence for a mile or so.

"Siarl," the officer said. "I've seen him fight. He's a whirlwind. Seen him duel nearly a dozen times, always before a battle. No fight has lasted more than one swing."

Adhira just grunted in response.

"So, you were a soldier, then?" the officer asked.

"Something like that," Adhira said.

"You mentioned 'your side of the war.' Which war are you referring to? King Tanas has the Coalition campaigning all across the north."

"You see them as separate," Adhira said. "But I assure you, there is only one war. It's between mankind and monsters. You are fighting for the wrong side."

"I took an arrow to the knee," the officer said. "I am no longer fighting for anyone."

"That we have in common," Adhira said.

"You are wrong, though."

"Oh?" Adhira said.

"King Tanas is a savior to mankind. He seeks only to unite the kingdoms so that what happened with Ba'altose in the north cannot happen again. Mankind must stand united."

"Oh," Adhira said. "He is killing people to *save* them. I think I see where I was confused."

"Entire kingdoms were wiped out by the army of the undead. Every man, woman, and child slaughtered. We fight now to prevent that from ever happening again."

"I heard," Adhira said, "that there were cities in Moriah that bowed to Tanas. Then, they were burned to the ground, and the people were thrown through one of his shadow gates."

The Road to War

"I was not part of that campaign," the officer said. "I heard the fighting there was the most brutal of all the fronts."

"Is that so?" Adhira asked.

"They say the battles there are what keeps the dragons away from the fighting now."

"What do dragons have to fear from man?" Adhira asked, though he knew. "I thought they were invincible."

Another guard rode up on Adhira's other side. "Ah, the four Dragon Slayers," the man said.

"They apparently have arrows that can kill a dragon," the officer said.

"And so, the dragons hide while men and monsters kill each other," Adhira said.

"I don't blame them," the guard said. "They say one of the Dragon Slayers can summon lightning to fight for him."

"The Shedim were nearly all destroyed in the final battle at the capital of Moriah, Uru, I think it's called," the officer said.

Adhira remembered the battle for Moriah vividly. Victoria had used her gift to hold up Alya, the Chayyoth homeland, which was nearly the size of a small moon. When the pieces of Alya were flung away from the city, killing the Shedim was merely a happy accident.

"When they told me I was guarding the most dangerous prisoner in the world," the officer said slowly, "I thought that maybe we had captured one of the Dragon Slayers."

"And what do you think now?" Adhira asked. The answer was a while in coming. Adhira turned his face that way in case the man was looking at him.

"I think if someone caught one of them alive, they would have sent him on the back of a Shedim. You could travel to where we are going in weeks instead of months."

Adhira had wondered at that himself. Maybe the enemy didn't know all the Chayyoth had fled across the ocean. A Chayya could easily outfly a Shedim. Whatever the reason, it helped Adhira now. It was important they didn't think he was at all formidable if he was ever going to have an opening to escape.

The conversation died as one of the Soulless dropped back near Adhira's cage. The smell of sulfur was very distinct. Something would have to be done about the two Soulless soldiers. They were very loyal watchdogs for Tanas and wouldn't allow him an opening, he was sure. But what could he do from his cage to kill two souped-up soldiers?

Weeks later, he thought he had an opportunity.

Chapter 10

"Then, we go that way," the Soulless said in his rumbling voice.

"That's not our route," one of the guards said. His feet scraped across the dirt, shifting his feet nervously, most likely. "We filed our trip with the Travel Master, and the scouts know to look out for us on the trade road. If we go off course, we could miss our resupply."

"What's the problem?" the officer asked, walking up. Their conversation was at the edge of Adhira's hearing, but he could make out everything they said. Not for the first time, he wondered if his hearing was getting better.

"Sir, Leon wants us to go off chart," the guard said. "He wants to go across Daggers Pass, no less."

"It is ten days faster than our current route," the Soulless said.

"Let me see the map," the officer said.

"The passes through the mountains there are dangerous, sir," the guard said. Paper could be heard rustling. There was silence for a minute.

"I was given travel vouchers for this trip. We could resupply at the fort instead," the officer said. "And I wouldn't mind being ten days closer to a nice comfortable bed, either. Your concerns are noted, Rind, but I agree with Leon."

"Yes, sir," the guard said, though his voice was tight. "I will pass the word to our point men." He walked away to where other men could be heard laughing and talking.

"Continue your watch," the officer said to the Soulless. He also walked away. Adhira thought he heard the telltale scraping of his limp.

Silence settled in the immediate area. That was common when the Soulless were on watch, which was often. Adhira imagined Leon just standing there watching him. He needed to use the chamber pot but didn't want to do it with the Soulless on guard. It was bad enough trying to use the bathroom with his arms bound tightly behind his back.

"So, what are you exactly?" Adhira asked. There was no response.

He used his gift many times over the last week, but the Soulless didn't like to talk to him. He figured he'd hold his side of the conversation anyway, in case the conversation eventually led to anything.

"I bet you are one of the Lesser Shayatin. Ba'altose used your kind to control the bodies of the dead. Are you what happens when a Lesser Shayatin enters a living body?"

Still, no answer.

"So, compared to a full Shayatin, you are like a little baby."

There was still no answer, but Adhira smiled when he heard leather creaking. He was sure it was the Soulless making a fist. Good, that was progress. The Soulless had a little pride. That, he could work with. Now, he just needed a way to use it to his advantage.

The next morning brought a steady rain. There was no top to the cage, so the water poured in. Adhira was gladdened by it. After several hours of rainfall, he felt nearly clean for the first time in months. Then it rained all day the next day. And then the next. And the next.

He was dozing against the cage as the cart moved through thick mud, which made a distinct squish as the horses pulled it along. The loud clang of metal on metal woke Adhira from his half-sleep. Because of his gift, it actually spoiled his rest fifteen seconds before it happened. He turned his face toward where he heard laughing.

"Oh, I'm sorry," Roan said. "Did I interrupt your beauty rest?" He laughed as he struck the cage again with his cudgel.

"Be careful near the edge there," the officer said from behind the cart.

"It's okay, sir; my horse is as sure-footed as they come."

For the next hour, every time Adhira was about to get anything resembling sleep, the guard would bang the cage. Adhira was already miserable because of the constant rain. The weather had grown almost cold with their rise in altitude. Sleep had eluded him for the past couple of nights.

"Your shift's up," the officer said at length. "Send up Leon to watch over the prisoner."

The guard's horse fell back, leaving Adhira alone for the moment. The Soulless would let him doze, at least. He woke up sometime later feeling no different. His ears popped as he yawned, and he could feel a breeze coming from the left side of the cart. The wind had a distinct upward push to it. He sat back on his heels, facing that way, wondering what it looked like.

He could smell the Soulless guard to the rear of the cart. Adhira moved away so he was at the front of the cart on the side with what he hoped was the ledge.

"I wonder what the real Shayatin are doing right now," Adhira said after a while. "I once saw a Shayatin with arms like a bear and fangs like a snake. Now, that would be a formidable fighter."

There was no response.

"The Shayatin that could fly are almost majestic when they fight. Could you fly? You know, before stealing that body."

No response.

"I once saw a group of Shayatin fighting an entire platoon of soldiers. My, but it was a terrifying sight. One Shayatin could breathe fire like a dragon! There was another one that had four arms and six legs. It held a weapon in each hand and fought several men at the same time without breaking a sweat. These, of course, were real Shayatin, not a half-breed like you."

The Shayatin spurred his horse forward; his voice came from the side of the cart, inches from the Indian's face. Adhira smiled at finding the chink in the Soulless' stoic demeanor. "I am every bit as powerful as the Free Ones!" the Soulless said. "You will never speak to me so again, human!"

Adhira's chance had arrived. Now, he just needed to capitalize on it.

Rolling onto his side, Adhira kicked through the bars as hard as he could, pushing off the bottom of the cage with his shoulder. His foot hit nothing but air.

He tried again.

This time, when he kicked, he aimed lower. His foot jammed into the cage bar.

He tried again.

His foot went high and thudded against something solid and unmovable, the Soulless' armor most likely.

Again.

He kicked the horse in the side, but it just whinnied slightly.

Again.

He kicked a leg.

Again.

He kicked the horse in the head. It turned, whinnying in pain, but the rider got it under control.

Adhira tried several more times. What felt like several minutes of attacks to him was just a few seconds of him sitting still in reality. He was beginning to think about giving up when he finally got the reaction he wanted.

In real time, Adhira rolled onto his face and pushed off the bottom of the cage with his shoulder. He kicked out as hard as he could and felt the heel of his foot strike the horse in the eye. The horse whinnied in pain, the screech rising into the air as the horse reared up. There was a deep howl from the Soulless that faded quickly as he fell down the cliff. The yell continued for a few seconds until it abruptly ended.

The cart came to a sliding stop. All was quiet except for the drumming of the rain and a few angry huffs from the horse he'd kicked. Adhira didn't know what the repercussions would be, so he sat in the center of the cart with his legs crossed. To anyone who'd witnessed his attack, it had happened and was over in a second.

"Sir," one of the guards said after a full minute of silence. "Um, what should we do?"

The answer was a while in coming. "Well, we can't retrieve the body. We can hold a memorial for him tonight."

"I mean, what should we do with him?"

"What can we do? He's already a prisoner on his way to be executed."

"We could beat him," the guard said, though there was obvious hesitation in his tone.

"Sure, let's beat him. You go ahead over and open the cage." The guard didn't respond. "I guess there's nothing for it but to keep going."

With that, the cart lurched forward. Another guard was ordered up from the back of the party to watch him, though the man traveled a respectable distance behind the cart.

The rain finally let up as they descended the mountain. Adhira turned his face to the sun, which felt low on the horizon. By the time the sun set, his hair was dry, and his clothes were merely damp.

He shivered in the cool night air as he listened to the fire crackle nearby. The guards didn't seem at all shaken up at losing the Soulless. They even forgot to hold a memorial for him. The other Soulless didn't seem to care at all. He even laughed when he found out how Leon died.

It was the Soulless who watched him that evening. Adhira was just starting to think he was dry enough to sleep when he heard feet crunching at the rear of the cart. Warmth spread there. The lanterns the guards used burned hot.

"Why didn't you kill me?" Roan asked, closer than anyone else had stood since the Soulless' death.

"What are you talking about?" Adhira asked, though he knew.

"I've been nothing but horrible to you. I've hit you several times. I keep you from sleeping when I'm on guard. I even spit in your food." Adhira hadn't known about that last one. "I was riding next to the cart, near the edge of the cliff, for hours, harassing you. You could have done to me what you did to Leon. Why not?"

"I don't like killing men," Adhira said, moving to sit with his legs hanging out of the cage near the man. "There are enough monsters in the world," he said, nodding toward where he thought the Soulless stood guard. "We need to stop killing each other."

"Well, I brought this to keep you warm," Roan said. Adhira could hear him set the lantern on the hook on the corner of the cage.

"What are you doing?" the Soulless asked, coming to stand beside Roan.

Feet shuffled, and then Roan could be heard from further away. "I was just checking on the prisoner."

"You can talk to him when it is your guard," the Soulless said. He was standing right next to the cart.

It couldn't possibly be that easy, could it? Adhira used his gift to try out a few quick scenarios before he found one that worked. He kicked as hard as he could, twisting slightly to get the trajectory right. He received a burn on his heel when his foot struck the lantern, sending it flying off the corner of the cage. There was a flash of heat as the lantern burst open, igniting the oil.

The Soulless' screams rent the night as he was covered in the flaming oil. The camp was chaos as men yelled out, and the officer called for water. The ball of heat moved one way and then the other as the Soulless ran around screaming. The screams suddenly choked off, and the ball of fire stopped moving. Water splashed over and over until the heat from the fire was gone. The only sound this time was the panting of the men who'd run for water.

Adhira held up his foot. "Does anyone have any ointment?" he asked innocently. "This burn really burns."

Chapter 11

That was how Adhira ended up with his legs bound by thick rope up to his knees. He could no longer sit cross-legged or with his feet hanging out of the cage, so he leaned his back against the side with his legs laid out before him. It was awkward with his arms tied behind his back the way they were, but he didn't have many comfortable positions left. The officer was whistling idly behind the cage as they traveled.

"You seem mighty chipper for someone who just lost two guards," Adhira said.

The whistling stopped abruptly.

"Admit it," Adhira said. "You don't like the Soulless any more than I do."

"They are fighting for the same cause I do. That makes them allies."

"I have a friend who would say the end rarely justifies the means." Asa had been great at debating morals and philosophy with people, but it was beyond Adhira.

"Is your friend as dangerous as you are?" the officer asked.

Adhira fought the sorrow that came with the memory of his friend.

"What happens if your arms are unbound?" the officer asked before Adhira could answer. Other soldiers, who were riding to the sides and behind the cage, suddenly stopped conversing. Everyone was listening.

"Well," Adhira said quietly, as if he were revealing a big secret. "There is this itch on my nose that has been bothering me for a month."

The officer roared with laughter, and several of the men joined him.

"I think you and I could have been friends if the world was different," the officer said.

"It can be," Adhira said more seriously. "Well, it could have been," he corrected. What could be done now? Everyone who could have stopped the dragons and the Beast from the Abyss was dead or blind.

The Armor of Light

The officer left him to his thoughts, calling a halt for the night. As they often did, his last sights replayed in his mind. The Beast, Chemosh, rising from the shadow gate. His friends capsized, then crushed by the waves. And Neviah. Always her. Waving to him as she fell into the Abyss.

He lay on his side and watched the replay over and over until he fell asleep.

✶✶✶

He was jolted awake. All was quiet in the small camp, save for a couple of snoring guards. There were no conversations, which sometimes went late into the night. It had to be near morning. He felt a poke in his shoulder. That's what had woken him.

"Do you promise not to kill anybody?" Roan whispered.

"How would I do that?" Adhira asked. He liked where the conversation was about to go.

"If I free you, do you promise not to hurt any of the guards? Or the cart driver," Roan added quickly as if he were afraid of leaving a loophole.

"I promise not to hurt anyone. Tell me why, though. Why would you free me when it's a death sentence for you?"

"When I saw my first Shayatin a few months back, I was nearly paralyzed by the evil I saw in its eyes. I instantly saw everything differently. With all the wars and conquering. The alliances with Se'irim, Shayatin, and now the Soulless, it all sunk in. We are the bad guys. You were right. There is one big war, and I'm on the wrong side."

"I wish everyone was as smart as the guards I've met since being captured," Adhira said.

"It's all the time we have to think," Roan said. "It's the curse of a boring job. Here, take this."

He was handed, or more accurately, something was placed in his lap, a cloth-covered item tightly wound with string. It couldn't possibly be what he thought it was.

"Hurry," Adhira said. He saw what was coming and needed every second. There was a moment's hesitation; then, he could hear sawing on the ropes. The tightness of his bonds slackened, and he pulled free of the ropes. It felt so good to be able to move his hands again despite the pain that flared up in his shoulders, protesting so much movement after so long.

The Road to War

"What are you doing?" one of the guards asked from the night. The question turned to alarm when he yelled, "The prisoner is unbound!" He cried, "To arms!" which was quickly cut off by the sound of a thud. Then, there were sounds of a struggle. Had Roan tackled the guy?

The camp came to life with shouts and running. In the initial confusion, Adhira dug his stiff fingers into the string holding the clothbound item. The string didn't budge. Then, he had a thought and willed the book of prophecies to become the sword. He felt the package shift as torn cloth and string fell. In his hand, he grasped the Sword of Re'u!

"Oh, I've missed you," he said, and with a quick swipe of the sword, the cage door was opened. Another freed his legs from the rope, and for the first time in a while, he was completely free to move.

"The prisoner is free!" the guard wrestling Roan yelled.

Adhira took a defensive stance. How was he going to do this without killing anyone? How was he to do anything blind? There were six guards, including his rescuer, and one driver. Roan was keeping another guard busy, which left four for Adhira to deal with if the driver stayed out of it. Feet pounded around him before coming to a stop, one on each side of him.

"Where did he get the sword and shield from?" one of the guards asked, voice higher pitched than it should have been.

"Take control of your fears," the officer said from in front of Adhira. "He is only a man. A blind man."

A blade pierced Adhira in the back. He let the shield disappear so he could reach behind him. The guy behind him had a spear. He held the shield up when he heard the guard on his left approach. The man beat on the shield with his short cudgel. Adhira swung instinctually to his right and cut through a weapon with a metallic ring. Probing with his foot found the edge of a sword. Another sword was quickly held tight against his throat.

He was facing two swordsmen, a spearman, and a…cudgelman? Was that a word? A guard with a cudgel. Using his gift, he was able to respond to each attack.

Without turning, he swung the Sword of Re'u over his shoulder and chopped the spear in half before spinning to kick the man's legs out from under him. Side-stepping allowed him to trip up the man with the cudgel as he overcommitted to his swing.

The Forest Shield expanded as he turned to block one of the swords. He stepped to the side to avoid one of the men he'd knocked down, who was about to grab his legs. The attacks paused, and the men regained their feet with grunts. He heard a sword leave its scabbard. Now, he was facing three swords and maybe a cudgel.

Two swords came at him at the same time. With foreknowledge, he blocked the one going for his midsection with his shield. He sliced the other one in half. A third sword sought to take off a foot, but he raised his foot and quickly rushed in with his shoulder to knock down the off-balance man. He knelt atop the man, who was face down, while he waited for the next attack.

He heard a strangled cry, then a gurgling sound. He stumbled over in that direction. His hands fumbled over a body, finding a gash in the throat. When a knife was held to his own throat, he realized the body was likely Roan's.

"Stop!" Adhira yelled, turning in the direction Roan was in. "Don't kill him."

"Traitorous scum!" a soldier said. "I saw him free you so you could kill us!"

"No," Adhira said. "When he freed me, he made me promise not to kill anyone."

"Liar!"

"Everyone calm down!" the officer said from Adhira's left. "Roan, why did you free him?"

"I wanted to be the good guy for once in my miserable life," he said, out of breath.

"The good guy?" the officer said. "But you betrayed us. You aided the enemy."

Roan was quiet for a moment.

"I was in the Lush Planes when they were excavating a mountain there," Roan said, his voice becoming steadier as he spoke. "I was a camp guard, watching over hundreds of prisoners, mostly women and children. I guarded them for weeks while they dug atop the mountain. When they uncovered it—the shadow gate—I watched as every man, woman, and child was fed to the gate. Tell me, do good guys murder people so monsters can escape the Abyss into our world? I didn't aid the enemy! *We* are the enemy!"

"Tell me, Sky," the officer said slowly. "Why didn't you kill Sid? You knelt over him. We were not close enough to save him. Why didn't you stab him?"

"I promised Roan I wouldn't harm any of you," Adhira said.

"If you don't give up your sword and shield, we will kill Roan," the

The Road to War

officer said.

Adhira let his sword turn into a book before the shield shrank down so it looked like a tattoo on the back of his wrist.

"That is the best I can do," he said, placing the book of prophecies on the ground. He then held his arms behind his back for binding.

"You would really sacrifice yourself so this man can live?" the officer asked. "He's been horrible to you!"

"I believe all men deserve a chance at redemption."

"What do you expect us to do?" the officer asked, exasperated. "Most of us have families."

That was when Adhira began to realize something. The questions the officer asked, he was wrestling with a decision.

"There is a place called Esdraelon," Adhira said. "It…"

"I am familiar with the place," the officer said. "It is an ancient stronghold at the southmost end of the Via Maris trade route. Our enemies, that is to say, Tanas' enemies gather there." Tanas already knew about Esdraelon and the people gathering there. Adhira supposed it was inevitable. Thousands of refugees couldn't just go unnoticed.

"Do you expect us to take our families to be slaughtered there?" one of the guards asked incredulously.

"Do you think anywhere will be safe if Tanas defeats the force gathering there?" Adhira asked. "He will not stop until all mankind is extinct. The more people who take a stand against him, the better our chance of success. Do you want to fight for what is right?"

No one said anything.

"If you are nodding or shaking your head, I can't tell. I'm blind, remember?"

Everyone laughed, though nervously.

"We all nodded," the officer said. His sword slid into its scabbard. "You don't fight like a blind man. I can only imagine what the fight would have looked like if you actually were trying to kill us. Men, pack up camp. Unhook the cart, we'll make better time without it. Sky, you can come with us. Our families are to the north. Once we gather them, we'll head to Esdraelon."

"Where are we?" Adhira asked.

"We are just to the west of the Via Maris."

"I am heading in the opposite direction," Adhira said. "I plan to move south." He needed to tell the Moriahns there the other Dragon Slayers had fallen, that and Tanas knew where they were.

"Can you ride a horse?" the officer asked. "Thanks to you, we have a couple of spares."

"I should be able to manage a horse, I think."

He was left alone while the camp was packed up, and everyone mounted their horses. He used the time to stretch sore muscles and walk around. He could feel the myriad of scars crisscrossing his body as he stretched.

"Here you go," the officer said as he walked up with a horse clopping beside him. "And you'll need these, too," he said, handing Adhira a pair of boots. "Sorry if they smell a little smoky."

After putting on the boots, which oddly enough fit him rather well, Adhira used his gift to find the stirrup and easily swing up into the saddle.

"Are you sure you're blind?" the officer asked. He could be heard pulling himself onto his own horse.

"I am," Adhira said. "I have a gift given to me by Re'u. It helps me manage."

"I'd say so. Well, your saddlebags have enough food and water to last you a week. There's also a blanket and some flint to help you make a fire. I figured you didn't need any candles or lanterns."

Adhira smiled. "I suppose I don't."

"Well, Sky, I guess this is goodbye."

"Goodbye, sir," Adhira said. "And thank you."

The men moved off at a quick trot. He turned his horse the opposite way and heeled it into a slow canter. Hoofbeats crunched dirt beside him.

Chapter 12

"Don't you have family?" Adhira asked.

"Yes, but I don't know where to find them," Roan said, riding on his right. "My parents are merchants, and there is no telling where they are. I doubt they'd want to see me anyway."

"Why is that?"

"I ran away to join the army when I was thirteen. When none of the academies would take me, I decided to become a guard until I was old enough."

"You're old enough now," Adhira pointed out, placing him near his own age.

"You don't know this, but I have what they call a baby face. I'm only sixteen anyway."

"Oh," Adhira said. "You sound older."

"Thank you. If you don't mind me asking, how old are you? You talk like a gnarled veteran, but you don't have any facial hair yet."

"I think I'm around seventeen or eighteen by now," Adhira said. "I've kind of lost track of time the last few years. Also, where I'm from, most men of my lineage don't have much in the way of facial hair."

They rode on for a while, Adhira glad to have the other horseman to help keep him on the path. How would he have ever fared alone?

"Are you one of them?" Roan asked, tone reverent. "One of the Dragon Slayers."

"I was." Adhira didn't have the heart to tell him the Dragon Slayers were no more. He doubted he could speak the words if he wanted to.

"And you fought Siarl."

"Yes."

Roan whistled. "I couldn't imagine facing him. They say he is the best swordfighter there has ever been."

"I believe them," Adhira said. What could anyone do about the creature? He could dodge arrows easily, and no one could beat him in a fight. If Victoria were alive, she could fry him with a lightning bolt. Could she still be alive? If the ship had gotten far enough from the shadow gate for her to use her abilities, maybe. He couldn't even force a spark of hope.

They rode until the sun was getting low on the horizon. Roan found them a spot off the trail clear enough to build a fire and let the horses graze.

"Can you make us a fire?" Adhira asked as he walked out a way into the field.

Pulling out the Sword of Re'u, he took an aggressive stance, holding the sword over his shoulder, point forward. Then he started going through the sword forms Mordeth had taught him, slowly at first. For every possible sword defense, there was an attack that could overcome it. For every attack, there was a defense that could stop it. In his mind, Adhira saw his opponent. In the past, during his training, it had always been Tanas he pictured. Now, it was Siarl.

As his muscles began to remember the forms, Adhira sped up. He flowed seamlessly from attack stances to defense stances as the battle progressed in his mind. Pausing long enough to remove his shirt, he continued. Sweat soaked the bandage around his eyes and ran down his chest and back.

His arms burned with fatigue, but he pushed on, forcing himself to move faster the more exhausted he became. He needed to be faster next time, needed to train until he was beyond getting tired again. Next time. The thought taunted him. The last time he faced Siarl, he still had his sight. How was he going to defeat the greatest swordsman who ever lived now that he was blind?

Still, he pushed himself further until his arms simply refused to obey him anymore. Putting the sword away, he knelt on the ground to catch his breath. The cool night air was welcome and quickly dispelled the sweat. He gathered his shirt and moved toward the fire and the smell of beans and sausage. He found his saddle to lean against, and Roan handed him a bowl of food.

"What were you doing?" Roan asked around a spoonful.

"It's called sword art. It is the best way to train without actually sparring, and sparring is only good if your fighting partner is your equal or better."

"Can you teach me?"

The Road to War

Adhira shook his head. "Technique and form are crucial to sword fighting. How can I correct you if I can't see you?"

"You could say the same thing about a lot of things you do. How can you kill two Soulless? How can you fight off four guards? How can you ride a horse? I'm not asking for you to turn me into a sword master. I just want to learn how to fight."

"Actually," Adhira said after blowing on a piece of sausage to cool it. "The horse-riding part is much easier than I thought it would be."

"What harm could it do? Teach me. You can't see it, but I'm making the saddest eyes you've ever seen."

That made Adhira smile. "You don't have a sword," he pointed out.

"I'll use a stick until I can buy one. I've got money. I've been saving up for years now to buy one."

"All right," Adhira said. "I'll teach you the best I can, but I make no promises."

The next day was pleasantly warm as they continued the downhill trek. According to Roan, they had a couple more days of travel before they found the trade route heading south. They decided traveling the Via Maris was the safest and fastest way to cover a lot of ground. Hopefully, it would be weeks before anyone realized he and the guards were missing.

The evening found Roan and Adhira standing across from each other. He'd used the Sword of Re'u to cut them a couple of sturdy branches into practice sticks.

"There are eighty and a half primary attacks and the same number of defenses," Adhira said.

"Um, how do you have half an attack?"

"Like this," Adhira said and quickly stepped forward, sword swinging. Roan yelped in surprise and shuffled back, but Adhira had stopped.

"See, I got you to react, but I only feinted an attack."

"I see," Roan said, sounding embarrassed.

"It is like a game of chess. For every move, there is a perfect defense and counter. I will train you in the two-handed sword art first. When you are proficient in this, I'll teach you how to fight with sword and shield."

"Great, but what is chess?"

"Never mind that," Adhira said. Somehow, he still forgot he was in a different world. "Now, pay attention. The first four attacks are these."

Adhira slashed down, slowly but fluidly, so Roan could see. Then he slashed horizontally from left to right. He did the same from right to left. He ended with a stab.

"Now, watch me again." He started through the basic attacks again.

"Look at my elbows. Do you see how I'm not swinging with my full arm?"

There was silence.

"I'm sorry," Roan said quickly. "I was nodding."

"Do you see how I'm swinging?"

"Yes."

"Try it yourself a few times. Just the down slash." Adhira got beside Roan and reached out and touched his shoulders and elbow to get an idea of placement.

"You are not chopping wood," Adhira said. "Turn like this so you present a smaller target. Good. Now, watch my feet."

He moved forward as he slashed. After doing this several times, he did the same attack but taking a step back each time. This was repeated, stepping to the right and then to the left.

"Watch my feet closely," he said. He pulled off his boots and went through the motions again. "Look how I balance on the balls of my feet. This will be hard to do in stiff boots, but this is how you should be moving." He glided through the movements, slashing down only. "Now, you do it with me."

Adhira slowed down, going through the basic foot movements, first with the down slash, then the two horizontal slashes, and lastly, the stab.

"Do this on your own until you are too tired to hold the stick up," Adhira said.

"What about blocking?"

"One step at a time," Adhira said. "It will take you a week to get your muscles used to these simple attacks."

"A week," Roan said, surprised. "What if we meet bandits on the road, and we need to fight?"

"Then, I recommend being very aggressive so you don't have to block. That stick isn't going to block a sword anyway."

With that, Adhira moved off a bit and began going through more advanced forms, using his stick instead of the Sword of Re'u. The soreness from the previous night's exertion soon disappeared and was replaced with a satisfactory burn as the muscles were worked. His battle with Siarl was back, and Adhira continued to fight the impossibly strong and fast adversary. Pushing his body to move faster and faster, he ignored the protest of muscles that were already doing their best.

He was still too slow! Siarl's strikes were effortless. He never tired, never faltered for a second. Adhira continued until he could no longer hold up the stick. When he sat near the fire, the food was almost ready.

"You train like a man who doesn't care that his joints will no longer work when he's old," Roan said. "I was exhausted in just a few minutes, but you…" Roan whistled.

"I don't think any of us need to worry about getting old," Adhira said. Even if the southern kingdoms and refugees united against Tanas, there was no one left who could kill a dragon, Siarl, or Chemosh. It always came back to that.

"They are dead, aren't they?" Roan asked softly. "The other Dragon Slayers."

Even with his gift, Adhira's surprise was enough that it took him a while to answer. "I think so." He couldn't say more.

"At least we still have you," Roan said.

"There was always the four of us," Adhira said slowly. "Everything we faced, we faced together. We almost died countless times, barely making it from one catastrophe to the next. And that was with all four of us. I wasn't even the most powerful. Now, it's just me, and I can't even see!"

"Can you tell me about them?" Roan asked.

Adhira took a breath to steady his voice. "We all met soon after we died," Adhira began. He spoke well into the night. They didn't go to sleep until after he told Roan the part where they'd slipped away from their first confrontation with Ba'altose and fled across the river.

Chapter 13

He had never told the entirety of their adventures before. It felt wonderful to relive the moments again, even if just in memory. Days passed before his stories brought him to his time with the blade master.

"You're lucky," Adhira said. "I didn't even touch a sword during my first two weeks of training."

"Me either," Roan said, tapping his stick loudly on something.

"I didn't even get to hold a practice sword," Adhira clarified. "I had to balance things on my head while I walked, stand on tall poles on one foot, and separate a pile of salt from a pile of pepper that had been mixed together."

"Why?" Roan asked with a laugh.

"To teach me patience or some such," Adhira said.

"What was it like training with a blade master?" Roan asked. "I can't imagine someone teaching you. I thought you were born with a sword in your hand."

"He was a wonder to behold," Adhira said, remembering the solid figure of his teacher going through the sword forms for hours. "He never tired. He was fast but fluid, almost like a dancer."

"I know what you mean," Roan said but didn't explain.

"I never touched him with a practice sword. Not once. Even as I got better and faster, I was never a match for him." And the blade master hadn't been a match for Siarl.

"We are catching up to that caravan I saw earlier," Roan said. "Will you be okay for a bit while I ride up and talk to them?"

"Of course," Adhira said.

Roan rode off, leaving Adhira alone with his thoughts. Telling stories had been a welcome distraction.

While imprisoned, he had a very distinct and attainable goal: to escape. Now, he was heading south. To do what? Warn the Moriahns they wouldn't be able to stop the dragons? That there was a monster the size of a mountain that could trample cities? He no longer planned to go to Esdraelon. There was no point. Let the people there hold to whatever hope they had left. The truth was, he was moving south because he just wanted to keep moving.

Adhira was pulled from his thoughts when he became aware of the dirt crunching beside him.

"You seem troubled," a man said.

"You surprised me," Adhira said. How had he not known the man was there? "I thought I was alone."

"You sound confused," the man said.

"I don't usually get surprised. Never, actually."

"And how could someone never be surprised?"

Adhira hesitated. He was usually free to talk about his gift, but who was this guy?

"I was given the ability to see the future a little. It was a gift from Re'u. I know what will happen a few moments from now." Adhira waited for the usual questions that followed his revelation, but they didn't come.

"It seems to me," the stranger said as they started down a slight decline, "that if someone was powerful enough to give you the ability to see into the future a little, allowing you to react and change what will happen, what do you suppose they would do if they could see days, months, or years into the future?"

Adhira had never really thought about that. If Re'u could give a gift to see part of the future, could Re'u see even further? "If someone could see years into the future and could see how their actions would change things, they could really plan ahead."

"There were two beggars," the stranger said. "They each begged on the same street but on opposite sides. Each day, they would ask for food. The people of the city were generous and gave them plenty to eat. The foolish beggar gave no thought beyond the day and enjoyed the bountiful nourishment that came his way. The wise beggar planned for the future and hid away much of his food.

"One day, a great famine came to the city. The foolish beggar wailed and cried for food, but there was none to be had. The wise beggar had food to eat to get through the lean times."

The man grew quiet, so Adhira finished the story for him. "And so, the foolish beggar died."

The stranger waited to speak. He waited fifteen seconds.

"No," the man said. "The foolish beggar cannot help but be foolish when he cannot see beyond the moment. The wise beggar shared his food and they both lived. So, you would have to assume this Re'u would know you would be right where you are, right now, in your current condition."

"That doesn't change my situation at all, though."

They walked in silence for a little while.

What if Re'u had known everything would happen the way it did? Could his friends still be alive? Victoria had the power to save her ship. It had to be possible. But Neviah had fallen into the Abyss. The Abyss!

"Who are you?" There was no answer. He knew there wouldn't be. Feet no longer crunched the dirt alongside his horse.

A horse approached, and Roan said, "We will reach a trading outpost before midday. We should be able to resupply our food there. The merchants I talked to said there might even be a weapons merchant there."

Adhira didn't bother asking about the stranger he'd talked to, knowing what Roan's answer would be. They rode for a couple more hours before the telltale signs of the town could be heard.

When they reached the town, it didn't take them long to locate a man selling weapons.

"What about this one?" Roan asked a short time after they'd dismounted. Adhira reached out, and Roan put the sword in his hand. It was heavy and had jewels on the crossguard.

"No," Adhira said, handing it back.

"Here's a good blade," the merchant said. If he thought it strange Roan was using a blind man for advice on swords, he gave no indication.

Adhira hefted the sword, giving it a few swings; it was well-balanced. He swung it down at the wooden table as hard as he could. The blade bent, and a chunk remained embedded in the wood.

"No," Adhira said, giving the sword back.

He went through the process with several more. All were horrible excuses for weapons.

"Where are your good swords?" Adhira asked.

"Sir, I am offended."

"I'm sure you are," Adhira said flatly. "My friend here needs a sword made by a real blacksmith." A woman beside them snickered.

"Sir, these weapons were made by the finest smiths in…" The man cut off when Adhira grabbed him by the collar and pulled him so their noses were touching.

"Do I look like the kind of man you want to swindle?" A sword was laid on Adhira's shoulder against the side of his neck. This was what he was working toward.

"I recommend you let go of my boss," a voice said from behind him.

Without warning, Adhira let go of the merchant, spun, and slapped the sword out of the man's hand. There were gasps from those nearby as he caught the sword by the pommel right before it struck the ground.

He swung the sword through the air to test its weight and balance, then slammed it down on the table to test its edge. This brought more gasps and a startled yelp from the sword merchant. He slowly ran his finger across the edge of the weapon. There was no damage at all to the blade.

"We'll take this one," Adhira said, laying the sword on the table in front of him.

"Um, but, sir," the man said, voice more than a little shaky, "that is my guard's sword. It is not for sale."

"Give him one of these," Adhira said with a smile, waving his hand generally over the table.

"I'm not using that junk," the guard said from beside Adhira.

Roan stepped up on Adhira's other side. "How much for this sword?" he asked.

"I need a sword," the bodyguard whined.

"Oh, give it a rest, Tad. I'll get you another sword," the merchant said to the guard. He turned his attention back to Roan. "I'll sell it to you for two coppers."

Adhira let his smile disappear.

"Did I say two coppers?" the man asked nervously. "I meant a copper and a half."

Adhira let the smile return to his face. "If you like the deal," Adhira said, "pay the man and take your sword."

Was Roan giggling?

After the coins were handed over, Adhira turned his face back to the merchant. "Now, you wouldn't happen to know where I could buy a good scabbard and a shield?"

The man swallowed audibly.

✼✼✼

"I can't believe it," Roan said as they rode down the Via Maris.

They both agreed staying in the small town wouldn't be a good idea after angering the guy who sold weapons. They headed out shortly after buying some food.

"Do you realize that I got the sword and shield for less than I expected to pay for just the sword? I like your bargaining technique. 'We'll take this one,'" he said with a deep, threatening tone.

"I didn't sound like that," Adhira said with a laugh.

"No, but I'm sure that's how he heard it."

"Those swords he's selling are going to get someone killed," Adhira said, shaking his head.

"It's getting dark," Roan said. "I'll find us a good spot to camp."

It was a cloudy day, so Adhira wasn't able to tell what time it was by the sun's heat. Not for the first time, he was glad Roan had come with him.

That evening, Adhira taught Roan the basics of how to block with both the sword and the shield. They were both exhausted from going through their individual sword art when they sat down to eat. During their meal, Adhira showed him how to care for the blade and the best way to sharpen it. Though Adhira had never owned a sword needing that kind of care, he'd spent a lot of time around soldiers and had picked up the gist of it.

The rest of their time on the Via Maris settled into a routine of traveling until the sun was low on the horizon, then practicing their sword art until they were exhausted.

"Are you sure you no longer want to stop in Esdraelon?" Roan asked several weeks later.

They had traveled to the end of the Via Maris, which led through a wide valley. Esdraelon was at the top of the plateau on their left, though Roan said he couldn't see more than the cliff face. If people had taken over the old fortress, there was no obvious sign from the road.

"What good would it do?" Adhira asked. "If they knew the Dragon Slayers were no more, they would lose any hope they still have."

"There is one Dragon Slayer who still draws breath," Roan said.

Adhira didn't respond. Yes, he was still alive, but he'd already failed the Moriahns once. What good would it do to show up in his crippled state and tell them they were likely doomed.

"So, we just keep heading south?" Roan asked. They'd already discussed this, but Roan seemed to be having doubts.

"You can stay, you know," Adhira said. "When the world war comes here, they will need every soldier they can find."

"No," Roan said at length. "I'm confident my place is with you. I don't know. It's just that I feel a strange pull to this place."

Adhira nodded. "I feel it, too."

"It has a monumental finality to it," Roan said. "Like this is the destination I didn't know I was looking for."

"Mankind's fate will be decided here," Adhira said. He looked to the left, though he couldn't see anything.

"We need to tell others of this place," Roan said. "Then, we can come back."

That was Adhira's reason for bypassing the stronghold. The southern kingdoms likely didn't know the scope of what was happening in the world. Someone had to tell them. Adhira tried to convince himself that was the real reason for leaving Esdraelon behind.

Chapter 14

"There're unharvested crops everywhere," Roan said as the horses trudged through the mud on their way to a village in the middle of the plains. "The weather will start turning cool soon. What are they waiting for?"

"Well, let's go ask." Adhira set his horse into a slow trot. Roan quickly caught up and took the lead.

"Go ahead and slow down," Roan said. "We are at what barely passes for a gate. It looks like they hastily threw up some defenses."

Adhira heard something being dragged across the ground.

"They are opening the gate for us," Roan said. "These people look to be nearly starved! Let's dismount, there are a lot of children about."

Adhira swung out of the saddle and led his horse through the muddy streets. Many whispers passed around him, but Adhira couldn't catch what they were saying. Roan halted him with a hand on his shoulder.

"Welcome to Druan," a woman said from in front of them. "I hope you were not planning to leave."

"Do you mean to take us prisoner?" Roan asked.

"No," the woman said quickly. "I am sorry, but what I meant to say is, now you are trapped here with the rest of us."

"Trapped?" Roan asked.

"The shadow wolf stalks the fields," the woman said. "I'm surprised it let you into Druan. It has killed everyone who has attempted to leave."

"If it's a wolf, why don't you hunt it?" Roan inquired. "You do have hunters, don't you?"

"It is not an ordinary wolf," a man said from the gathering crowd, who continued to whisper among themselves. "It is as tall as a man with claws that can cleave stone!"

"Oh," Adhira said, joining the conversation. "You are dealing with a

Se'irim."

"They don't have those in the south," Roan said.

"They do now," Adhira said. "It has attacked the village?"

"Yes," the woman said.

"At night?"

"Yes. It took old Conlin when he was on guard last night. We found large paw prints."

"With six toes on each foot?"

"Yes."

"See," Adhira said, turning his face toward Roan. "It's a Se'irim." To the woman, he said, "Is there a place we can stay for the day?"

"Sure," she said. "There's plenty of empty houses now. We don't have any food to spare, though. We've been rationing for weeks."

"A place to lay our heads is all we ask," he said.

They were led to a small cottage on the edge of town. Apparently, all of the houses at the perimeter were abandoned.

"My name is Sharia," the woman said as they gathered their saddlebags to take into the house.

"I'm Roan, and my blind friend here is Sky," Roan said. "Ma'am, my intentions aren't meant to be rude, but um, the horses. Will they be safe?"

"We haven't gone so far that we're eating horses yet," Sharia said. "Yet," she emphasized before walking away.

After they brought their things in, Roan found a couple of buckets and went to find them some water. Adhira felt around the house. There were two beds in one room, several wicker chairs in another, and the last room had a stove at the center.

Roan returned with the two buckets full and set them in the room with the stove. "I traded the last of my jerky for a couple of bars of soap," Roan said. "The woman tried to give me half her store for it," he said with a chuckle.

Adhira took a bar of soap from him and stripped down to his underwear.

"How many battles have you been in?" Roan asked. "I've never seen that many scars before."

Adhira ran his fingers over a few of the scars. "I've been in a few, but after Asa healed me, even my oldest scars disappeared. These," he said, waving over himself. "All came from Siarl."

Roan whistled when Adhira removed the bandage from around his eyes.

"That bad?" Adhira asked.

"Do you really want to know?"

"No," Adhira said before dunking his head in the bucket.

After washing up, they used the wash water to clean their clothes before hanging them to dry. They ate a little bread while lounging in the wicker chairs. When he was dry, Adhira was about to wrap the bandage around his eyes again.

"Use this," Roan said. "I got you a scarf."

Adhira held out his hand and received a thin scarf. He wrapped it around his head a couple of times and turned his face toward Roan.

"What do you think?" he asked.

"It actually looks quite fetching," Roan said.

"It's not a pink scarf, is it?" Adhira asked.

"No, it's not pink," Roan said. Adhira continued to stare at him. "It's not! I swear. It's black."

After a while, Adhira walked into the bedroom and lay on one of the beds. Though he couldn't close his eyes to go to sleep, his mind still went through the process of thinking he was closing his eyes.

"It's not even close to sundown," Roan said from the doorway.

"We might be up late tonight," Adhira replied.

"Oh, I see," Roan said. He took the other bed. "Have you ever killed a Se'irim before?"

"Once," Adhira said. "With an arrow. When I could still see."

"Any advice?"

"Don't bring the shield."

"Why?"

"If you're blocking, you're already dead."

✸✸✸

"The sun is below the horizon," Roan said as his bed creaked.

Adhira rose, found his dry clothes, and got dressed before walking out the front door. All was quiet except the flicker of fire all around him. The town was likely covered in torches and lanterns. They made their way to the front gate, which Roan told him was merely a sturdy table that had been laid on its side.

"We need to leave," Adhira said to the man at the gate.

"But the shadow wolf," the man said in shock.

"Would you rather the Se'irim eats us or see if you are as lucky as the last guard?" Adhira asked. The table was quickly moved aside, and they stepped into the open night.

"It's pitch-black out here," Roan said as they distanced themselves from the village.

"I didn't think about that," Adhira admitted. He pulled out the Sword of Re'u. "Does that help?"

"I didn't know your sword could make light," Roan said, amazed.

"I have to want it to," Adhira said.

"We are at the intersection," Roan said. "Which way do you want to go?"

"This is fine," he said and sat in the middle of the road with his legs crossed.

"Do you fear anything?" Roan asked, sitting beside him. "I'm doing my best to be like you, but I have to admit, I'm terrified."

Adhira thought about it for a moment. Roan was right. He wasn't feeling any fear at all. Did he even care if he died anymore? The answer didn't really surprise him. He didn't.

"Fear is normal," Adhira said. "Channel it into staying alert. The table is set; we only have to wait for our dinner guest."

"I don't know," Roan said with a laugh. "The town guard seemed like a much easier meal than you do."

"Thankfully, Se'irim are dumb and often give in to animal instincts. It has many claws. From its point of view, you and I only have one each."

After nearly an hour of sitting motionless, Adhira jumped to his feet. Roan was about to cry out.

"I see eyes in the night!" Roan said. "To the right." Adhira turned that way and held his sword at the ready.

"Se'irim are bigger than us and will strike down with their claws from above, but at an angle. Remember what I taught you about stepping away and to the side. It will protect you and give you an opening to strike."

"Me?" Roan said, suddenly alarmed. "I thought you were going to kill it!"

"I will if you have trouble, but this will be a good experience for you."

The Se'irim could be heard walking on the path, its heavy breathing sounding like a low reverberating growl.

"Sky, I don't think I'm ready," Roan said.

"Take an aggressive stance!" Adhira ordered. Roan's feet shuffled instantly. "Trust your training and use your brain. I'll be right behind you. Don't let it lunge at you. Now attack!"

Roan ran forward, Adhira using his gift to stay close behind without tripping them up. A roar split the night. Roan yelled back at the creature as he changed course quickly.

Adhira stopped and used his gift to follow the fight as best he could. Roan circled around the Se'irim, yelling out with each slash. Good. He was keeping up the attack. The creature barked a short roar, and Adhira heard the wind as the claws swung through the air.

Nothing. Good. That meant Roan had dodged the attack. Several more claw strikes followed. Roan was about to yell out in pain.

"Get back on the offensive!" Adhira yelled. "Don't let it gain momentum!" Adhira could smell the rotten breath as the Se'irim turned its head toward him, distracted by the yelling. It immediately yelped in pain as Roan struck while it was distracted.

Adhira jumped on the creature and ran his hands along it as fast as he could.

It had a gash across its ribcage. Roan should have stabbed there instead of slashed. The human was on the offensive again, and from the sound of it, he'd gotten a couple more hits in.

"My sword!" Roan yelled. "It's stuck!"

Adhira stepped in with the Sword of Re'u and stabbed the Se'irim under the base of the skull. It collapsed to the ground dead.

"How did you get your sword stuck?" Adhira asked, holding up the Sword of Re'u so Roan could see better.

"I don't know," Roan said, breathless. "I tried to cut off its arm, and when the Se'irim pulled back, my sword went with it."

"And what did you learn?" Adhira said.

"Not to follow you into the dark," Roan said with a grunt as he retrieved his sword.

"The Se'irim is covered in scars," Adhira said. "There's a lot of hair missing."

"Yeah, he's pretty beat up. Do you suppose he fought Siarl, too?"

Adhira laughed. "No, but it's a good sign. It means we aren't dealing with a pack."

"How do you know?"

"A lone Se'irim with claw slashes all over usually means it challenged the pack leader and lost," Adhira bent down and cut off the head. "They rarely kill their own, but the rest of the pack would have given him the boot."

"How do you know this stuff?" Roan asked as they each grabbed an ear and carried the head between them so they wouldn't get blood all over themselves.

"The Moriahns were thorough in their lessons. You likely would have learned the same if you'd been allowed to become a soldier."

When they got back to the gate, the guard was gone. He must have heard the roars and run. They let themselves in and walked through the deserted streets with the head in tow. They stopped at a small statue of a farmer in the center of town.

"Perfect," Roan said as they stepped back. "The head is sitting on the farmer's hand like he's presenting it to the people."

"Perfect," Adhira agreed. "Now, let's go practice our sword art."

Chapter 15

"I hope you are ready for this," Adhira said from his wicker chair the next morning.

"Ready for what?" Roan asked as he opened the front door and stepped out. He was met with cheering, whistles, and shouts of praise.

When Adhira moved to the door, he heard Sharia talking to Roan. "What can we do to repay you for saving us?"

"We don't need payment," Roan said, voice hesitant.

"Do you have a wife?" a woman yelled from the gathered crowd, which brought a round of laughter from everyone.

"Tonight, we are having a feast in your honor, Roan," Sharia said, which garnered more cheers from the crowd.

"I don't know," Roan said nervously. "I think we might have to get going."

"Nonsense," Adhira said, still standing in the doorway. "In fact, we will help with the harvesting."

"And we should get to it," Sharia announced. The crowds steadily broke up to get to work.

That night found Adhira seated at one of many tables that had been brought out for the feast. It felt good to relax a little after a long day gathering in the fields. The festivities stretched late into the night, and Roan was a favorite to dance with. He kept trying to sit by Adhira, but every time he came near, another young woman caught him up in a dance.

"I keep telling them," Roan said to Adhira, out of breath as he finally sat down. "They just won't listen. When I say we killed the Se'irim, they just say, 'Of course,' but they obviously think I did it by myself."

Adhira smiled. "It's quite all right. I can understand why they wouldn't think a blind man would help much against that thing."

"Without the blind man, I'd be giving that beast a stomachache right about now."

"Speaking of which," Adhira said, rising. "We need to practice."

"What?" Roan said incredulously. "But I'm exhausted from dancing all night. I don't think I'd get much out of it."

"You need to practice again while the fight with the Se'irim is still fresh in your mind. There is nothing better to practice your sword art with than a recent opponent."

An image of Siarl flashed through his mind. The Imprisoned One was always his opponent when he practiced with the sword.

Adhira took a couple of steps away before Roan rose and jogged over. "Good," Adhira said.

"I know. My sword training should always have priority."

"No. I meant good because I have no clue where our house is."

When they arrived, Adhira launched directly into the night's lesson.

"The only new technique I'm showing you tonight is the horseshoe step."

He demonstrated it a few times, turning to the side and making a quick C motion with his foot, which brought him from in front of Roan to his side, still facing him.

"This move allows you to dodge, close the distance, and break your opponent's offense, forcing them to defend themselves. If you had known to use this against the Se'irim, you could have broken its momentum, allowing you to go on the offensive sooner after its attack."

They both practiced the move for several minutes, Adhira incorporating some of the strikes he'd previously taught the other man. When Roan was comfortable with the new movement, Adhira moved several steps away. The night had turned cool, but he went ahead and took his shirt off anyway. Beginning slowly, he went through several moves to warm up his muscles. Then, in his head, the battle with Siarl began anew.

From the last warmup swing, he exploded into an offensive stance. His muscles strained to keep the initial pace he set, but he forced them into further motion. He needed to be faster. As his sword cut through the air, he pictured Siarl easily parrying and sidestepping the assault. Faster. His blade never came close to the enemy.

Now, he was on defense. Any attempt to break the enemy's aggression was met with bone-wrenching power and speed. He blocked with the shield, then his sword. It was always barely in time. He used a trick he'd been practicing, and just like that, he was back on the offensive. As usual, he had no clue how long he practiced for. It ended the same way it always did. His arms grew too tired, his movements too slow, and the fight ended with Siarl's sword against Adhira's throat.

Awestruck murmuring met his ears, and for the first time, Adhira realized they had drawn a crowd. He used his shirt to mop the sweat from his face and neck before finding water to quench his thirst.

"I don't think they believe I killed the Se'irim by myself anymore," Roan said. "What was that one move you did? You usually used it when you moved from defensive stances to offensive stances."

"It's something I'm working on," Adhira said, taking a defensive stance. "When you block an overhand strike, you can counter-strike quickly by stepping forward and swinging down. This normally leaves you open to their strike while they sidestep and strike at your midsection. But," he said, emphasizing the word, "if you swing down with your arms but rotate your blade sideways and then back up, you can catch them off guard."

"Even if you hit them with that strike, won't you still take their blade to the gut?"

Adhira smiled. "You are learning. Good. This move is meant to be used against an opponent who is much better than you."

"So, if I'm going to die and want to take them with me, then use this trick," Roan said.

"Exactly."

"So, I should use it if I have to fight you, then," Roan said with a laugh.

"It wouldn't work against me," Adhira said.

"Why's that?"

"To trick your opponent, they'd have to see it coming."

"I would think it wouldn't work because you know what is going to happen in the next fifteen seconds."

"There's that, too," Adhira said.

Chapter 16

"There's a messenger," Roan said, walking over to where Adhira was pulling excess foliage off of potatoes. "Sharia said we should hear what he has to say."

Adhira let Roan lead him back to Druan. The town wasn't too far from where the farmers were packing the produce onto carts. Apparently, the merchant trains from the south were long overdue to come purchase the food.

"We were hoping to go west from here and head to Ombo," a man with a crisp, hurried way of speaking was saying as Adhira and Roan walked up. "Someone has to warn them."

"Of what?" Roan asked.

"Orm has been besieged by Se'irim," Sharia said.

"Se'irim don't siege unless they are following someone or something strong enough to hold them in check," Adhira said.

"There are several Shayatin," the messenger said.

"Another myth come to life," Sharia said angrily. "Where did all these creatures come from?"

"Tanas is making war in the north," Adhira said. "It was only a matter of time before he turned his attention to the south."

"Making war against who?" Sharia asked.

"All mankind," Adhira said. "He has opened shadow gates and is setting Shayatin loose to kill."

"I don't know if this is part of anything bigger," the man said. "But regardless, when Orm falls, those creatures will be everywhere. You folk aren't safe here."

"Where can we go?" Sharia asked.

"You can come west with me," the messenger said. "I'm going the long way to Ombo, which is over the Axe Blade range, as I'm sure you know. I doubt you could make it with your carts."

"Are you saying we would have to leave everything?" Sharia asked, her voice rising.

"What about your other cities?" Roan asked.

"Orm is the major thoroughfare through the country. You can't go anywhere without going through there."

"Smart," Adhira said.

"What?" the man asked.

"By sieging Orm, the enemy has split your country. Where is your army?"

"Each city maintains their own militia," Sharia said. "The southern countries don't war among themselves like the northern ones do."

"Then Esdraelon is your only choice," Adhira said.

"The old fortress?" Sharia asked.

"Any who oppose Tanas gather there. If you finish your harvest and show up with all your carts full of food, they will surely take you in."

Conversations broke out among the gathered crowd. Most seemed eager to follow Adhira's advice. It was easy to agree with a choice when there weren't any others.

"Roan, Sky, will you come with us?" Sharia asked.

Adhira shook his head. "I will continue south." He didn't really know why. South originally seemed like the best direction to avoid the enemy. His fighting days were over, or so he thought, but he couldn't leave the people of Orm at the mercy of monsters.

"And I'll go with him," Roan said. "Maybe there is something we can do to help."

"We would feel much safer if you two came with us," Sharia said, her voice pleading.

"Feel secure in the fact that we will be between you and the enemy," Roan said smoothly.

The townspeople were more than generous when they parted, trying to give them more food than they could possibly carry. They were packed up and riding onto the south road when two horses rode up to them.

"My brother and I would like to come with you," a man said. His voice sounded thick with thinly veiled emotion.

"We want to fight," a second voice said, much younger.

"How old are you?" Roan asked.

"Nineteen," the younger one said, saddle creaking.

"Try again," Roan said.

"Okay, I'm fifteen."

"But he's really strong for his age," his brother said.

The Road to War

"Where are your parents?" Roan asked.

"Dead," the older brother said.

"You don't have weapons," Adhira said. "We will have to find you some."

"You're letting them come with us?" Roan asked.

"You used to spit in my food, and I let you come," Adhira said.

"I told you I was sorry about that," Roan said. "All right, guys, you can come with us."

That night found the four of them holding practice swords, going through basic forms and attacks. The younger brother, Ivan, had questions about everything they did and had to eventually be forbidden to speak for the remainder of the lesson. The older brother, Xan, didn't speak much, but according to Roan, he picked up the forms quickly.

While the brothers went through basic sword art, Adhira pulled Roan to the side. He'd finally decided Roan was ready to begin sparring.

"Remember," Adhira said. "I know what's coming, so don't hold back. I won't hurt you, and you won't hurt me."

Adhira couldn't help but feel a little pride as they fought. Roan was quick of arm and quick-witted. He was constantly trying something new, even trying to get Adhira to trip over one of their saddlebags as their sparring match moved across the camp.

"How much are you holding back?" Roan panted after they'd been at it for a while. He'd paused to catch his breath. Adhira was still breathing normally.

"Don't feel bad," Adhira said. "This is still a student-teacher relationship. No offense, but we are a long way off from being equals."

"Why is it," Roan said, "that when people say, 'No offense,' it is always followed by something that makes me feel bad?"

"That looked like something from my grandpa's stories," Ivan said with a hint of boyish wonder.

"No talking," Roan said. "Now, back to your sword art."

Adhira moved off to work on his own sword art, which only ended when he was too exhausted to continue.

It wasn't until the fifth day of travel that Adhira smelled smoke on the wind. A couple of hours later, Roan confirmed there was smoke billowing on the horizon.

"Is that Orm?" Roan asked.

"No," Xan said. "Orm is still over two weeks of travel. I think that is one of the other farming towns like ours is. Was."

Adhira didn't know if the "was" applied to the man's own town or the one that was burning. Roan said he could see burned houses and barns throughout the fields.

"I see people," Ivan announced as they neared the village. "Not all the houses are on fire."

"Who goes there?" an old voice croaked as they neared.

"We are the Foundlings," Ivan answered. "We have come to help."

"The what?" Adhira asked. At the same time, Roan said, "I told you we haven't decided on a name yet." Adhira turned his face toward Roan and waited.

"Sorry, Sky. The three of us were sweeping around a few ideas for what our force should be called. We were going to approach you with some options."

"Force," Adhira said with a laugh. "Four guys, two without swords, is hardly a force." The fact that they wanted to name their merry band underlined how young they all were. That was definitely a product of too many adventure stories.

"Well, Foundlings," the old man said after having been momentarily forgotten. "You boys had better head back the way you came. You might be able to outrun them since you have horses."

"Can you tell us what's going on?" Roan asked.

"You wouldn't believe me," the man said.

"Se'irim," Adhira said.

"Okay, so you would believe me."

"What's going on?" a woman asked, her feet crunching dirt as she walked up.

"A blind man, two farmers, and..."

"That sounds like the beginning of a bad joke," the woman said. Adhira decided he liked her already.

"Anyway," the man said. "These lads just came from the north."

"From Druan," Xan added.

"How are the roads north?" the woman asked.

"Clear," Roan said. "We killed a Se'irim before leaving Druan but haven't encountered any more."

"That will change if you stay here," the woman said. "We were just about to make a break for the north while we have time."

"What do you mean?" Roan asked.

"The fire saved us," the woman said. "When the smithy went up, we saw the monsters run away from it. I had the idea to set more buildings on fire, and the Se'irim retreated to the other side of Baker's Hill."

"She pointed southwest," Roan said to Adhira.

The Road to War

"Now that the fires are dying down, we know they'll be back," she said. "If we stay, we'll be killed. If we try to flee north, we'll be killed. We don't know what to do. We've already lost so many." Her voice grew distant at the end.

"How many Se'irim are there?" Roan asked.

"Dozens," the woman said. "We managed to kill a few, but we aren't fighters."

"How many weapons do you have?" Roan asked.

"More weapons than people now," she said, her voice breaking slightly.

"Get two swords for my men," Adhira said. "Then grab anyone who can hold a weapon and meet us on the west side of town. Close-quarters fighting favors the Se'irim. You need room to swing."

"What? Who are you to give orders? We'll be killed."

"I would listen to him if you want to live," Roan said. "Besides, you said yourself that your other two options ended with you dying anyway."

"If you want any chance to live through the day, meet us at the west side of town," Adhira said. He turned his horse and waited a moment for Roan to lead the way before they rode around the buildings.

They didn't have to wait long.

"There are eight men coming from the town. The woman we spoke with is with them," Roan said. "They all have spears, though it looks like they brought swords for Ivan and Xan."

"Good," Adhira said. "Spears are much better for fighting Se'irim, especially if you are untrained."

He waited until everyone was close.

"Now that we are all here," Adhira said. "We need to litter the battlefield with anything available: chairs, barrels, anvils; it doesn't matter, it just needs to break the enemy up into bite-sized chunks. Pick a spot to leave clear. That will be where you make your stand."

"'Your stand?'" Roan asked when the men began fetching debris to throw onto the field.

"I am going to pull away as many as I can," Adhira said. "Our best chance is to split the group."

"That's suicide," Roan said. "I know you're good, but you can't take a whole pack."

"If I get into trouble, I'll cocoon."

"Cocoon?"

Adhira let his shield grow into a giant bowl and then let it shrink again. "If I get overwhelmed, I'll hide beneath this." He didn't mention that someone could lift the edges of the shield and get to him.

"I'll go with you," Roan said. "If we get into trouble, you can fit both of us under that thing."

Adhira shook his head. "I'm blind, remember. If I lose you in the fight, and trust me, I will, you'll be killed. I'm hoping to pull enough away that you can help hold the lines here. They need someone in charge who won't panic when the fighting starts."

"Speaking of fighting, I think I see a group of Se'irim at the top of the hill."

They dismounted. Their horses would panic for sure.

"Lead me out beyond the debris," Adhira said. "It wouldn't do us much good if I went off in the wrong direction."

"I count twenty-five Se'irim and what looks like a Soulless on the back of a massive black horse," Roan said. "Are you sure you aren't just trying to die heroically or something?"

Was he? "No. I really think this is our best option."

"We're free of the junk they are laying out," Roan said. "Any last words?"

"'Feel secure in the fact that I will be between you and the enemy,'" Adhira mocked before turning and walking out a little further.

"You should have seen how the women swooned when I said those words," Roan called out with a laugh.

Chapter 17

Adhira waited. He suppressed the urge to walk toward the enemy. His muscles were like ropes with too much tension, begging to be loosed. Emotionally, he felt, well, nothing. That was still new to him. There had always been some fear in past fights, though he'd never let his friends see it. Now, he didn't feel any at all. Was Roan right? Was he out there to get himself killed?

No, though death would be an escape in some ways, there were others who depended on him at the moment. Despite organizing the town's meager defense, they would all be slaughtered if he died. He needed to kill as many as possible.

Still, he waited, mostly because he didn't want to walk the wrong way. Hoofbeats hammered the ground in front of him, accompanied by the heavy thumps he now associated with the Se'irim. He was just a blind man standing in a field with a book in his hand. An easy target. The horse outpaced the Se'irim as the hooves beat more rapidly, making a straight line for Adhira.

A quick burning sensation spread across his face, and everything went black.

He tried again.

This time, he brought up his sword to block the strike he knew was coming. The burning sensation spread across his face, and everything went black again.

How did the enemy blade make it around his defense?

He held up his shield, but again, the enemy blade made it through.

The enemy's weapon could pass through his defenses as if they weren't there. He ducked and rolled away from the horse, escaping the reach of the weapon.

The Vapor Blade! Neviah had been cryptic about the future, but she had told him to look out for an unblockable blade that could turn to mist. That probably meant the enemy soldier had the Abyss Shield, too. According to Neviah, the shield was a lesser shadow gate.

Claws raked across his back.

He spun quickly, bringing up his sword to severe arms. A howl of pain split the air before Adhira decapitated the Se'irim. The rest of the beasts surrounded him then, claws tearing at him from all sides. He protected his left side with his shield and wrought death with the Sword of Re'u on his right. He was being struck from so many directions at once, it was a wonder the Se'irim weren't clawing each other to death in their frenzy. Maybe they were.

Adhira pushed himself to his limits, blocking and striking as fast as possible. He needed to be faster. Looking ahead, he saw several times he should have died, but somehow, he managed to be quick enough, making corrections that put off death a little longer.

His footing was no longer secure as he clambered up the back of one of the beasts he'd just killed. He even helicoptered his blade once, which wasn't really a fighting technique but worked well in his present situation. Several times, he felt the slightest of tugs that told him his sword had passed through multiple enemies.

Jumping to the ground moments before the beast he stood upon was to be snatched from beneath his feet, he landed and quickly rolled to the side to avoid being crushed beneath one of the Se'irim as it tried to tackle him. His head was nearly torn off as he came to his feet, but he managed to sidestep in time. He needed to be faster.

Stabbing the Se'irim nearest him, he moved around it as it nearly fell on top of him. Another was stabbed, which turned into a slash as he pulled the Sword of Re'u free of the one beast to cut another in half. His blade whirled through the air, his training in complete control of his muscles as he focused on the immediate future and planned his next moves. The ground was growing increasingly muddy, which made his stances more difficult to maintain and less fluid.

He continued to whirl his blade about, always moving, lest he be smothered by the sheer mass of the Se'irim as they climbed over the dead to get to him. His heel struck something solid, which gave him enough footing to push off and run a few steps before turning and killing another of the beasts. They were no longer coming at him from all sides as he backed away faster, killing any who would have touched him.

There was a break in the attacks, which let him get his bearings. A chorus of howls went up from the field as the wounded cried out in pain. Then, the hoofbeats returned but stopped a little way off. Maybe the rider didn't want to risk fighting from horseback among all the scattered bodies. When feet struck the ground with the metallic ring of someone in full armor, Adhira moved around until he found a place with better footing.

"Sorry, I killed all your pets," Adhira said.

"I assure you, this was only the thinnest edge of the blade," a deep voice said as he came near Adhira. The Soulless, whose voice came from slightly above, was at least a head taller than the Indian, and being a Soulless, he was likely faster and stronger.

"Well, in that case, I'm sorry you have to face the embarrassment of being killed by a blind man," Adhira taunted.

The man grunted as he swung. The strike would have hit Adhira on the shoulder, but he horseshoe-stepped to the side opposite his opponent's shield. Stepping close, he swung low and took off the Soulless' leg and followed it up with a short horizontal swing that decapitated him as he fell.

"Well, that was a little disappointing," he said.

He felt around until he found the Vapor Blade, which had turned into a book. That seemed to be a pattern with the blades of power. The Abyss Shield was on the dead Soulless' wrist, and like his own shield, it rested at the size of a watch, though the Forest Shield couldn't be removed. It was like a tattoo.

After removing the Abyss Shield and attaching it to his own wrist opposite the Forest Shield, he stood and began picking his way among the bodies until he was free and standing on firm ground again.

"Marco!" he yelled out when it wasn't obvious to him which way to go. Smoke from the fires filled the air, but he couldn't pinpoint its origin.

"Who?" Roan yelled from across the field.

Adhira started walking that way. "It's a game kids play where I come from," he said loudly as he approached. "One kid walks around blindfolded yelling, 'Marco,' while the other kids run around yelling, 'Polo,' until he catches them."

"I have a comment," Roan said from right next to Adhira. "But it is rather insensitive considering your present condition."

"Thank you for sparing my feelings. What happened here?"

Roan grew serious. "Three Se'irim broke off from the pack and came this way."

"Only three?" Adhira said. "Where are the rest?"

"Wherever Se'irim go when they die. When you dodged away from the horseman's initial charge, he turned around. All the Se'irim except three stayed with him and attacked you. Sky, you killed them all. The only thing left standing out there is that giant horse."

How was that even possible? Even with his sight, he couldn't have fought twenty of the beasts. The press of bodies alone should have overwhelmed him.

"How did things go here? I'm assuming the three Se'irim are dead."

"They are. Not without cost, though. One of the men from the town got mauled pretty badly. His family is with him now, trying to bandage him up, but the others don't think he will last the hour." Roan spoke the last part in hushed tones, which told Adhira they were close to the town.

Adhira felt a pang of sorrow, not only for the man who lay dying but for his friend Asa. He could have easily healed the man. Any time he thought about healing, whether others or himself, he would picture the countless times he'd seen his buddy healing people. Hundreds were alive and well thanks to Asa.

"There was only one other wound. Ivan will have a mean-looking scar across his face when it heals. He got cut from forehead to cheek over his left eye. Thankfully, the claw missed his eye somehow. A few of the spearmen are tending to him. The boy and his brother brought the beast down, though."

"What about the other two?" Adhira asked.

"I killed the one that got a hold of the spearman who's going to, um, that got badly wounded. The other spearmen and the woman ganged up on the third and stabbed it to death. That woman is pretty feisty. The entire fight seemed to last only a moment."

Nearby, crying turned to wailing as the spearman died. Adhira had Roan lead him to the horses to get a drink from his canteen. That and he couldn't take the sounds of grief.

"I got something for you," Adhira said, holding up the sword of power he'd retrieved from the dead soulless. "This is called the Vapor Blade, I think."

"That is the evilest-looking sword I've ever seen," Roan said. Adhira was positive the man took a step back. "It looks like it's made of black oily smoke. Thank you, but no thank you. It is probably cursed."

"I don't believe in curses," Adhira said, tucking the sword away as a book in his saddlebags.

Several footsteps approached after he and Roan had stood there talking for an hour or so. Being blind wreaked havoc on his sense of time.

"Who are you?" the woman asked. Her voice was still strained but lightened considerably from their conversation earlier.

"I am Sky, and this is Roan," Adhira said.

"No. I mean, who *are* you?"

"You move like lightning made flesh," a man said from the gathering crowd.

"How can a single man stand before a flood of monsters like that and come away without a scratch?" the woman asked.

"Twenty is hardly a flood," Adhira said.

"I think I counted more than twenty," Roan said. Could Adhira hear him smiling? No, but that was how he imagined him. Smug and smiling.

"And a Showllessss," Ivan chimed in, voice slurred.

"Ivan!" Adhira said. "How are you doing?"

"He's fine," Xan said. "I gave him wine to help with the pain."

"I like wine now!" Ivan said, partially muffled. Xan was likely trying to quiet him.

"Can we come with you, Sky?" the woman asked after Ivan had been settled.

Adhira shook his head. "We go toward danger. A traveler told us that Orm is under attack. If the city falls, the entire country could be overrun by swarms of Se'irim and worse."

"What can we do?" the woman asked, pleading. "Our town is lost. Half our people are dead. Even if we could rebuild, what would be the point? Another band of monsters would come along and finish us off."

"Go north," Adhira said. Then, he told them about Esdraelon and the people gathering there. He explained about the war in the north and how Tanas was conquering the world.

When his group went their separate way from the townspeople, it was with four more recruits for the Foundlings, though none of them had a horse. One was an old man, and the other three were barely into their teenage years, and none of them had families anymore.

Chapter 18

"It's still following us," Roan said when the sun was shining on them from directly above. Their travel was slowed due to half the men having to walk and Adhira took advantage of the opportunity to walk some himself. In some ways, sitting in a saddle day in and day out was more tiresome than walking was. Without his sight, sitting in a saddle didn't feel much different than when he sat in a cage all day.

Adhira almost looked over his shoulder but stopped himself. Old habits. He was walking beside Roan, with whom he now shared a horse.

"But still not coming close," Adhira said.

"If I had a fish or a cooked egg," Roan said. "I bet I could get it to come over." Adhira shook his head with a smile. Since coming to that world, he'd marveled at the similarities to Earth, but sometimes, it was the little differences that were the most striking. Horses loved to eat fish and eggs more than anything.

"I don't want that thing to come over," the old man, Lux, said from Adhira's other side. "That horse scares me more than the Se'irim."

"Why do you suppose it's following us?" Roan asked. "You killed his master. I thought warhorses were trained to return home when their riders were killed."

"Its home is in the Abyss," Lux grumbled. Adhira liked having a grumpy old man along. It was nice having someone around without a filter to say what everyone else was thinking.

"I'll check it out," Adhira said and stopped walking. "You guys go on ahead a little."

"Be careful, Sky," Roan said. "Lux might be right. That horse could be some type of Shayatin."

The sound of his friends faded behind him while he faced the way they'd come. Hoofbeats slowly approached before stopping a few steps away.

The Road to War

"It's okay," Adhira cooed, holding up a hand for the horse to smell. "I won't hurt you. Just don't bite off any of my fingers."

The horse slowly approached but didn't sniff his hand. Instead, it brought its head low so Adhira's hand rested on its snout.

"You can talk," Adhira said before the horse's words exploded in his mind.

"Finally, one worthy!" Adhira fought the instinct to snatch his hand away. If he hadn't seen it coming ahead of time, he would have. *"There are none who can stand before us. We can subjugate kingdoms!"*

"First off," Adhira said, cutting off the horse's speech. "That was a boss use of the word subjugate. I think I know what it means. Secondly, I'm in the business of protecting kingdoms. I'm on my way now to kill a few more of your Se'irim friends."

"Imbecilic animals," the horse said. *"The Lesser Shayatin that led them was less than worthless."*

"I knew it," Adhira said. "The Soulless really are soulless. They have been taken over by Shayatin."

"I will enjoy killing more of their kind with you."

"I kill them just fine by myself," Adhira said. "Why do I need you?"

"You fight like a whirlwind, but like a whirlwind, you strike everywhere. You severed claws where you could have severed arms. You wounded when you could have killed."

"So, you're saying I fight like a blind man."

"Yes. But I have eyes."

"Are you saying I can see through your eyes?"

"That's ridiculous. Of course not. But as my rider, I can talk to you, even if you are not touching me."

So, telepathic communication was easy, but seeing through its eyes was ridiculous? Adhira let it go.

"And with me comes the Vapor Blade and the Abyss Shield." Adhira didn't point out the fact that he was already in possession of both. *"That idiot you slew wanted to use the shield to summon an army of imps! They are like rabbits in the Abyss."*

"So, you are a Shayatin."

"Yes, but I choose my own path. The rest of them are beguiled by dragons, but I am no fool. When man is gone from the world, the dragons will kill or enslave the other races."

"Beguiled? You need to chill it with the big words. Asa or Neviah might..." The horse jerked at the mention of Neviah's name.

"Is she here?" the horse asked. Was it scared?

"No. Why?"

"*She told me if she saw me again, she'd kill me.*"

Neviah had met this horse before? Why hadn't she said anything? Why mention the sword and shield but not the Shayatin? He thought she'd told him everything.

"That sounds like Neviah, all right. You know, I should probably kill you, too. You are a Shayatin."

"*I told you, I'm not like the others.*"

"Right, you don't want to kill and destroy because dragons want you to. You want to kill and destroy because you want to."

"*What is a weapon but a tool? The purpose for its creation and its use need not be synonymous.*" Created. Were Shayatin created? There was still so much he didn't know.

"We are a few mounts short." Adhira felt around until he found the stirrup. The horn was nearly out of his reach as he pulled himself onto the giant horse. "What's your name?" Adhira asked.

"*Euroclydon,*" came the response.

"Of course, your name would be a mouthful. All right, Clyde, they call me Sky. I want to ride up to my friends now."

"*There is a waist strap behind the saddle. I recommend putting it on so you do not fall from the saddle when I run.*" The horse lumbered forward at a quick trot. Adhira didn't know what to do with the reigns after strapping himself to the saddle. He'd never ridden an intelligent, talking horse before. Would Euroclydon even respond to his guidance?

"I like these guys, so no killing."

"*Okay.*"

"I want to hear you say it. Say, 'I will not kill your friends.'"

"*I will not kill your friends.*" No questioning or annoyance at the command. To the horse, it was as simple a request as someone asking a friend not to eat the last cupcake.

"It let you ride it," Roan said as Adhira came near.

"Guys, this is Clyde. He can talk in your head if you touch him." No one moved. "Go ahead, try it."

Roan's saddle creaked as he reached to touch Euroclydon. There was a fast, swishing sound as he snatched his hand back.

"The horse said it would bite my fingers off if I touched it again."

"Play nice," Adhira said to his mount. "Let's go," he said, and they all started off again. Roan helped him transfer his saddlebags from his old horse to his new one. "How long until we reach Orm?"

"About eight days or so," Lux said; he was walking much further away from Adhira than he had been.

"*I can have you and me there by nightfall.*"

"Well, that won't do much good to everyone traveling with me."

"What?" Roan said.

"I was talking to the horse. I guess you'll have to get used to me having one-sided conversations."

"*We don't need them,*" Euroclydon said. "*This rabble will get slaughtered anyway.*"

"You are wrong," Adhira said sternly.

"What's he saying?" Roan asked.

"Clyde says you have beautiful eyes."

"And you disagreed?" Roan said with mock anger.

"*That is not what I said.*"

"Don't you know what a joke is?"

"We have trouble up ahead," Xan said, riding up to Adhira. "It looks like a merchant train. What used to be a merchant train."

When they drew close, Adhira had Euroclydon describe the scene to him. There were eight carts, all ransacked, with one turned on its side. The horses and people were gone, but the amount of blood everywhere made it certain Se'irim were to blame. They never left behind a good meal.

"I can follow their trail," Lux said from atop the cart. "They went off that way."

"*The old one is pointing east,*" Euroclydon said. "*Don't these fools know you're blind?*"

"This was a large group, though," Roan said. "I see many boot prints mixed with hooves and Se'irim. This force is much larger than the one we fought yesterday."

"Then, we will keep heading south," Adhira said.

"Enemy scout!" one of the men shouted.

"Enemy scout!" Adhira shouted.

Before he could kick Euroclydon into motion, the horse was galloping away from the other men.

"*Be ready with your sword on the right. I will let you know when to swing.*"

The wind whipped at Adhira's clothing as they zoomed along. Though he couldn't see, he'd galloped a horse before, and this felt several times faster than what he thought possible.

"*He is riding over a hill in front of us. We will catch him before he descends the other side.*"

Adhira leaned forward with his sword ready as they climbed a steep incline. Euroclydon's hooves hammered the ground, nearly drowning out the sounds of the fleeing rider. A horn sounded just ahead of them, three quick blasts. When they reached the top of the hill, the large horse came to a sliding stop.

Adhira already knew what Euroclydon was about to say and cut him off. "Get back to the men, now!"

They flew across the ground to where his group waited.

"There is a large force just over that hill. Hundreds. The scout made it to the top before we could get to him and signaled his buddies. You guys set up the best defenses you can here. Clyde and I will try to draw their attention." Without waiting for a response, he heeled Euroclydon, and they quickly made their way toward the enemy.

"*What's the plan?*" the horse asked as they raced up a hill.

"We need to pull the enemy in the other direction. If you and I can be enough of a nuisance, hopefully, they will forget about the others."

"*Se'irim are much faster than normal horses,*" Euroclydon said as he crested the hill and turned right. "*We can separate their force into smaller groups if we lead them on a long chase.*"

"Do it. Go slow enough to keep them interested, but keep us from getting bogged down."

"*Then we can kill them all!*"

"I appreciate your enthusiasm, but you need to think a little less murdery. Tell me what you see."

"*In front of us is a force of about 300. Nearly half are Se'irim. Most of the rest are men and men with the Lesser Shayatin in them.*"

"We call them Soulless."

"*Fitting. There are many Soulless. There are only a handful of Shayatin. No shadow shifters, though. They see us.*" What was a shadow shifter?

"Let's get closer before turning. Hopefully, they will all focus on the chase."

The shouts of men and the howls of Se'irim met them as they neared the enemy camp. Euroclydon turned sharply to the right. Angry and shocked voices yelled after them as they rode away, keeping the enemy on their left.

"*They have archers lining up.*"

Adhira raised the Forest Shield, letting it grow large enough to protect them both. They were traveling so fast that the wind nearly pulled him from the saddle, the shield acting as a brake. The waist strap held him firmly in place. The metallic ring of metal-tipped arrowheads told him the first volley had landed.

"*We are out of bow range now.*"

Adhira was happy to put the shield away as he leaned low on Euroclydon's neck. They picked up speed. Shouts flowed around them on the left and behind. Then, the shouts came only from behind.

"*The Se'irim are following, but the men are forming ranks, facing the way we came.*"

"The scout. He told them about the others."

"*They are preparing defenses. Their scout must not be good at counting.*"

From anyone else, Adhira would have thought the statement a joke. The horse, though, was just stating a matter of fact. The enemy was preparing to be attacked, which bought his friends some time, at least.

"*When we engage the enemy, you will be able to guard my flanks better with two blades.*"

Adhira reached back into his bouncing saddlebags and pulled out the Vapor Blade. With a sword in each hand, he tested the waist strap. It let him stand in the stirrups but held him firmly. He rode like that, knees bent slightly, blades ready.

"*There are a dozen Se'irim behind us, but the rest were restrained.*"

"Let's turn and kill them," Adhira said, more vehemently than he intended. "We need to draw more attention toward us," he added.

Euroclydon turned so sharply that Adhira would have come out of the saddle if he wasn't strapped in. Within a couple of strides, they were eating ground at a breakneck pace again. Howls and barks met them as they neared the Se'irim.

"*I'm going to turn so they are on the right. I will keep them off us. Ready your sword to swing like a scythe.*"

A sharp turn and Adhira swung. Even without his gift to help, Euroclydon's suggestions would have been adequate. He felt the slight resistance over and over as they flew past the small group of Se'irim. Euroclydon took several more strides before turning around again.

"*Aim a little lower this time. The Se'irim are not as large as I am.*" No boasting. Just another fact. The average Se'irim stood at nearly six feet tall.

When they reached the Se'irim again, Adhira swung low. Several more of the beasts fell to his blade. Euroclydon slowed and turned around immediately.

"*Only half remain.*"

"Let's finish them!" Adhira yelled. The urge to kill was stronger than he'd ever remembered it being.

The Indian blocked a claw meant for him with his shield and cut down a Se'irim who came at him from the other side. Euroclydon jerked as he kicked out with his hind legs. A bone-splintering crack resounded, followed by the thump of a Se'irim striking the ground several feet away. Euroclydon reared, raking the air with its forehooves before crunching down onto another creature.

Adhira swung out with both swords at the same time. Where the Sword of Re'u sliced cleanly with a slight ringing sound, the Vapor Blade sizzled, leaving an acrid smell behind. A Se'irim fell to each sword. The horse spun and kicked out again, ending the life of another beast.

"*That is the last of them. The enemy has sent out riders toward the hill that hides your friends.*"

"Let's cut them off," Adhira said. Euroclydon rocketed across the hills.

"*There are four horsemen. We are coming upon the first now. Swing right.*"

Adhira leaned out and cut down the first rider. They quickly caught the next two, and both times, Adhira eagerly struck out with his swords. When they reached the last rider, the man was screaming in fear. There was a metallic thud as Euroclydon collided with the other horse. Adhira could hear the rider and mount tumbling on the ground as they were knocked over.

"*The soldiers are sending the force of Se'irim out front,*" Euroclydon said. "*They have begun to fear us!*"

"Good," Adhira said. There was an eagerness he wasn't used to. Above all else, he wanted to keep fighting. "We charge! Straight at them."

Without hesitating, Euroclydon turned and galloped down the hill. Adhira stood forward in the saddle, ducking his head behind Euroclydon's mane. The swords were held out to each side, extended to their full length. Two giant broadswords wielded from the back of the massive horse struck out mercilessly as Euroclydon crashed into the Se'irim. Those who tried to stand their ground were trampled beneath the oversized hooves.

Hissing followed them on the left as the Vapor Blade burned its way through countless Se'irim. The Sword of Re'u, however, was more silent but no less deadly. Eager howls turned fearful as the Se'irim realized the thing in their midst wasn't prey after all but a predator from their worst nightmares.

There was no time for the enemy archers. Thumps turned metallic as Euroclydon breached through the Se'irim and smashed into the row of soldiers. The men fared no better than their furry friends. Adhira laughed as he reached low, cutting down the men and Soulless as they tried to hold their lines before the pair.

They broke free of the fray, and Euroclydon turned and ran along the rear of the formation before plunging into the formed ranks again. If their initial charge was effective, hitting the enemy from behind was nothing less than devastating. Euroclydon no longer moved in a straight line but zigzagged around the battlefield. His footing was always sure as he zoomed around, never pausing or slowing in the slightest.

A horn blasted, two clipped blasts. The battle changed as the press toward them became a race away. Adhira could no longer swing indiscriminately but had to listen to Euroclydon's advice. They chased down one after another, men and Soulless mostly since the Se'irim fled much faster.

"The Shayatin are fleeing, too," Euroclydon said. *"Pity."*

It was a pity. Suddenly, his glee at the destruction struck him as odd. What was he doing? He hated killing men. Why was he taking such joy in it now?

"Clyde, stop."

"Why stop? We two can slaughter hundreds! Ballads will be written..."

"Stop!" Adhira yelled, pulling back on the reigns awkwardly with the two swords crossed in front of him. Euroclydon slowed his mad dash, slowing but not stopping. "The enemy is broken. We need to get back to the others."

"But we can kill them all."

Adhira shook his head to clear it. They *could* kill them all. Two against three hundred, and they'd won! But no. So many served Tanas out of fear or ignorance. How many had he already convinced to stop following the dragon? He needed to let these go now, even if he did have to fight them again later.

"We need to get back to the others. They need to know we are safe."

"They are standing at the top of the hill," Euroclydon said a few moments after changing directions.

No one spoke when Euroclydon stopped among the Foundlings. Had they watched the entire fight?

"There should be a few horses down there," Adhira said. "We stopped a couple of riders who were trying to get to the top of the hill."

"A few horses?" Roan said. "Sky, there are dozens of horses running around down there. The entire camp's been abandoned."

"I've never seen anything like it," Lux said solemnly. "Once, as a boy,

I saw a honey badger walk into a nest of vipers. I thought, surely this badger has made a fatal mistake. The honey badger slaughtered every one of them. That's the closest experience I've ever had to what I just saw." He sounded shaken. "There has to be sixty bodies down there."

"They are lucky you didn't kill them all," Ivan said. "I wish you had."

Lucky indeed. Adhira didn't know what had come over him, but if he hadn't been able to break free of the battle frenzy, he really would have killed them all.

Chapter 19

They continued south with an army's worth of supplies. They'd found nearly fifty prisoners, mostly civilians. Four joined the Foundlings, and the others were sent north with all the supplies they could carry on the six carts they took. Each of their growing crew, aside from Adhira, drove a cart, and there was a long line of riderless horses tethered to each other, following. At the moment, Adhira sat on Roan's cart. Euroclydon was out scouting the surrounding country. It had been days without enemy contact.

"I'm still not so sure about that horse," Roan said, probably for the tenth time.

"Would you rather fight against him?" Adhira asked.

"I would rather we just kill it."

Adhira shook his head. "I'm learning so much about the Abyss and the creatures that live there. Did you know there are actually five types of Shayatin?"

"I thought there were only three," Roan said, cracking a small whip to keep the horses moving.

"Everyone thinks there are only three. I knew there were Lesser Shayatin that could take over corpses or willing people. We all know about the regular Shayatin and the little imp ones that sneak out every now and then."

"What other kind are there?"

"Apparently, when an animal crosses from our side to the Abyss, they aren't always killed by the Shayatin there."

"So, they will kill people who enter but have mercy on animals?" Roan huffed.

"I wouldn't call it mercy. Over time, the Abyss turns the animal into a Morpho Shayatin."

"Is that what Clyde is?"

"I don't know. He doesn't remember."

"Does it really matter?" Roan said. "He's still a Shayatin now."

"If something can turn into a Shayatin, then maybe it can turn back."

"Let's just hope he doesn't kill us in our sleep before we find out."

A sound like a distant avalanche met Adhira's ears. Euroclydon was coming back.

"*I'm back,*" the horse said as it neared.

The horse could be heard in his head from several feet away now. Adhira transferred from the cart to the horse, strapping himself into the saddle.

"*There are several enemy encampments around the valley ahead, most holding a few hundred troops. There is a large group of more than two thousand holding a position in some ruins at the bottom of a mountain to the east. The city you seek is still a day's travel at your current speed.*" Euroclydon said the last with disdain. The horse hated moving slowly.

"Is Orm still intact?"

"*For the most part. The front gate is gone, lying in splinters. Debris is clogging the entryway. A battle was fought there. There are bodies all along the base of the wall. There is siege equipment smoldering in the field.*"

"Aside from 'killing them all,' are there any good options for reaching the city?"

"*It's a siege. The enemy won't willingly let anyone in or out.*"

"What angle of approach is least likely to get us all killed?"

"*The largest gap between enemy camps is to the west. Still, we will not be able to go unseen. If one camp sees us, the others will be alerted.*"

"And if we try to lure them away, it will be like before. They'll send a few to chase us and then take up a defensive position," Adhira relayed the information to the others.

"What if we set up a decoy," Roan said. "We have lots of horses and carts full of armor and weapons. Could we attack one of the camps with a bunch of armor strapped to horses? When the other camps come to their aid, maybe we could slip through."

"Great idea, but I'm sure Orm could use those supplies. We don't want to give them back to the enemy just to get into the city."

"*We could break their will to fight like we did before,*" Euroclydon said.

"I told you," Adhira said. "I don't want to kill a bunch of people like last time." Was that true? He felt it, a hunger to take up his swords again and fight. This was war, and he was good at it, even blind. Could he really avoid more killing? A lot of killing?

"Isn't that the point?" Roan asked. "I admit what we saw last week was extremely sobering. The war fantasies from my youth have been shattered. But if we don't kill them, they will kill us, or worse, they'll keep killing innocents."

He was right. Adhira knew it, but he didn't like what he was becoming when he fought. It was almost as if someone else was taking control of him. What if he didn't stop next time?

"*They are the enemy,*" Euroclydon said, the simple statement rendering Adhira's fears inconsequential.

"Let's stop here for the night," Adhira said. "We shouldn't get any closer without having a plan, and I want everyone's input. We need a plan. A good one." Of course, Asa would have been able to come up with something brilliant. Unfortunately, he wasn't around to help.

Before calling a meeting to discuss a strategy for reaching Orm, he had them run through the training routine he'd developed. Lux, the only one with any real experience with the spear, took the other seven spearmen through drills. Roan taught the brothers another sword technique and set them to practice their sword art before sparring with Adhira.

"I wish I could hit you just once," Roan said, collapsing to the ground to chug at his water skin after their match. The man was lasting much longer and fighting far better.

"I've never hit you either," Adhira pointed out, walking away a bit so he could begin his sword art.

"Yeah, but you choose not to hit me," Roan said. "There's a difference."

Later in the evening, with the heat of the fire at his back within the ring of carts, Adhira addressed the group. After explaining what Euroclydon had seen, he asked, "If any of you have ideas or suggestions on how to get to the city with all these supplies, I am all ears."

There was silence except for the crackling of the flames and the horses wandering around as they grazed nearby. It was a lot to process, and they were all new to combat. Adhira gave them time to think. Several minutes passed without anyone saying anything.

"Roan wants to put suits of armor on horses and send them at the enemy to draw their attention," Adhira said.

"That's the kind of thing heroes would do in a children's tale," Lux said with a laugh. "Why would we want to give them their horses back? Do you know what a good warhorse is worth? I don't know either, but I'm guessing a lot."

"Hey, I was just thinking out loud," Roan said. "I don't hear any other ideas."

"Could we set up an ambush?" Ivan asked. "I'm sure they send out patrols. We could whittle them down like a block of wood."

"But there are thousands of them in all," Rixen, one of the spearmen, said. "If we kill them ten or twenty at a time, it would take us, what, a year to whittle them down to nothing."

With that, the ideas flowed, some good, others not so much. Overall, their planning session led them to one unfortunate conclusion: making it to the city would be nearly impossible, not with everyone and everything in tow. After the ideas stalled out, they were back to quietly thinking.

"Do we really have to reach the city?" Ivan asked. No one answered immediately.

"Do we?" the old man echoed after some thought. "We could harry the enemy from out here. What good would we do in the city anyway?"

"They need the supplies," Roan said.

"They seem to have done just fine without them so far," Adhira said. "They were able to repel the attackers."

"What if we travel to the surrounding towns?" Xan asked. "We can recruit the able-bodied men and arm them. Build our own force from outside."

"*It won't work,*" Euroclydon said. "*All the towns I saw were abandoned or destroyed. Everyone outside the walls of Orm is gone, dead, or being held prisoner.*"

"They have prisoners?" Adhira asked. "Why didn't you say anything?"

"There are captives?" Roan asked. "How many?"

"Hundreds in all," Adhira said before the horse could speak in his head again. The men began talking at once, exclaiming anger and determination to free their countrymen.

"Everyone shut up for a minute," Lux said. Everyone obeyed. "Roan, what was that one idea you had playing dress up."

"I said we should dress up in their armor and uniforms and just travel in the open straight to the city. But we determined there were a bunch of problems with…"

"I know what we said," the old man said, cutting him off. "This is different. What if we impersonate the enemy to infiltrate them?"

"We could march right into their camp," Roan said excitedly. "With all these weapons, we could arm the captives before we free them."

"They will never think I'm one of them," Rixen said. "I don't speak any of the northern languages, and the humans are likely all from there."

"Not even all the northerners speak all the northern languages," Adhira pointed out.

"It doesn't matter," Roan said. "Sky and I speak the northern languages just fine. We may need to bring along some 'prisoners' anyway, if you know what I mean."

"Good thinking," Lux said. He was not one for compliments.

"My brother and I speak a few of the northern tongues," Xan said. "Merchants traveled through our town all the time."

"That gives us four soldiers and eight prisoners," Roan said. "It could work."

They planned long into the night. The next day, they trained, planned, and went over contingencies. It wasn't until the following day that they continued their trek south wearing the enemy's armor and insignias, the red horse on a white background. By early afternoon, they came into view of the camp holding the most prisoners.

"Are we crazy?" Roan asked as they neared the enemy camp.

The helmet Adhira wore clinked when he nodded. "Of course we are. Twelve guys trying to infiltrate and capture a camp with a couple of hundred entrenched troops and Se'irim; yeah, we're completely nuts. If anyone could pull it off, though, it would be us."

"Why is that?"

"We have nothing left to lose. We've all already lost as much as a man can."

"*There is a spiked wall circling the entire camp,*" Euroclydon said. "*Dozens of small one-man tents are within the wall. Five larger tents are at the center of the camp with another spiked wall around it. At the south side of the camp is a fence with maybe two hundred men, women, and children tied together. There is a pen with about fifty Se'irim near the front gate.*"

"Halt," a soldier said from the front of their column. The carts rumbled to a slow stop. They'd left all the extra horses picketed in a wooded area near their last camp.

"*A man is walking down the line of carts with a Se'irim, letting it sniff each of you. They can smell fear. These men are wary.*"

Adhira knew Se'irim could smell fear but didn't think of someone using one to detect infiltrators. He could hear the beast sniffing as it reached him. When it passed him, it growled near the cart behind him.

"Why is this man afraid?" the soldier asked, walking back over to Adhira, who was wearing the wings of an officer. With his visor still shut, Adhira looked toward where the voice came from.

"He is a prisoner," Adhira said off-handedly, trying to act the part. "Why wouldn't he be afraid?"

"You let your prisoners drive carts? And unshackled?"

Adhira let a little irritation into his voice. "As you can see, we are a little shorthanded. These eight," he waved off-handedly, "they are earning their lives. I made a good example of a ninth. They obey."

"Your orders?" The man's tone had become less abrasive, less sure.

Adhira handed him the rolled parchment he had tucked inside his breastplate. The forgeries were entirely the work of Roan. He'd found a few papers with the correct letterhead and some high-ranking stamps.

"Oh, you are here for resupply," the man said, his voice turning eager. "I thought we were going to have to start fighting with sticks. Our weapons are in horrible shape. Do you have a blacksmith?"

"No," Adhira said. He didn't know there was even such a thing as a traveling blacksmith. "He was lost with my other carts and many of my soldiers."

"Who attacked you? These people don't even have a standing army."

"You wouldn't believe me if I told you," Adhira said, fishing.

The man's voice grew quieter, almost a whisper. "Was it a ghost horseman?"

"How do you know about him?" Adhira asked. Ghost horseman?

"One of the raiding parties was attacked by a man on a horse that could pass through solid objects like a spirit. Apparently, the group camped on his grave or something, and the horseman killed them until they fled."

"He attacked us on the road," Adhira said. "We fled with most of the gear while my men held him off. My men never caught up with us."

"You're lucky to be alive," the man said. "Come on in, sir. Your detainees must be put in with the other prisoners until you depart. Camp regulations and all."

"Of course," Adhira said. "These eight have an acceptable mixture of fear and obedience. See that they are not fed to the Se'irim."

"Yes, sir."

They were led into camp. After, they set up their carts near the prisoner pen, which was the only cleared space. Adhira immediately became aware of why. The stench from the human pen was horrible.

The soldier who'd spoken with them at the front gate walked up to Adhira. "Sir, may I begin sending men to turn in their old equipment and get issued new?"

"In the morning," Adhira said. "I am in no hurry."

"Oh, okay. Sir, would you like to dine with me in my tent?" the soldier asked with all the nervousness that came with someone of lower rank speaking with someone considerably higher.

"I would love to," Adhira said, swinging from Euroclydon's back and walking after the man. The horse followed, telling Adhira where to go.

"Your horse is following," the soldier said from the left.

"He's very protective of me," Adhira said and had to duck to enter the tent, which thankfully had the entrance rolled up to let in the breeze. This let the horse see in and guide him so he looked less blind, sitting down and taking the glass of wine handed to him. He hated wine but took it anyway to be polite.

"Feel free to take off your armor and make yourself comfortable," the soldier said, taking the chair opposite Adhira.

"I can't," Adhira said. "Until I am out of the field, I am bound by the codes."

"Ah, you are Durnkian," the soldier said. Another benefit of having a former merchant in his inner circle. Roan knew a lot about nearly every people.

"Yes. You may call me Sky."

"Just Sky, sir?"

"Yes, we can skip the honorifics in private, don't you think?" As he always did when speaking with strangers, he used his gift to see ahead to mold the conversation into what he needed.

"Yes, sir. I mean, yes. I am Ivak. How did a man of your station end up leading a resupply unit?"

Adhira laughed. There was nothing as disarming as a good laugh. "I wasn't supposed to be leading anything. I was on my way here to help your superiors break the siege."

"Break the siege? The last orders said to secure the countryside. We just need to keep the southern countries from forming their coalition. This time next year, our entire army will be marching south."

"Plans change," Adhira said. "Tanas wants Orm as a foothold from which to launch his campaign here."

"So much for having it easy for a year," Ivak said. "Aside from the Se'irim and Shayatin, this has been the best duty station I've ever had."

"They make my skin crawl," Adhira said.

"But, sir, you ride a Shayatin," Ivak whispered.

"Yes, but my horse hates Shayatin too, so it's okay."

"Me too," the soldier said, still whispering. "When the war is over, I hope we send these things back where they came from."

"I wouldn't count on that happening," Adhira said. "Oh. Forget I said that last."

"What is it, Sky? It's okay. Anything you say will stay between us officers. What do you mean you wouldn't count on that? Them going back?"

"I'm not supposed to talk about it," Adhira said in a whisper, leaning over the table. "I could be imprisoned if anyone found out I spoke about it."

"Oh. Okay. I wouldn't want that." The hook was set. Now, he just needed to circle back to it.

"Are you using the prisoners here for what I think you are using them for?" Adhira asked.

"*He nodded*," Euroclydon said. "*He looks troubled*."

"What's wrong?" Adhira asked. "You look troubled." He waited patiently for the soldier to find the right words.

"I don't like it," Ivak said. "I've killed men before. I'd be lying if I said it didn't bother me, but this…. These are civilians. Half are women and children." Ivak seemed to remember who he was talking to. "I'm sorry, sir. You probably think I'm weak. I'll follow orders without question, I assure you."

This was better than Adhira could have hoped. Tanas' troops were already questioning their orders. He looked over both shoulders before leaning forward again. "Maybe you should question your orders."

"But sir, Sky, what you are saying is…"

"I know the weight of what I'm saying," Adhira cut him off. "Do you remember what the original mission was? The reason for the war?"

"King Tanas seeks to unite mankind so what happened with Ba'altose in the north can never happen again."

"Word for word, the ideology I've heard from countless soldiers." Adhira waved a hand toward where the prisoners were kept. "Does this fall in line with that mission? People, real people, are being forced through shadow gates. The land is being flooded with Shayatin. You are feeding women and children to Se'irim!"

"Just those who don't join our cause." Ivak obviously didn't believe his own words.

"Tanas has killed far more people than Ba'altose ever did. Dragons, Shedim, Shayatin, Se'irim, Soulless; Tanas is filling the world with monsters! How did we let ourselves be fooled?"

"What can we do?"

"I've been asked that question a lot," Adhira said. "Men sense something is wrong. Some outright know it, but no one knows what to do. And so, they keep following orders. We are like a bunch of sheep following each other off a cliff. We know the cliff is there, but no one is saying anything."

The Road to War

"But what can we do?"

The original plan was to sow descent for a few days while they found out as much information as possible. Then, they would supply the prisoners with weapons and stage a small revolt, hopefully winning over a few of the soldiers. What he found instead was a man who was more than eager to throw off the shackles of Tanas' orders.

"Do your men think as we do?" Adhira asked.

"*He shrugged.*"

"I am their commander," Ivak said. "I am the last person someone would tell if they were having traitorous thoughts. I do catch bits of hushed conversation from time to time, however. I think most want a way out. Not all, mind you. There are men who believe Lord Tanas is someone to be worshipped."

"Can you tell the difference? In your own men?"

"No, but I know a couple of junior officers I trust. They will have a better idea of the climate of the camp."

"Good," Adhira said.

"What exactly are we doing here anyway?" he said, suspicion creeping into his voice. "I haven't even seen your face. How do I know you aren't one of the Soulless? Or a dragon?"

Adhira hesitated. He was already way off script. The officer had been so ripe that he'd rushed along, helping the man draw conclusions to see his own doubt. It was time to make a big gamble. Standing, he slowly removed his armor, saving his helmet for last. He stood before the officer, wearing all black, the black scarf around his eyes.

A chair fell back as the man shot to his feet. "You. You're the ghost rider."

Adhira smiled despite himself. The *Ghost Rider* comics were some of his favorites.

They stood there for a while. Adhira needed him to put the pieces together and give the man time to process the information. Would Ivak cry an alarm, or would he join them? Before he could find out, a horn blasted outside, low and short.

"*Soldiers are coming down the road,*" Euroclydon said. "*Hundreds of them.*"

Chapter 20

Neither flight nor fight was a good option. His men would be slaughtered. Half were already being tied up with the other prisoners. Ivak remained still; whether from fear or indecision, Adhira didn't know.

"What should we do?" Ivak asked, at last, freeing Adhira of his own indecision.

Adhira quickly donned his armor.

"We need to know how many men feel the way you do," Adhira said.

"And then what? Will we desert?"

"No, we will do what soldiers do best. We will fight."

"We need to talk more," Ivak said, walking out of the tent. "Go back to your men and wait for me. Right now, I need to find out why a raiding party is at my camp." Adhira moved through the tents, walking beside Euroclydon for guidance.

"*The Soulless do not converse with the humans,*" the horse said. "*This alliance was already tenuous before our arrival.*"

"It's all a bunch of dry brush waiting for a spark," Adhira said quietly.

"That was quick," Roan said when Adhira walked up. "What's going on?"

"There is a large group at the gate. The officer I was speaking to, Ivak, went to go talk to them."

"I talked with a handful of guards when I dropped off the guys at the prisoners' pen. I barely mentioned the Soulless once, and the guards let out a rather impressive string of profanity, cussing every creature from Soulless to Shedim. I think we just jumped into a simmering pot that is about to boil. The men, those that are still human, are scared."

"Let's not get too eager," Adhira said, though he hadn't taken his own advice. "There will always be those who are blinded by their loyalty."

"It's already getting dark out," Roan said. "I've circled the wagons to give us a little privacy while we sleep."

"Good. Let's practice our sword art and figure out what we will be doing tomorrow. I think our original plans need some major tweaking."

"Especially since the number of enemies in the camp may have just doubled," Roan said, leading the way.

No one sought them out the rest of the night, giving them time to adjust their plans and make new ones.

✳✳✳

They had barely finished breakfast the next morning before Euroclydon informed him they had company. "*Ivak is coming with one of the Soulless,*" the horse said as Adhira walked out from between the carts in full armor.

"That Soulless outranks you," Roan said quickly. "Fair warning."

"Good morning, sir," Ivak said as he and the Soulless stopped in front of them.

"Good morning," Adhira said. "And to you, too, sir."

"You are Sky," the Soulless said, skipping pleasantries and not even giving his name. "This is a magnificent Shayatin mount you have."

"Yes, sir," Adhira said. "He's as fast as lightning and stronger than a bull."

"What's a bull?" Ivak asked. Oops.

"It is a strong animal where I'm from," Adhira said off-handedly.

"My current mount is under-sized," the Soulless said. "It will be reissued to you, and I will take this one as my mount."

"*If this Lesser Shayatin touches me, I will kill him,*" Euroclydon said, taking a step back.

"Of course," Adhira said pleasantly to the Soulless. "He has always been too much horse for me. But he is a highly temperamental war mount. Let me soothe him and explain that everything will be okay."

Adhira walked over to Euroclydon, making cooing sounds. When he got close to the horse, he said quietly, "I want you to take him on a ride around the countryside. Make sure he doesn't come back."

"*That, I can agree to,*" Euroclydon said eagerly.

Adhira stroked Euroclydon's flank to keep up the appearance of soothing as he led the horse over to the Soulless.

"I'll hold the reigns while you mount up, sir. I recommend you take him for a ride so he can get used to you." Once the Soulless was mounted up, Adhira removed his saddlebags and threw them onto a nearby cart. There was no need to put them on the other horse.

"You just gave him your horse?" Ivak asked incredulously when the Soulless was out of earshot.

Roan echoed him with, "What just happened?"

"Do you remember what we talked about last night?" Adhira asked, directing his question at Roan.

"Yes. And?"

Turning to Ivak, Adhira said, "We needed a way to even the odds a little better, you know, between human and not human."

"We are outnumbered two to one," Ivak said.

"Exactly," Adhira said. "But if you were worried about a force of marauders roaming the countryside, attacking scouts and such, you would send out patrols to combat them."

"Sky will lead out a patrol," Roan added. "But many won't come back. These marauders are quite fierce." In a whisper, he added, "I just winked for effect."

"Won't they notice only non-humans are falling in battle?" Ivak asked, catching on to their meaning.

"Not until after we have gone on a couple of patrols," Adhira said. "After the second patrol, I need you to conduct a field exercise with the entire camp."

"But what about your horse?" Ivak asked. "Is that part of the plan?"

"That, my friend, is a happy accident. I have a feeling our Soulless friend will be the first casualty of the marauders."

"And now we have the perfect excuse to send out the first patrol," Roan said. "Sky, you are a genius!"

"Time will tell. Now, we need to begin vetting soldiers. Find out who's ready to hear some hard truths."

"I have an idea where to start," Ivak said. "I'll meet with some of my officers now. Let me know when your horse returns." With that, Ivak walked away.

"I'll go talk with the soldiers guarding the prisoners," Roan said. "I'll talk to our men too and update them on the plan." Roan walked away, leaving Adhira alone. With tasks set and plans put into motion, there wasn't really anything left for him to do.

He thought about practicing with his sword, but it was best if he remained fresh for the patrol later. Wandering around the carts, he pretended to inspect their contents by lifting canvas covers. He did several circuits before sitting on the ground against a cart. He sat for hours as he felt the sun shift high overhead.

He was dozing when Roan ran up. "Sky, a couple of Shayatin are grabbing prisoners to feed to the Se'irim!" he said in a rush.

"Take me," Adhira said, hopping to his feet.

He was led at a run to where two women and a man could be heard screaming in terror.

"What's going on?" Adhira demanded as he slowed and walked up to them. He used his gift to feel around really quickly. The two Shayatin were dragging the civilians across the ground.

"We don't answer to you," one of the Shayatin said in a gravelly voice that could barely be understood. Adhira was already missing the horse's descriptions. Every Shayatin looked different with different abilities. It would be nice to know what he was up against.

"This says that you do," Adhira said, pointing to his rank insignia.

"That means nothing to us," the same Shayatin said. It tried to step around Adhira, but the Indian moved back in the way.

"Do you know the penalty for disobeying a direct order?" Adhira didn't know but assumed it was harsh.

"And who will carry it out?" the Shayatin asked, dropping his prisoner and stepping up to Adhira. "You?" This close, the smell of sulfur was almost overwhelming.

Great. He needed to hold this together for just a little longer, and these bozos were going to make him kill them. He was just about to reach into his satchel for the Sword of Re'u when his gift told him a horn blast was coming. Four quick blasts. Adhira waited. Before long, Euroclydon strode up beside him.

"*The Soulless put up a fight,*" the horse said happily. "*It made his death much more enjoyable.*"

As disturbing as his words were, the return of the horse set the next stage of his plan into motion. "Why is he covered in blood?" Adhira asked.

"His rider must have been killed by the marauders, sir," Roan said.

"What marauders?" the Shayatin asked.

"They've been roaming the area north of here," Adhira said.

"I have heard no such thing."

"Why do you think I showed up here yesterday with only three soldiers and a handful of prisoners? It is a sizable force."

"I heard the signal for possible trouble," Ivak said, walking up. "What's going on?"

"The horse came back without its rider," Adhira said.

"Do you think it was the group of marauders you told me about?" Ivak asked.

Adhira nodded. "I think I should take out a large patrol to track them down."

"How many do you need?" Ivak asked.

"I want 150 of your best warriors," Adhira said.

"The Shayatin are the best warriors," the Shayatin interjected.

"I agree," Adhira said. "How many Shayatin and Enhanced do you have in this camp?" Enhanced was what the Soulless called themselves.

"Twenty-seven," Ivak said.

"I would like to take all twenty-seven with me," Adhira said. "Along with seventy Se'irim and fifty archers. Do you have fifty archers that are any good?"

"Yes," Ivak said, reading the hidden meaning in Adhira's words. "But can you handle so many?"

"Yes," Adhira said. "I am confident I can. Have them report here as soon as possible." When Ivak walked away, Adhira turned back to the Shayatin. "I want my dogs hungry for the hunt. The Se'irim will feast on marauder tonight. Gather the Shayatin, Enhanced, and Se'irim." Without waiting for a response, Adhira walked off.

"Well, that almost went to the dung heap," Roan said.

"Yes," Adhira said. "Go grab the brothers and meet me outside of the northern barricade."

Adhira replaced his saddlebags and swung up into the saddle.

"*Who are we killing?*" Euroclydon asked, picking his way through the camp.

"Everything that isn't human," Adhira said.

"*Two of the Shayatin I've seen have poison quills. If you receive so much as a scratch, you are dead.*"

"What about you?" Adhira asked. "Can their poison kill you?"

"*I've been poisoned several times by Shayatin, but my resistance is high. If two of them poisoned me together, it could be fatal.*"

"Then we know who has to go first."

The archers, all human, were the first to meet them near the road leading north, easily within sight of the camp. The men were armed with short bows and throwing spears.

"They will listen to your orders," Ivak said. "All of your orders. Good luck." He rode back to camp, leaving them all to wait for the others. The monsters were a long time in coming, but eventually, the howls of Se'irim on the hunt filled the air as the other part of their group came out of the camp.

"We will head north until the Se'irim pick up the scent," Adhira announced. "I will scout ahead." To his horse, he said, "Take me to where your last rider was killed."

Euroclydon galloped swiftly north before cutting across the hilly terrain. Their speed took them far ahead of the patrol.

"*I killed him in a valley just ahead,*" the horse said. "*There is an overhang to the left and a steep slope to the right. The overhang hides what is below, but the hill gives a clear view of the small valley.*"

"It will have to do," Adhira said.

They moved back to the main road and waited for the patrol to arrive.

"*They are coming,*" Euroclydon said. "*But we have a problem. The Shayatin and Se'irim have outpaced the humans and Soulless.*"

"Just great," Adhira said. When the group reached them, he said, "We will wait here for the others."

"We will not," one of the Shayatin said. "The Se'irim smell blood that way. You can stay here and wait for the others if you want." The group moved on. Adhira saw that anything he said would be useless.

"*When they reach the body,*" Euroclydon said. "*They will see that there was no ambush. I don't know what conclusions they will draw, but there is nothing that points to a large group of marauders.*"

"What are we facing?"

"*The Soulless are back with the archers. Eleven Shayatin, and seventy Se'irim. There are actually three with poison quills, one that can breathe fire, two that can fly, and others with unknown abilities.*"

"We need to take out the flyers first," Adhira said. He quickly pulled off the helmet and other armor and dropped them to the ground. It was time for him to become the ghost again. "I will lead with arrows. You need to guide my aim. Let's go." He pulled out the Sword of Re'u and let it turn into a bow.

"*Both of the flyers are hanging low above the Se'irim, directly in front of us.*"

Adhira loosed an arrow directly ahead. Euroclydon told him to aim higher and to the right.

Starting over, Adhira loosed again. This time, his shot was just too low. It took several more tries before he dropped the first flyer.

By the time he zeroed in on and felled the other, the Shayatin and Se'irim were turning about to find who had shot the silver arrows. It wasn't a hard puzzle for them to figure out.

"Head on! Aim for the Shayatin." Adhira shouted, pulling out the

Vapor Blade and standing in the stirrups as Euroclydon rushed forward. With both blades poised, they bore down on the creatures, who were trying to form up just as the giant horse crashed into them. There was far less give than there had been against humans.

Adhira set about him on both sides as they slowed in the midst of the enemy. Twice, he had to raise his shield to stop poisoned quills from burying themselves in his neck and arm. Euroclydon pushed forward and out of the press.

"That was almost disastrous," Euroclydon said. "The Se'irim are running wild and chasing us."

"Lead them off a bit and circle back. We don't need one of the Shayatin getting wise and running back to camp."

Euroclydon slowed enough to keep the beasts interested, then circled back to the waiting Shayatin. "There are four Shayatin left. One with poison and another with fire."

Euroclydon veered right, and Adhira blocked a fireball with his shield. Cutting back left, Euroclydon strafed two of the Shayatin, allowing Adhira to kill them with a low swipe of the Vapor Blade. Before they could turn to the other two, the Se'irim caught up to them, forcing them to run away again.

Above the howls of the Se'irim, Adhira heard the shouts of men and the clang of metal on metal.

"The men and Soulless are above us on the overhang fighting each other."

"They will have to take care of themselves. If we go, a bunch of Se'irim will follow. Let's do like we did before."

Euroclydon led the Se'irim on a short chase and circled back around to the remaining Shayatin. The horse stumbled as a fireball exploded at his feet. The Shayatin was targeting Euroclydon instead of Adhira. A stream of fireballs followed. They were able to outpace the fire, swinging wide around the two Shayatin. The fireballs abruptly stopped.

"The archers are in place."

"Good, now let's see how dumb the Se'irim really are. Stay just ahead of them like before."

They ran in a large circle. Every time they came within bow range, arrows fell among the Se'irim. The creatures were so blind with blood lust that they never stopped chasing them, even when their numbers were diminished down to a handful. Not able to keep down the hunger for battle any longer, Adhira turned Euroclydon and charged into the remaining Se'irim, killing them with swift strikes from both swords.

"I think that's all of them," Roan said when Adhira rode up the hill to regroup with the archers.

"What happened up here?"

"When the Soulless saw what was happening below, we attacked them before they could ride down the hill. Even caught by surprise, those guys put up quite a fight. We killed them all but lost five of our own. We have a few wounded, too, but nothing serious."

"*Where did we kill...*" Euroclydon asked.

"We need to get back to camp!" Adhira yelled, cutting off the horse. The first Shayatin he shot, the flyer, was gone.

Euroclydon raced toward the camp. How long ago had the flyer left? Did it see the other humans turn on the creatures, or did it leave right after it was shot? If the two of them got back before the creature did, they might be able to stop its report. The smell of smoke met them when they crested a hill and galloped onto the main road. Most camps smelled like smoke, but this was stronger than it should have been.

"*Tents are burning.*"

Chapter 21

"*There is fighting. Men are killing men, and Se'irim are running wild, attacking anyone in their path.*"

Even if he could see, how was he supposed to know which humans were which? "We need to find Ivak." The horse took them into the fray.

A claw pulled him from the saddle.

He swung around, cutting off an arm before beheading the Se'irim. Men and women screamed on all sides. Howls pierced the air as Adhira rode among the fighting. He had no way of knowing who was winning.

"Where are my shields!" Ivak yelled from in front of them. "We need to stop the Se'irim from flanking us!"

"Ivak," Adhira said when he was next to the man who rode his own horse. "What's going on?"

"Good," the man said. "You are alive. One of the Shayatin flew in here wounded, screaming about how the humans were betraying them. When it said it was going to warn the other camps, I drew my sword and killed it. Men took sides, though many had no clue what was going on. All the fighting set the Se'irim into a blood lust, and they broke out of their pen. Without the Shayatin or Soulless to calm them, they are running wild."

"What's the plan?" Adhira asked.

"No plan. It's too confusing. We don't even know if everyone we are fighting knows what they are fighting for."

"They need someone to guide them," Adhira said, shaking his head to clear it. The urge to fight was growing strong again, but he had nowhere close at hand to channel it. "Call them to rally, and their training should kick in."

"With what? The signal horn is somewhere in this mess."

"We'll have to do it the hard way. I'll ride through the camp, yelling for the men to rally outside the camp. We need to disentangle them from infighting."

"The northern hill," Ivak said. "Tell the men to go there."

Euroclydon ran through the camp, with Adhira yelling at the top of his lungs, "All men to the northern hill! Rally at the northern hill! Everyone to the north! Rally! Stop fighting each other! Rally north!"

Adhira couldn't tell what people were doing in response to his words. Several times, he had to pause to kill Se'irim.

"*There is a large group of humans surrounded by Se'irim,*" Euroclydon said. "*Get ready to strike on the left.*"

With the horse's guidance, Adhira was able to slay several Se'irim as they rode around the beasts, which were too focused on the human buffet in front of them. His horse killed the last of them with a double kick from his back legs.

"Rally to the north of the camp!" Adhira yelled at the people they'd saved before kicking Euroclydon into motion again.

"*There are fewer men in the camp,*" the horse said at length. "*We risk getting bogged down here.*"

"We can't leave men behind to be butchered by the Se'irim," Adhira said. "Let's help anyone we can."

Adhira had to trust the horse's discretion as they rode from one skirmish to another, which were becoming more desperate with each passing moment. They were able to free a few groups, but the press of Se'irim was getting to be too much. He could still hear men screaming.

"*We have to go.*"

"No!"

"*They are already dead, and we will be, too. Besides, Se'irim are chasing people to the rally point. We can't save them all.*"

Adhira didn't protest further as the horse turned and galloped out of camp, leaving the screams of the dying behind them. If only he still had his sight. How could he be an effective fighter when he couldn't see?

The pair zigzagged across the plains leading to the hill, cutting down any Se'irim that had broken free of the slaughter in the camp. It was several minutes before the last of the people fleeing the camp made it to the rally point. There were heated arguments among the gathered soldiers when the pair of them rode up.

"They were going to kill us all!" Ivak was yelling at another soldier. "We had to act first!"

"You are a traitor! Our blood is on your hands, Ivak!"

"Shut up!" Adhira yelled at the pair. Then, louder, he said, "Everyone just shut up!"

"The Se'irim are gathering at the edge of the camp. When the pack is together, they will charge."

"Whatever the reasons, those Se'irim are going to come up here and kill us all if we don't stop fighting each other. Form up and listen to your officers!" No one moved and some of the arguments started up again. Adhira felt anger surge up inside of him. Their infighting was about to get them all slaughtered.

"We can put the prisoners up front!" the soldier who'd been arguing with Ivak said. "The Se'irim won't attack us once their blood lust is sated. They are trained to obey us."

Adhira couldn't contain the lust for battle anymore as his left arm swung around as if on its own. The Vapor Blade took the man's head off his shoulders. The arguments abruptly cut off in shock, which matched Adhira's own. What had he just done?

"They are coming."

"Form ranks!" Ivak yelled.

"They won't survive a charge this size. What do you want to do?"

Adhira was still dazed by what he'd just done. He just killed a man for speaking. They were evil words born from selfish and calloused thoughts, but they were still just words. And he killed the man.

"Sky, what do you want to do?"

"Break the charge," Adhira said, coming back to himself. "We need to hit them on the flank and try to draw their attention."

Euroclydon galloped down the hill before turning and picking up speed. *"Swing right."*

Adhira leaned forward with the sword of Re'u ready. According to Euroclydon, they hit the Se'irim from the side, passing in front of the charging beasts. So many in the front ranks fell to his blade that the others stumbled and broke apart. Another pass across the rear of the enemy sowed enough confusion that the momentum of the charge was broken.

Suddenly, there were other horsemen riding near them. Euroclydon described a scene with soldiers on horseback riding around the Se'irim, circling them as arrows were fired into the mass of creatures. With both blades ready, Adhira rode into the midst of the Se'irim, removing limbs and heads with ease. The beasts' howls changed, becoming more frantic. It was the first time Adhira had heard it from them. Panic.

Soldiers crashed into the Se'irim, biting deep into the creatures' ranks, what was left of them. Even afraid, the beasts were formidable, slicing at men and horses indiscriminately. Adhira saw none of it, but the sounds painted a very gruesome picture as man and beast alike screamed in fear, pain, and battle lust.

Adhira was increasingly unable to use the Vapor Blade for fear of hurting a human. Though a part of him wanted to keep fighting in the thick of it, he pulled Euroclydon back to focus more on the Se'irim as they began to flee. The pair of them rode through the hills, killing any of the escaping beasts they came upon.

Adhira was glad he could not see the carnage when they rode back to the battlefield. All the Se'irim were either dead or fled, though Euroclydon thought they'd gotten them all. Moans of pain and grief drifted across the hillside as Euroclydon picked his way among the dead and injured. How many would die still when Asa could have simply touched them and brought them back from the brink of death?

"What have we done?" Ivak asked quietly to Adhira as the man rode up to the giant horse. "So many…"

"You saved lives," Adhira said with more confidence than he felt. "This battle was going to happen no matter what you did. If you had waited for them to strike the first blow, not only would every man in this camp be dead, but all the men in all the camps everywhere."

"What do we do now?" Ivak asked. "This battle will not have gone unnoticed." Ivak was an officer in the military. Why did everyone always need to be told what to do?

Adhira put his swords away reluctantly and took a calming breath before answering. "Signal the other camps," Adhira said. "We won, so we can frame the events in whatever light we want. Call for help."

"They will send more than just humans," Ivak pointed out.

"I'm counting on it," Adhira said.

Some of the lower-ranking officers were organizing men and women into groups to help transport and treat the wounded. Ivak grabbed a passing officer and told him to signal the other camps for help.

"I need to take charge of this," Ivak said before riding away. "Meet me in my tent when I have this mess sorted."

"What's the plan?" Roan asked, riding up.

"So, you are alive," Adhira said. "How did everyone fair?"

"We lost Rixen, and the old man has a couple of new scars, but the rest of us are okay. We grabbed the horses and got here just in time to help you break the enemy charge."

"Just in time, indeed," Adhira said.

"I see you managed to arm the prisoners," Roan said. "Without the extra manpower, this fight would have looked very different."

Adhira hadn't even realized the prisoners were armed. Their planted "prisoners" must have been able to get the weapons to the captives somehow.

"What's the plan?" Roan asked again.

"We wait," Adhira said. "Ivak is having his man signal the other camps for aid."

"Smart," Roan said. "We need to stay out ahead of this thing. Are we going to attack the shadow creatures when help arrives?"

"No," Adhira said. "We are going to talk to them until the shadow creatures attack the men they come with."

"And how will you manage that?"

"Talking is what I'm best at," Adhira said.

"That is definitely not what you're best at," Roan said under his breath.

Adhira heard but chose to ignore him. "How many dead, do you think?"

"Humans?" Roan asked. "I would say nearly a hundred, maybe. More alive than dead, though. A lot more."

"Still, so many," Adhira said. Everything went so wrong. He should have made sure the flyer was dead.

"If we had done nothing, they would have kept feeding those people to the Se'irim. A lot of people were going to die regardless. This way, most of the women and children are alive."

"It still sucks," Adhira said.

"Are you okay?" Roan asked. "Your left arm looks odd."

"What do you mean?"

"It's darker than your other arm, and your veins almost look black. I noticed it looked odd this morning, but we were busy. It looks worse now."

"I feel fine," Adhira said. He flexed his left hand. It felt fine, but there was an odd sensation like something was missing, as if his hand needed to be holding something.

"I'm going to find an ax and cut down a tree or five for some wood," Roan said. "We have a lot of burning to do."

"Don't worry about the ax. I'll come with you," Adhira said.

"I'll grab a wagon then."

"*No need for a wagon,*" Euroclydon said. "*I can drag a tree back whole.*"

"No wagon," Adhira said. "Just get some rope. Clyde wants to show us how strong he is."

Darkness had descended before the pyres were lit. They burned the Se'irim separately from the humans. It seemed appropriate somehow.

The Road to War

✷✷✷

"Despite our loses, everyone is moving with purpose like I haven't seen in months," Ivak said later that evening. He paced his tent nervously. "I can't remember the last time I was in a camp that was wholly human."

"Now imagine if the other camps follow your example," Adhira said. He had redonned his armor, everything except the helmet, which rested on the table in front of him.

"Speaking of which, there are three forward bases sending aid. Our scouts report that the first will arrive shortly. It has somewhere around two hundred men and an equal number of shadow creatures."

"Do you want me to do the talking?" Adhira asked.

"Please," Ivak said. "I can give orders fine, but navigating the intricacies of persuasion and men's hearts is far beyond me."

"*The force is arriving now*," Euroclydon said from outside the tent.

"You are doing better than you think," Adhira said to Ivak before standing. Picking up his helmet and putting it on, he said, "It's time. Make sure your men are all in position. Let's see what happens."

Adhira drew both swords as he walked out of the tent. He resisted sighing in relief when he felt the sword hilts in his hands. Complete was the only way to describe how it felt to hold the weapons as he walked through camp. Euroclydon walked beside him, guiding him to where a group of soldiers were standing outside the camp's ring of spikes.

"Remember," Adhira said to Euroclydon. "Stay out of the fighting this time. When the battle starts, I don't want a human putting a spear in you."

"What is going on here?" The voice was deep, that of a Soulless.

"You know what is going on!" Adhira said, walking outside of the protective ring of spikes. As usual, he used his gift to help him choose his words and actions carefully.

"Who are you? Why are the prisoners armed? And where are the others?" There was no doubt who he meant by the others.

Adhira walked up to the speaker but talked loudly so everyone present could hear. "We found out about the Shayatin plans to betray us!" He didn't use Tanas as his example as he'd planned. Tanas' name would have been met with anger from the men who were still under the dragon's spell of deception.

"What foolishness are you speaking about?"

"Don't try to deny it," Adhira said. "The war is nearing its end. You don't need us anymore. The Shayatin and Se'irim attacked us. The only reason we survived was the prisoners came to our aid. You didn't factor that into your plans, did you?"

The Soulless he was speaking to drew a weapon. "I will not listen to this anymore!"

"I wasn't talking to you!" Adhira said, raising his voice even more. "Men. Look around you. Every day, the camp is filled with more of them and less of us. They have been waiting for the right time. That time is now. Look at the men around me. Every one of them will confirm what I've said."

"*Most of their men are backing away from the Shayatin, Se'irim, and Soulless,*" Euroclydon said. "*Your words are having an effect. Some of the men are staying near the shadow creatures, though.*"

"King Tanas wouldn't let that happen!" a man shouted.

"He isn't here," one of the other soldiers said. "I've seen the way they look at us. They hate us. Despise us."

"I've felt this coming for a while," another man said.

"Shut up, all of you!" the Soulless said. He stepped forward and swung at Adhira, who dodged easily.

"You can't silence the truth!" Adhira said, dancing back to avoid another swing.

This was good, but he needed to get the men involved. Ducking another swing, he backed toward where their men were gathered.

"I'm just trying to talk," Adhira pleaded.

"Let him speak," a man said from behind Adhira. More weapons were drawn, stopping the Soulless from advancing further. It was time. He raised his sword in the air.

"To arms!" men shouted all around him.

Adhira stepped forward to where the Soulless had paused. This time, when the Soulless swung at him, Adhira sidestepped the attack and cut off a hand.

"Help me!" the Soulless screamed. It was the final spark they needed.

"*The shadow creatures are attacking the humans now.*"

Adhira rushed into the den of war cries. Cutting down the first Se'irim that came at him, Adhira leaped over the beast and cleared an area just behind it. Barbs bounced off his armor before Adhira could cut down the Shayatin. He needed to be faster. Rushing through the ranks, he was able to carve a path through the confusion.

The enemies didn't see him coming until it was too late. Though the press of bodies threatened to overwhelm him, he found openings or created them so he never broke stride. Raising the Abyss Shield just in time, he was able to block a spray of acid that would have melted through his armor in seconds. Running at full speed, Adhira let the shield grow larger until it enveloped the Shayatin, sending it to the Abyss through its shadow gate.

Fighting from Euroclydon's saddle had been devastating for the enemies they'd faced so far, but nothing gave him more satisfaction than moving through his forms, dancing through the enemy with his blades of power. Anytime he drew near the humans as they fought the lines of shadow creatures, he would dive right back into the swirling mass of creatures. Euroclydon followed the fight and kept him updated.

The humans outside the wall held off the initial charge. Men from inside the camp hit the creatures in the flank, and their horse archers rode in to attack them from the rear. With fighting on three sides and having a wild honey badger in their midst, the shadow creatures were soon overwhelmed. It wasn't enough to extinguish the fire that had been building in Adhira. The battle lust had grown to an inferno, stronger than it had ever been.

A horn sounded in the night. Then another.

"*Men and creatures are attacking the camp from the north,*" Euroclydon said, riding up to Adhira as he finished off a soulless with a backhanded swing.

"Defend the camp!" Ivak yelled from somewhere. Others took up the cry.

"*What do you want to do?*" Euroclydon asked.

"It's time to be ghosts again," Adhira said, swinging into the saddle.

With that, Euroclydon rode off into the cool night. According to the horse, who could see rather well in the dark, there were hundreds of men and creatures assaulting the camp. Did the men not see what the fighting was really about?

"I want to focus mostly on Shayatin and Se'irim, but we need to protect the camp."

"*Only kill humans if they get in the way,*" Euroclydon confirmed, turning sharply. That wasn't exactly what Adhira said, but close enough.

"I'm going to hit them in the flank, near the front, so it disrupts their press against the outer defenses."

The horse picked up speed. When the first thump of metal rang off the horse's armor as he trampled someone, Adhira began swinging. He felt a satisfactory heat pulse through his veins with each kill. Instead of being sated, the battle lust grew. They passed through the enemy,

Euroclydon never slowing as he tore through the ranks from the side.

They had barely made it free of the press before circling around and hitting them again from another angle. Again and again, they hit them, but always there were more.

Suddenly, Euroclydon fell, sending Adhira flying. He landed on his side but pushed himself to his feet and ran over to the horse. One of the horse's legs was missing at the knee.

After running through a few scenarios in the split second it took for him to see the immediate future, Adhira dove from the horse. As he flew through the air, he sliced down with the Sword of Re'u, severing an arm, which dropped the sword it had been swinging at Euroclydon's leg.

He blocked a ball of fire with the Forest Shield before rushing into the crowd. With the armor he was wearing, it was impossible for those around him to know he was a foe until he attacked. Many fell to his blades as he moved among the rows. It was easy killing. Too easy. He hungered for a fight!

As he moved among the enemy, he put away the Sword of Re'u and began shedding his armor. Speed was gained with each piece dropped. At last, he removed his helmet, which he used to bash a Se'irim in the face before dropping it and taking up his other blade again.

The desired result came crashing in on him as the enemy saw him for what he was. Weapons and claws sought his flesh from all sides. He continued moving as he fought. This worked the Se'irim into a frenzy as they tried to catch him, breaking ranks and turning the force into a swirling mass with Adhira at the center. Without the armor to constrict his movements, he swung his swords with lightning speed. The shields saved him when he wasn't able to kill fast enough, but this fact infuriated him, pushing him to greater speeds.

It was impossible to tell if he was killing man or beast as he moved among the enemy. Whenever a weapon would have killed or wounded him, he would kill whomever it belonged to.

There was a sudden shift in the battle. The press of bodies toward him became a press away. Nothing sought to kill him but only to get away from him. He didn't let them. Couldn't let them. His thirst for blood had not been quenched. The retreat bogged down as men and creatures trampled each other in their haste to get away.

Adhira took full advantage, laying about himself with both swords, striking several enemies with each stroke. A few turned to fight him, but without the strength of numbers, they barely slowed him. Soon, none were fighting back at all, but he showed no mercy.

The Road to War

He cut through a Se'irim, shoulder to shoulder. Sprinting forward, he used the Vapor Blade to stab a man in the chest. Before the soldier struck the ground, Adhira spun to his right and swung at a man with the Sword of Re'u. The blade bounced off the man as a stick would against a brick wall.

Rushing ahead, he felt around, finding the man didn't have a shield or a blade of power. He swung with the Sword of Re'u again, but still, the weapon bounced off.

He struck out with the Sword of Re'u again in real time at a different target, but once again, the sword bounced off. Another target and another failed attempt. It was like beating a stick against stone.

The Sword of Re'u no longer worked as it should, but the Vapor Blade had no such restrictions. Quickly tucking away the Sword of Re'u, he moved through the enemies once again, cutting down any who came within reach. The den of battle had been replaced with cries of fear. A voice cried out his name, faint, though it sounded like it came from directly beside him. Still, he killed.

"Sky!" Roan yelled. "Stop! They are trying to surrender! Stop!"

Stop? He couldn't stop. The enemy wouldn't stop. They never stopped. Death. It was the only way to stop them. He would kill them all!

A hand grabbed his shoulder. For the next fifteen seconds, he saw himself kill the person who grabbed him. Over and over, he killed, but something deep within him screamed to stop. In real time, he paused his swing before it struck down the man who'd grabbed him.

"They surrendered! It's okay. You can stop now." It was Roan. He'd almost killed Roan! "It's okay," Roan said loudly, his voice changing slightly as he turned away from Adhira. "He's blind! He didn't know the fighting stopped!"

That wasn't true. The Sword of Re'u stopped working. Even caught up in the battle, he knew what it meant when the sword wouldn't hurt someone. And he'd killed anyway. Still holding the Vapor Blade, he walked off.

"Where are you going?" Roan asked.

Adhira paused and said over his shoulder, "I'm going to practice my sword art." The urge to fight was still strong, and only exhaustion would stop it. He hoped it would stop it.

Euroclydon caught up to him but remained silent as he led Adhira to the carts, which had remained largely untouched during the fighting. Walking to the center of the ring of carts, he started going through the forms. He went through the various forms as fast as he could while properly following through with strikes, though he didn't practice blocking. His stance remained offensive throughout his session, fluidly moving from strike to strike.

Chapter 22

When Adhira woke, he still held the Vapor Blade in his hand. He vaguely remembered falling asleep at some point in the night. The rest of the camp was already buzzing with activity.

"Sky, you okay?" Roan asked as boots crunched the dirt nearby.

Adhira slowly stood to his feet and grunted. "Yeah."

"Does the offer still stand?" Roan asked.

Adhira looked ahead at the conversation and didn't feel like going through it for real. "No," he said simply. "I should not have offered you this sword before. You are not ready for a blade of power."

"Maybe I can just take it to practice with," Roan said.

"Maybe you should let the boy practice with it," Euroclydon said. Why did the horse sound concerned?

"When he is ready," Adhira said sternly. "Tell me what is happening now," he said, waving his hand behind him to indicate the camp.

"Most of the men from last night's fighting have joined us. Ivak is preparing the men here to march on the other camps one by one," Roan said. "He's already sent riders to inform the human officers of what is going on."

"When do we leave?" Adhira asked.

Roan didn't answer right away. "Um, maybe you should stay here," he said slowly. "If the Se'irim or Shayatin who escaped last night attack the camp while we are gone, they will need your help."

"The stragglers will not be coming back here," Adhira said. "If anything, they are already at the other camps spreading their own tales of what happened. I will ride with Ivak. When do we leave?"

"Soon, but Sky, the truth is I'm worried about you. Your veins are black as oil, and there are tendrils of smoke rising off the left side of your body. You look half Shayatin."

"I feel fine," Adhira said, mounting up. "Let's go."

"*Ivak wants to see you,*" Euroclydon said. "*We captured quite a few Shayatin and Soulless. He wanted to know what to do with them.*"

"Why didn't he just kill them all?"

"*If an enemy knows there will be no quarter, he will fight that much fiercer. I gave him another option. I told him about the Abyss Shield you carry.*"

"I'm surprised you let him get close enough to have a conversation," Adhira said. "What you say makes sense, though. We give them a choice: death or the Abyss."

"That's right," Ivak said, walking up to him. "We should probably take care of this before we ride."

Adhira dismounted. "Just show me where." He was set up in a tent where he let the Abyss shield grow to its full size. His job was to mostly sit there, though he held the Vapor Blade ready just in case. One by one, the creatures were led into the tent and given the choice. A few chose to fight, but Adhira was quick with his sword and stopped them before anyone could be hurt.

"That's the last of them," Ivak said after an hour of the task. "Are you doing okay? You have what looks like black smoke following you when you move. I've never seen sickness like it before."

"I'm fine," Adhira said with more heat than he intended. "Now, let's go liberate the other camps."

The army, which was a nearly even mix of mounted and ground troops, moved out toward the closest outpost. It was one of the camps that sent troops the previous night, so they didn't expect there to be many left. While they rode, Adhira wondered what the men of Orm thought was going on. There was no way they missed all the fighting.

They were barely halfway to their target camp when a scout rode up with a dire report. "There is infighting in the other forward bases," the scout said, pacing his horse with Adhira and Ivak. "The humans must have gotten your messages first because they seem organized and are holding their own. Only camp eight is truly in danger of being overrun."

"Where is camp eight?" Adhira asked quickly. He waited painstakingly as the man described the place.

"*I can find it,*" Euroclydon said when the man was done.

"Help the other camps," Adhira said to Ivak and kicked his horse into motion.

With Euroclydon's speed, it wasn't long before they were near the target camp.

"*The humans are surrounded and doing little more than hiding behind their shields. One of the Soulless is waving us over. The fool believes we are one of them.*"

"Let's show him his error," Adhira said.

Euroclydon picked up speed as they crashed into the creatures pressing toward the humans. The next hour was a blur. Euroclydon never stopped moving. They rushed into the fray and back out again before they could get bogged down. Adhira didn't know how many enemies died before they realized what was happening. Even when creatures started targeting the pair, it was like trying to catch smoke. The two of them didn't stop moving until the enemy broke, fleeing away from the camp and the men trapped there.

"Why are you stopping?" Adhira yelled. "Let's kill them all!" He barely recognized his own voice. It sounded throaty, almost like an animal growl that was trying to form into words.

"*The other camps need our help*," Euroclydon said. "*Men will die if we hunt all those that flee.*"

"We must kill them all!" Adhira repeated. He felt like he was starving, and the only thing that could satisfy him was more fighting.

"*There are more to kill in the other camps*," the horse said.

"Then let's go!" Adhira yelled.

He lost count of the camps as the enemy broke before them over and over. The cadence of insects told him night had long since descended when he slumped to the ground at their own camp. It was the first time he felt truly exhausted in months without doing his sword art. There were still more to kill. The camps were free of the creatures, but they had all gone somewhere, and he intended to find out where in the morning. He closed his eyes.

✱✱✱

His eyes popped open. He heard a whisper, "eleven, ten."

Adhira tried to sit up, but dozens of hands grabbed him at once, pinning him to the ground.

"Grab it!" someone yelled.

"I can't; he has a death grip on it." Roan's voice. What was going on?

"Get off me!" Adhira yelled. At least, that was what he tried to yell. The words came out as more of a menacing growl.

Someone was trying to pull the Vapor Blade out of his hand. Adhira couldn't move any of his limbs, but he looked ahead and saw his opening. The grip someone had on his wrist was about to slip just slightly. He would be able to turn the sword in his hand and cut down those holding that arm. Then he could kill the rest.

"Release the blade!" Roan yelled. "Sky, you have to let go!"

A faint voice pulled at a memory buried deep in the back of his mind.

"Please," Roan pleaded. "Let go of the sword!"

"*Let go*," Euroclydon said.

The voice, the other one in his head, why did it sound so familiar? Roan said to let go again, but this time, he didn't hear it as Roan's voice, but Neviah's.

"There will be a moment, Adhira. The moment. You will have to let go. Choose to let go."

Adhira let go. He didn't expect the pain. It felt like his entire arm was being pulled off.

"Sky, open the shadow gate."

Men let go of him, and he let the Abyss Shield open in front of him. Suddenly, the pain was gone, and the sensation of loss was replaced by numbness. His head felt clear for the first time in weeks.

He rolled over so he was kneeling face down in the dirt and wept, though his eyes could no longer produce tears. How many had he killed? How many men had he killed? He remembered men trying to surrender to him, the Sword of Re'u choosing to spare their lives, but the Vapor Blade demanding their deaths. He'd killed so many. In the past, he'd always tried his best to avoid killing men. If the greater enemy was ever defeated, he wanted there to be as many people left alive as possible.

He'd killed hundreds over the past few days. How many had been men? He'd stopped caring, no longer making the distinction. So many men dead, and though they fought against him, it was due to trickery and deceit. How many would have joined him if they'd only known what he knew about Tanas?

His hatred for the dragon was renewed with great intensity. He didn't know how long he knelt there, but he became aware of a hand resting on his shoulder. Sitting up caused the hand to slowly pull away.

"Thank you," Adhira said. His voice sounded almost back to normal. No other words would come, however.

"You're welcome," Roan said. "I told you the sword was cursed."

Adhira nodded. "You did."

"How are you feeling?" Roan asked.

"Better than I've felt in weeks."

"You look better, too, though that half-Shayatin look was growing on me."

Adhira nodded but didn't trust his voice as his mind drifted.

"It wasn't you," Roan said.

"I know," Adhira said.

"Really, though. It was the sword. I've seen you offer to sacrifice your freedom to spare your captor. This wasn't you."

Adhira nodded. It may have been the Vapor Blade's influence, but he was the one doing the killing. "How did the fighting go?" Adhira asked after a while. "It's all a fog to me."

"All the camps are free of shadow creatures," Roan said. "All except Clyde, though he is looking more gray than black these days. We are all combining into one big camp here. Tomorrow, most of us are heading to the large stronghold in the ruins east of Orm. The ruins are the only place we haven't liberated yet. I think the locals call it the Fire Temple."

"Sounds like something from *The Legend of Zelda*."

"I would like to hear that legend," Roan said.

Adhira laughed, which started as a chuckle and grew to an uncontrollable burst of laughter.

Chapter 23

"Why is it quiet?" Ivak asked as they rode near the outer wall of the ruins of the Fire Temple.

"I don't know," Roan answered. "If they fought here as they did in the other camps, there should be someone, man or monster, manning the walls."

"It could be a trap," Ivak said.

"If so, it's not a very good one," Roan said. "They should know we would send in a scout first."

"I'll go," Adhira said.

"Okay, just report back everything you see," Roan said with a laugh.

Adhira smiled lightheartedly, but his heart still weighed heavily over the events of the past weeks. "Clyde can take note of what he sees," Adhira said.

"Makes sense," Ivak said. "Are you going now?"

"I might as well," Adhira said, and Euroclydon trotted toward the first archway, the doors of which had rotted off long ago.

The only thing barring their way was a couple of large carts, which the horse easily shouldered out of the way. He heard a horse following right behind him. That would be Roan.

"Stay close," Adhira said over his shoulder. "If I say run, you run."

"Will do," Roan said, riding up beside him.

According to Euroclydon, there were tents everywhere, enough to hold a few thousand troops. None aside from them stirred as they moved about the camp, scouting deeper into the ruins. According to Euroclydon, there were ancient buildings, some of which had been turned into kitchens, barracks, and war rooms. Straining his ears against the quiet, he was sure he heard whispers. They sounded faint but human. If the humans had won, they wouldn't like seeing a Shayatin walk through their camp, even with its rider being human.

"How did these soldiers let things go so far?" Roan asked in hushed tones. "From those I've talked to, most all but knew the monsters were planning to destroy all of mankind. They were too frightened to do anything about it, though. If it wasn't for us, I doubt they would have done anything before the Shayatin turned on them and killed them all."

"*Sometimes, men just need a rock to grab onto before they can even think about turning to fight the flood.*"

"Wow, Clyde. That was deep."

"What did he say?" Roan asked.

"Oh, I'm not going to tell you. That way, I can use it later as my own words."

Euroclydon walked sideways and nudged Roan's leg. "Wow. That was deep," Roan said after a moment. "And you're right. This lighting really does compliment my cheekbones."

The horse shook his head, walking away from Roan.

"*You should dismount,*" Euroclydon said after they'd taken a couple more turns. "*The way becomes low and narrow up ahead. Be on guard. I smell a dragon.*"

After relaying this information to Roan, Adhira dismounted and ascended some stairs ahead of the horse. It was a pleasantly warm morning, but the heat increased significantly as he moved higher into the temple. He was sweating when he came to a small door.

"It looks like that door takes you right into the side of the plateau. I won't be able to fit."

"I'll go in and check things out. Why don't you two look around a little more?"

"*And the dragon?*"

"I can handle one dragon," Adhira said confidently, pulling out the Sword of Re'u.

"*Dragons are not so easy a foe as Shayatin and Se'irim.*"

"I know. I've killed a few."

"*Could you see at the time?*"

"I'll be fine," Adhira said, opening the door, which creaked on hinges with the loudest screech he'd ever heard. "Now, go check out the rest of the camp and report back to the others," he said, stepping into a passageway.

"*If you die, I may take Roan as my rider. He is young but shows promise.*"

Adhira poked his head back out of the door. "Clyde, was that a joke?"

The horse was quiet for a moment. "*I suppose it was,*" he said slowly.

"*Though it is probably true as well.*"

The horse descended the stairs, leaving Adhira with a smile on his face for a moment. The crackling of torches welcomed him into the temple as he walked the narrow passageway. The only other sound was his footfalls as he made his way deeper into the temple.

Suddenly, the passageway opened into a large chamber. It was hard to explain, but he could feel the openness, the change from narrow corridors to a vast room. There was a roaring fire in front of him.

"It's beautiful," a deep voice said from beside him. "Of course, I'm partial to fire. It is a shame you cannot see its magnificence."

"Shouldn't we be fighting?" Adhira asked.

"I have lived for thousands of years. I would like to live for thousands more."

This was not how dragons were supposed to talk. After so many years of being invulnerable, there was an expected level of egotism.

"If we aren't going to fight, then what are we doing?" Adhira asked.

"My orders were simple, yet absurd. I was to wait here, guarding the temple until the four of you arrived, then kill you. I remember watching Re'u fight. If he had not gone into the Abyss, I do not think even Iblis would have been able to stand before him. And now there are four of you."

Four? So, the dragon didn't know what happened with the other Dragon Slayers at sea. Did he think the others were with him?

"Instead of catching a silver arrow through my heart, I would rather trade information for passage into the Abyss."

"You would rather go into the Abyss than die? Isn't that the same thing?"

"The Abyss is only death if there is something there waiting to kill you. I assure you, there is nothing on the other side of the shadow gate I fear."

Adhira's thoughts were spinning.

"Hypothetically, if a human were to go through one of the shadow gates, what would happen to them?"

"So that part of the report is true, I see," the dragon said contemplatively. "If someone went through *that* gate, they would find themselves afloat in a sea of poisonous water. Even within the Abyss, nothing dared go near Chemosh."

Neviah had fallen into a sea of poison? But she had been on a ship. Could she be alive? That was several months ago. Even if she had survived the initial plunge…

The Road to War

"You want something," Adhira said. "What is it?"

"Simply safe passage and your word," the dragon said. "In exchange for information."

"What is the information?" Adhira asked, though he knew it wouldn't be that simple.

"First, my terms. In a show of good faith, I dismissed the nonhumans to head north out of the southern lands. The humans, I put under house arrest until your arrival. You will find them unharmed. As for information, I can tell you war strategies, the current status of your allies, and even where to find the next piece of the Armor of Light. All I ask in return is for you to open up the shadow gate on your wrist and let me pass into the Abyss. It is quite a bargain I offer you."

"And you would betray your kind for entry to a barren wasteland?"

"You might not have known it, but we have frequented the same battlefield, you and I. I've seen you kill my brethren as well as other formidable adversaries. I've watched you these last few days decimate my troops, though, by all appearances, you are blind. If we fight, there is a chance I will die. If I fail to kill you but live, Iblis will kill me himself."

At last, Adhira understood. "So you choose exile. Why not just join us?"

The dragon laughed. "Just because I think you can kill me doesn't mean I think you can kill Iblis. Do we have a deal?"

"Yes. The information?"

"Since the Beast has been unable to make landfall in Tarsis, Iblis will likely divert it to its next target, which is Esdraelon."

"What do you mean, unable to make landfall?"

"The Beast's first task was to wipe out the entire island of Tarsis. After you were captured, Siarl led Chemosh toward the island, but your golden-haired friend has impeded its progress at every pass."

"Victoria!" Adhira said, not caring to hide his relief and excitement. "She's alive!" And Asa, he had to be alive too! She wouldn't save herself without saving him.

"Already, my information has proven valuable to you. How nice. Yes, at least one of your friends is in Tarsis."

They were alive! At least, Victoria was for sure. For the first time in, he didn't know how long, he felt hope. Asa could heal him, and together, the three of them could make a stand with the other humans at Esdraelon. Not three, but four. If Neviah was still alive, he would find her. Why hadn't he gone after her sooner?

He tried to calm himself. "What about the piece of armor?"

"That bit of information I will tell you from the other side of the shadow gate," the dragon said. "From your reaction to my news so far, I believe I have provided adequate collateral."

"Thank you," Adhira said. The Abyss Shield grew large enough for a man to pass through. The dragon's boots changed from the gentle slap of stone to the crunch of dirt as he passed through the shadow gate.

"The piece of armor is in the fire in front of you," the dragon called through the gate, followed by a laugh that faded as he walked away, deeper into the Abyss.

Adhira sat on the stone floor for a while after, facing the fire, though he couldn't see anything. Sweat slicked his bare skin where he'd discarded his shirt. He was drinking from his waterskin when Roan walked up behind him.

"Clyde told me you were in here fighting a dragon," he said, sitting down beside the Indian and handing him some jerky.

"No fighting," Adhira said around a mouthful. "The dragon chose to go into the Abyss, but not before telling me two of my friends were still alive." And maybe the third.

"Asa and Victoria?"

"Apparently, the Beast didn't kill them, and they are harassing it, keeping it from leaving the sea."

"Then, what are we doing here?" Roan asked. "Let's go get you healed!"

"First, what do you see in front of us? Besides the fire."

Roan could be heard walking the length of the fire and back again. "The entire ground and air for thirty feet or so is completely engulfed in flames. I think I see something in the middle. A pair of boots, maybe."

"I've seen myself enter the fire every way I can think of. Each time, I die in agonizing pain."

"There is a plaque outside the temple. It is weathered smooth, but I was able to read two words, peace and faith. Does that help?"

Of course, faith would be part of the test. Faith had been a major part of Asa's and Neviah's trials. How did peace play into it?

"It helps, I think. The faith part would seem simple if I couldn't see the future. I would have thought merely stepping into the fire would have shown faith. But I know that won't work because I can see what happens."

"But if you can see what happens, can you really have faith?" Roan asked.

"Don't get all philosophical on me."

"I'm serious. Just think about it. You are seeing what could happen; therefore, you don't have any faith you'll survive. You only see yourself failing."

"Yes, and failing means being cooked. What about the peace part?"

"Maybe you need to be at peace with your inner self."

"What does that mean?"

"I don't know, but it sounded good."

Adhira sighed and stood. He removed his boots and pants and set them aside.

"What are you doing?" Roan asked.

"Obviously, I'm going to step into the fire," Adhira said, taking a step closer to the flames.

"But why did you take off your boots and pants?"

"That's a good pair of boots," Adhira said with a smile. "After I'm dead, someone might need them."

"What about your pants? No one will want those."

"If you weren't here, the underwear would have come off too," Adhira said.

"We can't afford to lose you now," Roan said. "I think you'll get along fine without the boots in that fire."

Adhira thought before speaking. "Years ago, Re'u sent us on a mission to find his sword. After finding it, we realized there was a complete armor set. I think he means for us to find the full set."

"Well, go ahead and jump in the fire already," Roan said. He was trying to be flippant, but Adhira could hear the concern in his voice. Adhira took a deep breath and tried his best to ignore what he saw coming.

Adhira stepped forward, and the fire immediately seared his skin. He tried to scream, but the heat flooded his lungs, stealing his breath as he fell to the ground, writhing in pain.

The vision played over and over in his head as he chose to step forward, then changed his mind. He had to do this. Re'u had already given them his sword and shield. The sword could cut through anything, and the shield could block anything. What could the boots do? He had no clue, but he felt them pulling at him.

The need grew and grew as he stood there, as close to the flames as he could bear. He didn't know why, but his heart hammered with a sudden urgency. Those boots were needed, and they were needed immediately. He took a calming breath before wincing in anticipation of the pain to come as he took a step forward.

"Sky! Are you okay?"

"I—I'm fine," Adhira said in wonder, though the urgency was still there. He ran over to the boots and slammed his feet into them. The roar of the fire slowly dissipated, and with it, the sense of urgency.

"You did it!" Roan said, running up to him. "Oh, those are shiny. What do they do?"

"I don't know."

"Try running really fast."

"After I get dressed." The room was rapidly becoming cooler.

The boots retracted into ankle tattoos until after he donned his pants. Once he had all his clothes on, the boots reappeared on his feet. Adhira sprinted, though he saw ahead that he didn't have super speed. Next, he tried running, jumping, and even squatting with Roan on his back. Nothing felt different than it should have been.

"Well," Roan said after a while. "Maybe you just have indestructible feet now. Woah, where'd that come from? How'd you get a helmet?"

Adhira slowly reached up and realized he was wearing a helmet that covered his forehead, ears, and the back of his head, though it left the face open, aside from a nose guard. "I don't know," Adhira said, equally bewildered.

"Adhira?" a familiar voice spoke in his ear. "Adhira, is that you?"

"Asa? Can you hear me?"

"I thought you were dead."

"I thought *you* were dead."

"What's going on?" Roan asked.

"It's the helmet," Adhira said. "It's letting me talk to my friend Asa."

"So, he's really not dead!" Roan said, joining Adhira's excitement.

"How is this possible?" Adhira asked. "I saw Chemosh crush your ship."

"I thought we were goners, too," Asa said. "We were so close to the shadow gate that Victoria couldn't use her abilities. When Chemosh stepped on the ship, it must have pushed us far enough away because she was able to protect us with some kind of air shield. The ship was broken in half. Victoria somehow protected us from being crushed, held the ship together, and moved us to safety, all while underwater. We eventually found one of the other ships. It was wild."

"That sounds like quite a ride," Adhira said.

"Yeah, I felt like I was in a submarine made of wood. What about you? When we made it back to the island, you were gone, and there was blood everywhere. The last thing I saw was you fighting someone."

"It was Siarl," Adhira said.

"Was it his blood I saw?"

"No, it was mine."

"You okay?" Asa's voice was full of concern.

"I got beat up pretty bad, but I'm fine now. Better than ever now that I know you guys are okay."

"Where are you?" a quiet voice squeaked.

"Victoria!" It felt so good to talk to his friends, especially after months of thinking he'd never talk to them again. "I am very far to the south. I can't wait to see you guys." Actually see. "Where did this helmet come from?"

"It was in a deep cave full of obstacles and traps," Asa said. "Victoria has been keeping the Beast trapped while I hunted this piece of the Armor of Light."

"Me too," Adhira said. "Actually, I wasn't hunting for a piece of the armor. It's more like I kind of stumbled upon it."

"So that's where the boots came from," Asa said. "You saved my life."

"Saved your life!" Victoria said, louder than he'd ever heard her speak. "Asa, you said the helmet was lying at the back of the cave. You said it wouldn't be dangerous at all."

"I'm sorry," Asa said sheepishly. "I didn't think it was dangerous until the ground fell out from beneath my feet. "I was falling when the boots appeared on my feet, and suddenly, the ceiling was the floor. I had a rough landing, but other than a few bruises, I'm okay."

That explained the feeling of urgency Adhira experienced. Well, it didn't explain it, but he at least knew why he'd sensed what he did. Was Re'u still helping them, even after Adhira had all but abandoned their mission?

"So, these are gravity boots," Adhira said, filing his other thoughts away for another time and jumping to point both feet out in front of him. He quickly fell sideways until he landed heavily on the wall. It was a strange feeling. The boots weren't just sticking him to the wall. The wall actually felt like it was down. He walked around normally.

"That looks fun," Roan said, walking near him. "But what happens if you try them outside? Could you fly?"

"We will definitely do some experiments later," Adhira said. To Asa, he said, "What's the plan, then? Has your girlfriend killed Chemosh yet?"

"I can't," she said wearily.

"Victoria has hardly slept in three days. We spent months at sea leading the thing in circles before it came here, to Tarsis. We haven't found a way to kill it or send it back yet."

"My gift can't touch it," she said. "And keeping it in place is difficult."

"I've put several arrows into it, but the holes close up immediately," Asa said. "Maybe the three of us could attack it together. Enough arrows might kill it. Or maybe we could land on the thing and cut into it. We've really missed having you and Nev—sorry."

"And Neviah," Adhira finished for him. An idea occurred to him in the silence that followed. With renewed urgency, he said, "Neviah? Neviah, can you hear me?"

Everyone was quiet. "Neviah, please say something if you can." Still nothing. "Your ponytail is fake."

There was a low, rumbling coughing sound followed by a barely audible mumble and a static sound. They were definitely words, but Adhira couldn't completely put together what they were. There was another mumble, and this time, he was able to decipher one word.

"Idiot."

Chapter 24

"Neviah!" Asa shouted. "But you fell into the Abyss. How can this be?" There was no response.

"Neviah," Adhira said, forcing himself to be calm. "Hold on just a little longer. I'm coming." There was no answer, but he'd heard all he needed to. Neviah was alive. He didn't know how it was at all possible, but it was.

Adhira jumped to the actual ground, already speaking before his feet touched. "Roan, lead me out of here, now." Roan walked off swiftly, and Adhira followed his footsteps.

"I heard your part of the conversation," Roan said. "All your friends are alive. That's awesome! What's the plan?"

"Neviah's alive, but she's in the Abyss. I need to find her as soon as possible."

"Why don't you use the Abyss Shield? We can lead a search team through."

"I don't know how to traverse the Abyss," Adhira said. "If we entered the shield, we could show up hundreds of miles from her without a clue what direction to head in. I don't know where she is, but I know where she entered, and I think Siarl left the key to the gate there."

"I want to come with you," Roan said, though Adhira could already hear the defeat in his voice. There wasn't a horse alive that could keep up with Euroclydon.

"You are needed here," Adhira said as he exited the Fire Temple into the warmth of the sunlit day. "The Foundlings need a leader. The southern kingdoms need to raise their militia, and the deserters from Tanas' army need guidance. A final confrontation is coming, and it will be at Esdraelon. I will see you there."

"Your horse told me there was a dragon," Ivak said as he walked up to them.

The Armor of Light

"I guess Clyde's talking to everybody now," Adhira said off-handedly, stuffing his sword away in his saddlebags. "You have nothing to worry about. We dealt with the dragon."

"When we first met," Ivak said slowly, "even before you revealed yourself, I knew you were an imposter. I just wanted to see what your game was. I wasn't afraid of a handful of men. I see now that I should have been terrified."

"Wait until you meet my friends," Adhira said. "I am the least of us. When I return, I will have them with me."

"Farewell, Sky," Roan said as Adhira swung into Euroclydon's saddle. "I look forward to fighting with you again at Esdraelon."

"Thank you," Adhira said, pausing to turn his head toward his friend. "For everything." He kicked Euroclydon into a gallop and yelled over his shoulder, "Keep practicing your sword art!"

While they moved, Adhira caught Euroclydon up on what had happened in the Fire Temple and what their current objective was.

"We just need to make it to a port city and hire a ship somehow," Adhira finished.

"*Why would we need a ship? I am the fasted thing alive.*"

"Yeah, but can you run on water?" Adhira asked. He could feel mirth coming from the horse. What was he missing?

After they'd crested a hill and started down the other side, Euroclydon said, "*Sometimes, I forget how blind you actually are. I run across water all the time. Twice on this trip alone, I've run across lakes.*"

"How?"

"Physics," Asa said in his ear suddenly. "If your horse can move forward faster than he sinks, it seems possible. Or it could be a power your horse has. I've seen stranger things."

"You can hear my horse?" Adhira said.

"Yes, and it's really weird, like he's in my head. Are you guys on the way to Shipwreck Bay?"

"Yeah, I have to get her out of there somehow."

Euroclydon went over a hill so fast that Adhira felt himself rise out of the saddle slightly, held down only by the waist strap.

"What happened to you the last time we were all there?" Asa asked. "I heard Euroclydon say something about you being blind."

"Do you remember that one Finn Folk I spared?"

"Yes."

"It spit acid in my eyes. I can't see anything."

"You've been blind this whole time?" Asa said, shock and anger obvious in his tone. "How did you escape Siarl? How did you end up halfway across the world? How have you done anything?"

Starting with the fight with Siarl, Adhira recounted his entire journey. From his imprisonment on the ship, Roan freeing him, meeting Euroclydon, to all the fights and battles in between, he could barely believe the story himself.

"I look forward to meeting Roan," Asa said when Adhira was done. "Though he sounds like a carbon copy of you. I don't know if I could handle two of you. I do wish I could have helped."

"It's okay," Adhira said. "I've made new friends and learned what the enemy is planning."

"It will be nice to have the gang back together," Asa said, "when you get back from the Abyss."

"Did you notice if the key to the gate was still there on the island?"

"It is; at least, it was the last time I saw it. We didn't stay long, just long enough to confront the Beast, but that almost got us crushed again. Victoria isn't able to hurt it with her gift at all."

"How were you guys able to keep it away from Tarsis so long?"

"Victoria keeps trapping it in blocks of ice. It keeps breaking free, though, and faster each time. She's not getting enough sleep. I'm afraid she'll collapse any minute."

"Soon, we will have Neviah back, and together, we'll find a way to kill the thing. Has Siarl made another appearance?"

"I don't think he will as long as Victoria is able to fight. She could toss him into space if she wanted to. I'm worried about her. I've never seen anyone so exhausted before."

"She'll be fine," Adhira said. "What's she doing now?"

"I'm not sure. I'm on my way back from the Cavern of Whispers, where I got the helmet. I should get back tonight. There's one other thing you should know. I think the Beast is somehow poisoning the ocean. Fish are dying, and people who've eaten from the sea in the last few weeks have gotten really sick. I don't know how far it's spread, but if we don't kill this thing soon, who knows how bad it will get."

"*Sky, there is a pack of Se'irim ahead, five total,*" Euroclydon said. "*Do you wish to engage?*"

"Time is against us," Adhira said.

"*There are farms and small villages out here,*" the horse pointed out. "*I know we can't scour the countryside, but killing these five could save innocents.*"

Adhira was shocked at the change in the mighty warhorse. It had been a creature enthralled by power and death, but now he was actually concerned for people.

"Let's do it, then. I'll lead with arrows."

With Euroclydon's guidance, two Se'irim were killed with arrows before the armored horse plowed into them, killing another. Adhira beheaded one, while Euroclydon finished off the last. They had barely slowed and were soon back on track.

"Sky, huh," Asa said after a few minutes.

"It felt right," Adhira said, hoping his embarrassment didn't show in his voice. It was not an emotion he was used to feeling. "I thought I had lost everything. I didn't feel like the same person anymore."

"How about now?"

"I feel more like myself than I have in months. I'm just missing one thing."

"Your sight?"

"No. My girl. Though sight would be awesome, too."

"You'll find her," Asa said confidently.

Adhira could no longer feel the sun shining by the time he heard the crash of ocean waves. The horse stopped.

"Now is the time to eat and relieve yourself. I have never run on the ocean before, but I know I won't be able to stop until we reach land. Do we have a heading?"

Adhira dismounted and pulled out a large piece of bread while Euroclydon quickly grazed in the tall grass. Adhira thought back to his original voyage to Shipwreck Bay. There was nothing distinct he could think of.

"I don't know," Adhira admitted. "We should head northwest."

"The ocean is big," Euroclydon said.

"I know, but I have a direct line to the smartest guy I know," he said, tapping his helmet.

"You're going to make me blush," Asa said with a laugh. "I just got back to the city. Nearly everyone else has evacuated. I'll find some maps and star charts. We'll get you heading in the right direction. Meanwhile, you can probably head northwest like you suggested."

Adhira thought he would be able to tell the difference between riding on land and riding on water, but other than the hoofbeats becoming muted, the sound of moving water was the only real indicator. They rode on the hilly terrain of the gently rolling waves for nearly an hour before Asa spoke again, everything coming in a rush.

"The Beast is gone," Asa said in a panic. "I found Victoria asleep on the pier and the ice cage she made has been destroyed. It couldn't have made landfall. I was in the city, and nothing has been destroyed."

"Calm down, Asa," Adhira said. "I think it went back out to sea."

"Why would it give up after all this time?"

"A dragon told me the Beast was being sent to Esdraelon."

"Okay," Asa said.

"Really? Just an 'okay'? I thought that statement about talking to a dragon would need more explaining."

"You are currently riding a horse across the ocean, and I've spent the last hour walking up the side of buildings to look for maps. I've learned to just accept things."

"You should find a crew and meet me at Shipwreck Bay," Adhira said.

"I will, but first, I'm going to watch over Victoria while she sleeps. I have a bunch of maps with me. Once I decipher them, I'll give you directions to the island."

The sun was high in the sky the next day before Adhira began drifting toward sleep. He found he could will his helmet to go away. It became a necklace, tight against his throat, like a raised tattoo. Letting it become a necklace, he slapped himself in the face a few times to wake himself up. If he nodded off and fell, he would be adrift in the middle of the ocean.

"I miss energy drinks," he said.

"*What is an energy drink?*" Euroclydon asked. The horse had worked up a lather, and it was the first time Adhira had heard him breathing hard.

"It is a beverage where I come from that washes away all fatigue and makes you feel powerful, like you can do anything." He might be overselling the drinks a little, but at that moment, that's how he remembered them.

"*I want to try one of these energy drinks.*"

The sun had been down for hours before Adhira sensed a distinct decrease in their speed. They should have stopped to rest before setting out onto the ocean. The horse had already run for an entire day before they began the final leg of their journey. Even with Asa's guidance, they had no idea how close they were.

"Tell me what you see," Adhira said, trying to distract himself and his companion from their exhaustion.

"*The constellation of the shrub is still in front of us,*" Euroclydon said slowly. "*Though it is almost directly overhead. The other two constellations are to our left and right, which means we are on track. According to your friend, we have to be close.*"

"How are the waves?"

"*The water is smooth. If the waves begin to crest again, I don't know if I can keep us at an adequate speed.*" Suddenly, the horse veered right, then back the way they'd been traveling.

"A ship's mast!" Adhira said, not bothering to ask what they'd dodged in real time. "We have to be close."

It didn't take long for them to find the island after that. Euroclydon stopped as soon as his hooves struck the sand. Adhira jumped from his back and collapsed to the ground. He gave himself one minute before stumbling to his feet.

"*We should rest,*" Euroclydon said when Adhira walked up the slight incline toward the center of the island. Having been one of his last sights, the place was etched in his mind.

"I will not leave her there for a second longer than I have to."

"*If there is fighting, we will be at a disadvantage.*"

"It has to be now."

"*One hour,*" the horse said. "*We don't know how far we have to travel when we get to the other side. It will do us no good to go through the gate just to drown in a sea of poison because we were too exhausted.*" Adhira hadn't thought of that. He assumed she would be just inside the shadow gate. If the Abyss mirrored the human world, Neviah could have sailed anywhere.

"Okay," he said, slumping against the pedestal after confirming the key was still in it. "One hour."

✦✦✦

Euroclydon nudged him awake. He shook off the disorientation of sleep as he quickly rose to his feet. Feeling around, he found the key and wasted no time turning it. The roar of water met his ears as the whirlpool started sucking water into the gate.

"Are you ready?" Adhira asked, swinging up into the saddle. He had to shake off a wave of dizziness that came with the sudden motion. In answer, the horse galloped toward the sound of rushing water.

"*I don't know what is going to happen,*" Euroclydon said as they began their descent.

The rushing water of the whirlpool was deafening. Adhira had to lean heavily to the side as the horse ran at an angle down the whirling slopes of the whirlpool. Water splashed them from above, soaking them in saltwater. Then, they were free of the spray of water and running at top speed.

The first thing he became aware of was the smell. Everything smelled like rot mixed with a sulfuric haze that burned a little when he breathed in. Suddenly, the warmth of the sun was gone, as if a switch had been flipped.

"What do you see?" Adhira asked.

"*The water here spirals down into the world of man. There is sea all around us, though there is land ahead.*"

Adhira wondered how water could spiral into the gate from both sides, but he'd learned from experience to shrug off the unexplained.

"*I see the ship ahead,*" Euroclydon said soon after. "*It is docked at a large stone outcropping. When I get off the water, I should be able to traverse the terrain up to it.*"

Adhira was furious with himself. Why did they stop to nap for an hour? She had been so close. They could have rescued her and been back out of the Abyss already.

The horse slowed as he made his way up a rocky hill. The minutes were agonizing for Adhira, who jumped to the ground the second Euroclydon told him they were at the end of the stone pier. According to Euroclydon, the ship was tied to the jutting rock, which was at a nearly even height with the deck of the ship.

"Neviah!" he called out as soon as he jumped over the ship's railing. "It's me, Adhira!" After kicking in the door to the captain's quarters, he found the ladder leading below deck and slid down it, holding on to the sides.

"Neviah!" The ship was still completely filled with the gunpowder they had made, but there wasn't a soul on board. "Neviah!" he cried out once more, but he already knew she wouldn't answer.

Chapter 25

"Do you see anything?" he asked, climbing back onto the main deck.

"*There are no signs of struggle,*" Euroclydon said. "*Though there is a cave nearby.*"

"Let's go," Adhira said, hopping the rail and mounting up.

"*Caves here are far more dangerous than the ones in your world,*" Euroclydon said, starting forward at a trot. "*And these caves are likely home to the worst sort of creatures. No Shayatin with any sense would come anywhere near the Beast's prison, and not just from fear of Chemosh alone.*"

Adhira wondered who or what could have made a prison that could hold such a large monster. "Do you think there are ways in and out? You know, for creatures smaller than a mountain."

"*If so, the passageways would likely be through these caves or others. It will be impossible to see once inside.*"

"I'm not worried about that," Adhira said.

"*I also won't be able to see,*" Euroclydon pointed out. "*I can see well in the dark, but there has to be at least a little light.*"

Adhira pulled out the Sword of Re'u and let the sword glow.

"*That will be sufficient.*"

When they entered the cave, the smell of rot grew worse, born on the wind of a slight breeze that blew from deeper within.

"*Have you tried to contact her with the helmet? Now that we are in the Abyss, perhaps you will have a stronger connection.*"

Adhira let the necklace around his neck turn into the helmet again. "Neviah, are you there? Can you hear me?" There was no response. "Asa, can you hear me?"

"Barely," came a response so faint he could hardly make out the word. "Did you make it through the shadow gate?"

"Yes, but Neviah is not with the ship."

"You will find her," Asa said with a yawn. He sounded as exhausted as Adhira felt, but his words were confident. "I almost pity any Shayatin that crosses her path."

"How's Victoria?"

"Resting. I'm going to let her sleep a little longer. With Chemosh gone, sailors are starting to return. Hopefully, we can catch up to the Beast before it reaches Esdraelon. Let me know when you find her."

The rotten smell was becoming almost unbearable. The further they traveled, the worse it got. He wondered if they should go back and find another tunnel. They curved around a bend, and the horse immediately froze.

"There is a giant cave spider ahead."

"Two adventurers traveling through a dark cave in a strange land; why wouldn't there be a giant spider?"

"*It's just sitting in the path, waiting.*"

Adhira fired an arrow directly ahead of them in the span of a heartbeat.

"*You missed, but it didn't even flinch.*"

They sat there waiting for the creature to make the first move, but after a minute, Adhira grew impatient. He gave the horse a light kick on his flank. Euroclydon slowly moved forward.

"*It's already dead,*" he said. They'd found the source of the rotten smell. "*It is missing a leg, and there are holes covering its body that match holes in the stone behind it.*"

"Neviah," Adhira said with a smile. "She came this way."

"*This has been here a couple of weeks,*" Euroclydon said. "*At least we are heading in the right direction.*"

"And let's get on with it before I throw up all over you."

It took much effort to hold his excitement at bay. The trail had just turned from cold to warm. The air was still stale and rotten as they moved away, but it was less so. Several turns later, Euroclydon stopped again.

"*This spider is larger than the other and is certainly not dead,*" Euroclydon said.

"Guide me," Adhira said as he rolled backward off the horse pointing his feet to the sky. The ceiling immediately became the ground, and he landed in a crouch. With Euroclydon's help, he ran across the uneven surface, quickly closing the distance to the giant spider. His imagination tried to picture a multi-eyed fanged monstrosity, but he forced himself to picture a large, doe-eyed plush stuffed spider.

The loud click of pincers came straight for him. A leg smashed into him from the right, knocking him against the cave wall. The pincers enveloped his waist and snapped closed.

Adhira couldn't suppress a shudder as he ran forward in real time, unable to imagine a worse way to die. The sound of pincers came at him again, but this time, he dodged by running along the wall for two strides before doing a flip and landing on the other wall, raking the Sword of Re'u along the creature's side and severing legs.

It fell heavily to the ground, where it thrashed around. Adhira sprang from the wall and drove his sword through its back as he landed on the beast. It rolled over in its death throes, but Adhira had already jumped to the ground. It let out a horrible screech as it died. Euroclydon walked up behind him.

"*Do you think Re'u had magical armor for a horse, too?*" he asked. "*The spider looked confused when you started running along the ceiling. I don't think it was accustomed to its prey trespassing in its shadows.*"

Several clicks could be heard coming from their right.

"*Which way?*" Euroclydon asked when Adhira quickly jumped into the saddle.

"I still feel a breeze. Let's continue toward it." The hammering of dozens of spider legs grew louder as the two navigated the caves and caverns. Despite the spiders dogging their steps, the horse was forced to slow at every turn, and some of the tunnels were barely tall enough to give them passage.

"*I can see the lead spider now,*" Euroclydon said. "*He is about fifty feet behind us. They will likely catch us if we are forced to squeeze through one more narrow corridor.*"

Adhira loosed a few arrows over his shoulder but couldn't tell if he struck anything. Then, he remembered those arrows would pass through just about anything, even the winding stone tunnels. Turning around completely in his saddle, Adhira sent arrow after arrow behind them. Every few seconds, he would hear a screech of pain, sometimes near, sometimes much further behind. He imagined the arrows passing through the stones and hitting the spiders several turns behind. Less than a minute after his decision to turn in the saddle, the clicks faded, the spiders retreating or dying.

Facing forward, Adhira leaned low in the saddle to avoid archways and stalactites. "I think the spiders gave up," he said.

"*Good,*" Euroclydon said. "*Hopefully, we don't run into anything worse.*"

"What could possibly be worse than a horde of giant spiders? On second thought," he added quickly to cut off what the horse was about to say. "I don't want to know."

After several more curves in the rock, the breeze became steadier, if not a little stronger. A little further, and suddenly, everything felt different. It was as if a weight had been pressing in around him and was suddenly removed.

"Do you know where we are?" Adhira asked.

"As good as one can know a place they've only seen on a map. We are at the base of a mountain. I believe we are to the north of the Beast's prison."

"Remember where the cave is. We will likely come back through here. Any indication Neviah came this way?"

"No, but there is a fortress at the end of the valley. I believe it is one of the gate arenas."

"What's a gate arena?"

"In your world, most of the shadow gates are buried, hidden, or lost. On this side, the Shayatin have no way of knowing which ones will be activated. The toughest Shayatin from all corners of the Abyss come to the arenas to fight for the right to be the first through should the gate be activated."

"What you're telling me is, not only is that fortress filled with Shayatin, but it's filled with the toughest and meanest Shayatin around."

"Most likely. Now that a few of the gates have been activated, it is possible some have set off to earn a slot at one of those arenas instead. Though, I can't see the toughest throwing away a high position here to fight their way up the ladder again."

"You need to learn to end your statements on a positive note," Adhira said. "What do you think? Should we head for the fortress or around it?"

"If she has been captured, she will likely be there. If she was starving and looking for food, she will likely be there. Unless she had those magnificent boots when she came this way, she is likely there."

"I feel like you are trying to tell me something," Adhira said with an exaggerated slowness. "But I just don't know what."

Ignoring his joking, Euroclydon said, "We need a plan. There will likely be thousands of Shayatin there. Tens of thousands possibly."

"How many do you think you could take?" Adhira asked. The horse didn't answer. "Okay, okay. What are our chances of sneaking in? We could go in under the cover of night."

"Our chances are not good. One: I'm a horse and can't sneak. Two: You're blind and can't sneak. Three: It is always dark here. There are Shayatin that can see in the dark, pitch dark, and some that don't need to see at all to know you are there. They may have a freshwater well, though."

"What does that last have to do with anything?"

"*You told me to end my statements with a positive note.*"

Adhira laughed. He was really starting to like the new Clyde.

"All right, then. No sneaking and no direct assault. That leaves us with one option. The Trojan Horse."

"*The what?*"

"It is a legend where I come from. Some people gave some other people a gift, which was a big wooden horse. Only, the horse was filled with enemy soldiers. They attacked and killed the people after the gift was taken into the city."

"*And what will our gift be?*"

"Me," Adhira said. "Do you still look enough like a Shayatin?"

"*I am a Shayatin,*" Euroclydon said with pride. "*I mean, yes. I am not as dark as I used to be, but being back here is bringing back the miasma that rises from my skin.*"

"That's not a good thing, but it will help us now. Just don't get all murdery again."

"*What's your plan?*"

"I will be your prisoner. You take me to the fortress and hand me over. Say I was sent here by Iblis or something, and no harm is to happen to me. Convince them not to kill me, and hopefully, I can get near where they are keeping Neviah." He really hoped she was there and, more importantly, that she was okay. "When things get crazy, and they will once I start cutting through walls, I'll meet you somewhere along the valley coming this way."

"*It is a bold plan. There may be a chance it will work.*"

"I love the confidence. Well, let's be about it."

While riding toward the fortress, he willed the helmet to become a necklace and put his book of prophecies inside his shirt, tightening it with his belt. After managing to tie his hands behind his back, he sat drooped in the saddle, trying to look weak and defeated. They'd been traveling for several minutes before the rotten smell grew strong again.

"*There are several dead Shayatin on the path ahead. The cuts through the armor are too clean to be anything but a blade of power.*"

"The Sword of Re'u," Adhira said. "She's been here, then." By the smell, they'd been dead a while.

Less than a minute later, Adhira heard the sound of unoiled metal hinges groaning, echoing loudly through the valley as the main gate was opened.

"*A handful of riders are coming from the front gate. They have a truth seer. He will know if I'm lying. I'll talk to you and him at the same time so you will know what is happening."*

"What is another human doing here?" one of the Shayatin asked, voice so gravely it almost sounded like he was speaking in clicks.

"*I am giving him to you as a prisoner,*" Euroclydon said after moving close enough to touch the Shayatin. "*He is one of the Dragon Slayers.*"

This brought surprised grunts from the small group of Shayatin.

"And how did you come by him?" the Shayatin asked.

"*He fought Siarl.*" This brought grunts of awe. It was the most animated Shayatin had ever been around him. "*When Siarl defeated him in combat, he was blinded and taken prisoner.*"

Adhira was impressed. Euroclydon seemed to be a master at lying with the truth.

"And what is he doing here?"

"*I was told to bring him to this fortress and that no harm was to befall him. If Iblis wanted him dead, he would have been executed by Siarl.*"

"Does Iblis want him to be turned, too?" Turned? Too?

"*Too?*" Euroclydon asked.

"We captured a girl a couple of weeks ago. Lord Draven was impressed she killed eight Shayatin. He wants to wait until she becomes one of us." That's what turned meant. If she was in the Abyss too long, she would become a Shayatin, much like Euroclydon. "Are we supposed to wait until he becomes one of us?"

"What do you think?" Euroclydon asked. "*Now, pull this filthy human from my back, and let's find some food.*" Grunts of approval preceded rough hands that pulled him from the horse's back.

He cleared his mind and focused on where he was and where he was taken. When they moved through a creaking gate, they immediately turned right, went down a set of stairs, and turned left. Down a hallway and left again. Then right. After several steps, they stopped, and more hinges groaned when a latch was raised and a door opened. Adhira was pushed into a cell to his left.

Right, stairs, left, left, right, and the cell is on the left. He went over the directions several times in his head, keeping in mind when he broke free, he'd have to reverse everything. As soon as the feet moved away from the door, he quickly moved around the cell and found a prone form lying in the corner.

"Neviah," he whispered, untying his own hands. "Neviah, it's me, Adhira."

"Why won't it stop?" she sobbed, and though her words were muffled because she faced the floor, he could tell her voice was unnaturally low and deep, almost guttural.

"Neviah," he said, gently reaching out to touch her. She pulled away when his hand made contact and sat up in a flash, backing up against the bars.

"No, no, no," she said in a rush. "I can't take it anymore. How are they doing this? His voice. That's all I hear, his voice, but I know it isn't real. It can't be real. Am I real?"

"Neviah, you are talking like a crazy person," he said, trying to speak lightheartedly, but his concern was too strong. "It's really me."

"Nope. Can't be. Adhira is killing. Killing. So much killing. Did he let go? Please, Adhira, let go. Let go!" She screamed the last part loudly before devolving into mumbles.

"I did, Neviah. I let go. Asa found a piece of the Armor of Light. It's a helmet that lets us talk to each other. That's why you've been hearing my voice."

"Asa!" she screamed. "Don't go to the tower. You won't come back, Asa. Don't go. But you have to go. But you can't go. Only, you have to go."

"Asa is fine," Adhira said.

"Asa," she said quietly. "Who's looking for me?" She paused for a moment, and Adhira realized she was listening to something. The helmet! She was still wearing her helmet.

He let his necklace become the helmet again. Asa was speaking, and though faint, his voice sounded thick. "…going to get you out of there. It's really him. I have to go now."

"Asa, what's wrong?" Adhira asked.

"It's Victoria," Asa said in a rush. "She won't wake up. I've healed her and tried shaking her, but she stays asleep. I have to go. She needs a real doctor." With that, he stopped talking.

"She can't wake up," Neviah said. "The Nightmare Helm has been found. Dreams are not safe. She won't wake until Adhira enters the Abyss. We have to break the nightmare. We can't beat the nightmare without the Helm of Dreams. Don't sleep. Can't sleep. No more sleeping until the helmet is found. Only Asa can get the helmet, but he can't get the helmet without Adhira, but Adhira can't be there when it is found, or all will be lost. What does it mean? Adhira, you have to let go. Just let go."

"Neviah, we have the helmet," Adhira said.

"Three go into the Abyss, but only two return. What does it mean?"

"Touch your head, Neviah. You're wearing the helmet."

There was silence until he heard a slight ring as she knocked on the side of her helmet. "Adhira?"

"Yes. It's really me."

He felt her fingers caress his cheek, tentatively at first, then she grabbed his face roughly in her hands, pulling him close.

"I can't see," she whispered. "Where has all the light gone?"

He pulled out the Sword of Re'u and let it illuminate the cell for her. She screamed and hissed. After whimpering in the corner for a minute, she scuffled back over and took his face in her hands again. She gingerly touched the cloth around his eyes.

"Your beautiful brown eyes," she said and began to sob again.

He grabbed her and pulled her against him, hugging her tight. She wrapped her arms around his waist. Holding her head against his chest, he let her cry as long as she needed to. If only he could.

Chapter 26

Adhira opened his eyes and stretched as he stood. Then, he froze, slowly raising his hand to his face. He could see his hand! Looking around the cell, he saw Neviah standing nearby. There was a faint light that shone from nowhere yet was everywhere.

"Good," Neviah said. "You're asleep." Her voice had lost the deeper bass that made her sound like a Shayatin. She sounded like herself again. A white formal evening gown hung on otherwise bare shoulders and flowed down loosely around her body to her ankles.

"You are the most beautiful thing I've seen in months," he said. "But how is it that I can see? And what do you mean asleep?"

She waited an annoying fifteen seconds before answering. "We are asleep. In a shared dream, I think. The Helm of Dreams allows us to be conscious in our own dreams while we sleep."

"You don't have to wait fifteen seconds to respond to me anymore. I stopped skipping conversations months ago." Turning in a circle to inspect the dank cell, he said, "You would think we would have dreamed ourselves someplace a little nicer," he said.

"I don't know exactly how it works," she said. "It is still a dream, but we are here more fully, so we are limited in many of the same ways as we are in the real world."

"So, if we explore the fortress, will it look how we imagine it to be or how it really is?"

"I think we will see it how it really is," she said.

"But first we need to leave the cell," he said and looked around for the Sword of Re'u, but it wasn't there.

"This might help," she said with a smile. Oh, how he missed that smile. In her hand was a large iron key.

"How did you get that?"

"I was hoping to find a way out of the cell and was wishing I had a key. Then, it was in my hand as if I'd been holding it the whole time."

With a smile on his face, Adhira wished for a cheeseburger with all the fixings. He held up his hand and was holding a cheeseburger with steam still rising from the patty. Taking a bite, he groaned in ecstasy as the flavors exploded on his tongue.

"I don't think I'm going to bother waking up," he said around another mouthful of burger.

Neviah rolled her eyes, then paused and smiled mischievously. "I didn't know you liked tofu burgers," she said. The flavors in his mouth changed, and he spit the contents on the ground.

"I didn't know you liked to dress up like a chicken," he said. Her beautiful gown turned into a chicken costume.

"Truce!" she yelled as her gown quickly returned.

"Don't ever mess with a man's cheeseburger," he said with an exaggerated scowl.

"Okay," she said, scowling back. "It appears we have some control over our dream. So, if I imagine the cell door open." The door slowly screeched open on its own. The key in her hand disappeared as they strode into the narrow dungeon hallway. "Which way?" she asked.

Adhira went over the directions in his head and quickly led them to the right. After taking two more turns, he realized he must have gotten one of the turns wrong. They exited the dank hallway into a large room with weapons piled in barrels and on tables.

"I think I went the wrong way," he said, looking over his shoulder. Neviah was eating a chocolate candy bar.

"What?" she asked innocently around a mouthful of chocolate.

"We need to backtrack," he said. "We have to be able to find our way out in the real world." The thought made him shudder. In the real world, he would go back to being blind.

After finding their cell, which took quite a while, they set out again. After a few more course corrections, he found the stairs he was looking for. Running up and exiting the door at the top, he was relieved to find himself standing at the front gate.

"That's the way I came from," Neviah said, pointing to an enormous looming mountain at the end of the valley.

"Yeah, we found the giant spider you killed," he said.

"I killed three giant spiders," she said. "And a stone worm almost killed me. The stone worm was terrifying. And what do you mean by 'we'?"

"Euroclydon is with me," Adhira said.

"The Shayatin horse? I've been waiting to see him again." A sword suddenly appeared in her hand.

"No killing Clyde. He's changing, actually starting to care about people."

"But he's Shayatin," she said, covering the word in as much disdain as possible.

"Promise me you won't kill him."

"But I promised him that I would kill him if I saw him again. You wouldn't want to make me a liar, would you?"

"Promise," he said sternly.

"Fine. I won't kill the horse." The sword disappeared.

"At least it shouldn't be too difficult to escape. Once we meet Clyde outside the fortress, nothing will be able to catch us."

"There's one small hiccup," she said, turning to look at the giant fortress sitting in the midst of the massive walls. "When they captured me, they took my book of prophecies. I'm not leaving here without the Sword of Re'u."

Adhira sighed. "Just once, couldn't something be easy?"

"Where would be the fun in that?" she said with a smile and a punch to the shoulder. "Now, follow me. We have to find out where they are keeping my sword." She set off across a small courtyard toward the inner fortress gate.

Catching up, Adhira said, "When you were, um, talking in the cell before we fell asleep, you said something about the Nightmare Helm. Does that have something to do with why Victoria won't wake up?"

"Yes," Neviah said, waving a hand in front of a large pair of iron doors. They swung outward to admit them. "It is similar to our helmet, but it allows someone to invade other people's dreams. If Victoria fell asleep without her helmet on, she could be trapped in a dream."

"Is she in any real danger?" he asked as they began opening doors and peering into rooms.

"Yes. The helmets allow us to be in our dreams so fully that the dangers are very real."

"But she wasn't wearing the helmet, so can she be hurt?"

"I don't know. If whoever wears the Nightmare Helm wanted her dead and had the power to kill her, she'd be dead. But without the control our helmet gives us, she may be trapped in a nightmare of their making."

"Can we help her, you know, from the dream world?"

"It's not really a dream world. We are either in my dream or your dream. I think we could help her, but we would have to enter her dream.

The Road to War

And to enter her dream, I think we need to get to her."

"So, we need to find a way out of the Abyss first," he said, walking up a narrow stone staircase.

"Precisely," she said, walking up the steps behind him.

They searched the upper floors, one at a time, slowly climbing higher into the keep.

At the top of one set of stairs, Adhira paused, staring at the silhouette of someone standing in a doorway. The person slowly stepped into the dim light of the hallway, staring menacingly at them. It was a clown.

"Um, Neviah," he said to get her attention. For the first time in months, he felt fear. He had no fear of clowns the way some people did. His fear, he realized, was due to Neviah being in danger. Had it always been that way? He couldn't remember the last time he was afraid for his own life.

"Oh, no," Neviah said when she saw the clown, who was walking forward, wiggling his fingers menacingly. "We are definitely in my dream, then. Most of my nightmares involve clowns."

"Then, can you make it go away?" Adhira asked. They slowly backed away. He'd faced monstrosities far worse than a clown, but he wasn't sure what a dream clown was capable of.

"I'm trying," she said. "I'm terrified of clowns." As soon as she said the word, four more clowns jumped out from behind the first. Standing shoulder to shoulder, the five of them filled the hallway and continued their slow advance.

Adhira tried to imagine them gone, but nothing happened. Pulling out a dream Sword of Re'u, he let it become a bow and quickly shot an arrow at the original clown. The arrow passed through the air in slow motion, which the clown easily ducked under.

"Sorry," Neviah said from beside him. "In this nightmare, I often run away, but I always move too slowly."

Adhira smiled. His favorite comic book was *Green Lantern*. In it, the power of a person's will could create constructs they could then use to battle the forces of evil. He already knew he could create things like keys and cheeseburgers; why not something bigger?

Adhira imagined the floor beneath the clowns was lava. It became a bubbling pool of lava. The clowns sank slowly beneath the surface, eventually disappearing from sight. With a thought, the floor became stone again. Looking around, he was glad to see they were clown-free.

"For the rest of the dream," Adhira said, turning to look at a very embarrassed Neviah. "You are not allowed to think about anything except for food and puppies. Leading the way, he took them into another room to continue their search.

Their search ended on the top floor, which had balconies overlooking a large arena with a shadow gate at the center. They had finished their search in a rather out-of-place plush bedroom before Neviah slumped into a chair that looked like it was made to seat something not quite humanoid.

"If we wake up before finding it, we'll have to try again the next time we fall asleep," Neviah said with resignation.

"We need to get you out of the Abyss as soon as possible," Adhira said. "In the real world, you are becoming more Shayatin every day."

"It's taken me months to get that bad," she pointed out. "I think I can hold out a little longer. Having you with me has already helped clear my mind." A chocolate milkshake appeared in her hand, and she started sipping it.

Its appearance sparked an idea in Adhira's brain. At a thought, a compass appeared in his hand.

"What's that?" she asked.

"It's a compass," he stated triumphantly. "And it only points towards your sword," he said with a smile, turning the way it pointed.

"You're a genius!" she said, tossing her milkshake across the room and jumping up. The smell of jasmine filled his senses as she pressed against him to look over his shoulder at the compass. "It's pointing that way. Let's go!" She ran off the way she'd pointed.

Adhira followed her out of the bedroom down a narrow hall that spilled out into one of many weapons closets.

"We already searched in here," she said, walking directly away from the compass he held. She pushed aside armor and threw weapons to the floor to clear the wall.

"Wait," he said suddenly. "When you threw that helmet, the needle on the compass moved. She bent over and picked up the helmet, which was shaped into a semblance of a crow's beak. Reaching her hand in, she slowly pulled out the book of prophecies. She held it to her chest and teared up as she looked at Adhira.

"I know this isn't real," she said, "but it feels so good to hold this again. We need these prophecies if we are going to win this war, and I've felt helpless without them."

"I haven't been able to read mine in months," he said, realizing for the first time that he could read the book again, if only in his dreams.

"Come with me," she said excitedly, taking him by the hand and rushing back to the room with the balconies. She pushed him into a chair and took the chair opposite him. "This is what we are doing until we wake."

"Shouldn't we be finding the best way out of here first?" he asked.

She looked at him as if he were stupid. "Yeah, duh. That's what I'm doing." She opened the book of prophecies and began reading.

He opened his own book, starting at the beginning. It had been so long since he read any of it, everything felt fresh and new, though he still didn't understand much. After reading for a few minutes, he was shocked to find he understood more than ever, though.

Some prophecies were now in the past. Like, "The enemy within the enemy will become your ally." Surely, that spoke of the humans who rebelled against the shadow creatures within Tanas' army, the beginning of what would likely become a full-blown civil war.

Another passage read, "Only the prisoner's friend can dispel the present darkness, halting the sway of shadow over that which is good." He was certain that spoke of Roan taking the Vapor Blade from him and throwing it into the Abyss. Roan would be excited to know he was mentioned in the book of prophecies. Or was it about him freeing Neviah?

What shocked him most was when he was sure he understood a passage that had not yet come to pass. "All things die, even that abomination from the pit. Its death will come suddenly, undone by fire and its own insatiable appetite."

He looked up with excitement, but Neviah wasn't there.

Chapter 27

When he woke, he could still feel Neviah's head on his chest. His back ached from leaning against the cold stone wall. The Sword of Re'u was still in his right hand, the light of which he could not see. A disappointed sigh escaped his lips.

"I know," Neviah said, tightening her arms around his waist. "I don't want to be awake." Her voice was thick again, but she sounded far less frazzled than she had before they fell asleep.

He ran his free hand through her hair, which felt dry and matted. Not caring, he slowly worked his fingers through the tangles.

"My hair is such a mess. I'm almost glad you won't be able to see me until I've had a few baths. What are you doing?" she asked when he pulled on a particularly tough tangle.

"Just checking to see if it's real," he said with a laugh. She pulled away and punched him in the stomach.

"You always have to go for the joke," she said, standing.

"Are you ready?" he asked, standing and walking over to the cage door. "I have a rough idea of where we are going, but I will have to rely on your eyes to lead us."

"Give me a second," she said. He heard her doing something with her hair.

Euroclydon chose that moment to speak to him. *I don't know if you can hear me or if the information helps you, but Draven, the ruler of this fortress, has taken me as his mount. We are heading through the plains opposite the valley we entered.* Adhira didn't know how that would help them. If they escaped the fortress, the horse would be in the wrong place to be of any assistance. He passed on the information to Neviah.

"Can you respond to him?" she asked.

"No, he can talk in my head, but I can't talk back the same way."

"Here, give me the sword," Neviah said. "Now, grab my ponytail. I'll lead us to my sword." Protesting was out of the question, and he quickly found himself being led out of the hole she cut with his sword. He had a firm grip on her ponytail, which he was surprised she was able to accomplish with her hair so matted.

"Turn here," he said when she was about to ask if they should turn. He guided them through the dungeon with a few whispered directions until they found the stairs. From there, he only had vague recollections of where they were going.

At the door at the top of the stairs, he gave her a boost so she could see out the bars at the top. She groaned before stepping back to the ground.

"There are hundreds of Shayatin moving around out there. Fighting is out of the question," she said quickly to squash any thoughts he had about battling their way to the top of the tower. "There are too many as it is, and when the alarm is sounded, there will be thousands of them. Even you aren't that good."

"I wonder if the underground passages run under the center keep," he said.

"We never explored them," she said. "And now is not the time to go off blind. No offense."

"We can go back to sleep and try again when we wake," he offered.

"I want to get out of here now," she said. "I already look more Shayatin than human. My voice makes me sound just like one of them. My thoughts are darker than they've ever been. I'm afraid in a few days, I may be one of them."

"That's it," Adhira said, an idea quickly forming. "Just pretend the transformation is complete."

"It could be weeks before they check to see if I've turned enough. They bring me food once a day and usually just slide it through the bars and walk away."

"I'm talking about something way bolder," he said.

"What?"

"They are waiting for you to become Shayatin, right?"

"Yeah."

"You sound like one of them. Do you look like one of them, too?"

"Do you think it will work?" she asked, understanding what he was getting at. "I think I look the part, but if I say or do the wrong thing, we'll be in a worse situation than we already are."

"That's the beauty," he said, rapping a knuckle on the side of his helmet. "I can hear everything you say. If something goes wrong, I can tell you ahead of time to do or say something different."

"That is just crazy enough it will only *most likely* get me killed."

"So, you're telling me there's a chance," he said with a smile.

"When did you get so smart?" Neviah asked.

"I always have good ideas," he said, crossing his arms. "It's just that Asa usually has better ones."

"Who should take the sword?" she asked.

"You take it," he said. "If no one comes to the dungeons, I should be okay. Even if someone comes this way, I'll manage."

"Okay," she said and took a steadying breath. "I just have to walk out like I own the place. I'll see you when I get back." The handle screeched as she turned it, ready to open the door.

"And Neviah."

"What?"

"Watch out for clowns."

"Always with the jokes," she said as she stepped through, then closed the door behind her. Through his helmet, he heard her mumble, "I have the worst taste in men."

His heart leaped at the words. She *did* like him. "Still talking to yourself?" he asked, unable to help himself, and smiled when he heard her barely bite back a curse.

Before she could say anything more, a deep Shayatin voice could be heard. "Who let you out of your cell, human?"

"Who are you calling human?" Neviah said, her voice sounding more Shayatin than ever.

"Who let you out?" the Shayatin repeated.

"Do you think they would have given me my sword back if I wasn't fully one of us now?"

"Who?"

"Neviah, say Draven," Adhira said. "I think that's their leader."

"Draven," Neviah said.

"What is your assignment?"

"Guard duty," Neviah said without hesitation.

"Which guard duty?" the Shayatin asked, sounding annoyed.

"The keep."

"The keep guard is full already."

"Draven wanted me close so I could teach him how to use this sword."

"What are you about, then?" the creature asked.

"I've been stuck in a cell for months. I want to stretch my legs."

"Get to the keep," the Shayatin said.

After a few seconds, Neviah whispered, "That went better than expected."

Any worse and she would be fighting for her life. Adhira felt exposed, sitting near the door at the top of the stairs. The feeling wasn't from sitting out in the open but from being away from his sword. If Neviah got into trouble, he would be all but powerless to help. He shook his head when a yearning for the Vapor Blade seeped into his mind. It would be nice to have a sword, but not that one.

A thought occurred to him. When they were lost in the dungeon in the dream, they'd come across a small armory. He might not have his sword, but he could find a sword. With half his attention on Neviah, he set off into the dungeon. The image from the dream was still fresh in his mind, allowing him to picture the tunnels as he ran his hands along the walls.

"I was assigned here by Draven," Neviah said. "Now, let me in."

Adhira paused, waiting for a response. After a minute, Neviah whispered, "I'm in and going up the first flight of stairs now."

"Okay," he said. "I'm looking for a sword in case things get messy before you find yours."

"Don't get lost."

He walked through an open door, and his foot struck a small shield. After feeling around the room with his gift, he walked over and picked up a thin sword with sharp ridges along one side of it. The weight felt okay. Giving it a few test swings, he shrugged.

"It will do," he said. "I found a sword."

Neviah didn't respond.

"I knew the girl couldn't have been fully transformed yet," a voice said from the doorway. It was the Shayatin Neviah had spoken to moments before.

Turning toward the door, Adhira took an offensive stance.

"I knew the girl was not fully transformed yet," the Shayatin said. That was by far the worst part about his gift. Everyone always repeated themselves.

"Is everything okay?" Neviah asked quietly.

"Just fine," Adhira said, rushing toward the Shayatin. The creature attempted to parry his strike, but Adhira changed his grip at the last moment, pulling the blade up at an angle and slashing the creature. There was a whistling sound followed by a loud pop. A flash of heat washed over him, and then it was gone. Adhira rushed in and sliced the creature across the chest and its arm, causing it to drop its sword.

"How are you unaffected?" the creature sputtered. "That was enough light to daze anyone."

"You have got to be the unluckiest Shayatin there is," Adhira said with a grim smile, raising his sword to shoulder level, parallel to the ground. "I'm already blind." He thrust his sword forward into the Shayatin's chest.

Adhira stepped over the creature into the hall behind it. There was no one else. Rushing through the passageways, he was able to find his way back to the stairs, which he climbed. He listened carefully, but other than his own breathing, all was silent.

Euroclydon spoke into the silence. "*A Shayatin just reported that Neviah was out of her cage on Draven's orders. After Draven refuted the orders, the messenger flew away to sound the alarm before I could stop him. I'm going to kill Draven and meet you where we discussed. Good luck.*"

"Neviah," Adhira said quickly. "The alarm will be sounded soon! Get your sword and get out of there!"

"Okay. I'm on the last floor now."

Voices could then be heard on her end, yelling something Adhira couldn't make out.

Neviah cried out suddenly. "There was one waiting around the corner. It got me in the neck with a needle from its tail." Her voice faded into incoherent babbling.

"Neviah duck!" he yelled.

She screamed and grunted. "That was close," she panted. "It's dead. Thanks for the sword."

A horn blasted through the compound, its force vibrating through the door he leaned against.

"I'm in the room," she said.

Looking ahead, he said, "Don't go to the left. There is a trip wire we didn't see last time." He didn't know what the wire did, but did know there would have been a lot of screaming from her.

"Got it!" she said. "I'm on my way back."

"Hurry," he said as someone tried to push on his door from the other side.

Reaching to the side, he slammed a crossbar into place. Shayatin beat on the door calling out for more of their kind to take a different way.

"I need my sword," he said.

"We have a problem," she said. "There are a bunch of Shayatin coming up the stairway. I'm trapped on the top floor."

"Use your boots. They change gravity somehow. Whichever way they face becomes down."

"What do you expect me to do?" she asked, but her tone made it obvious she knew where he was going with it.

"You have to run down the side of the building."

"That's not going to happen," she said. He heard the faint sound of fighting on her end.

"If you don't run down the building, they are going to overwhelm you and throw you off." That wasn't what was going to happen, but he needed to instill enough fear that she'd listen. "Remember, I can see what is going to happen. I won't let you get hurt. Now run down the side of the building!"

He cringed as she shrieked in terror. It did not let up until she said, "The courtyard below is filled with Shayatin. They don't see me coming." It was a wonder they hadn't heard her.

Pulling up the crossbar, he yanked open the door the Shayatin were beating on. The first two fell to his sword before they could recover from their shock. As the others tried to swarm in around their bodies, he used his shield as a ram to force his way into their midst. The stolen sword was much less effective than his own blade, but death still followed in his wake.

"I see you," Neviah said, the last word a grunt. "Catch!"

Reaching up, he caught the Sword of Re'u before it could smack him in the head. Though it had only been a few minutes, it felt like being reunited with a long-lost friend. Using it to clear a wide circle around himself, he yelled, "Let's go!"

"Follow me," she said, sprinting past him.

He sprinted after her but was slowed when he was forced to defend himself again and again. The attacks from all sides began to stall their flight completely.

"There is a ceiling above us now!" Neviah yelled above the shouts and roars from the Shayatin. He swung his sword in an arc to his right and held up his shield to protect his other side. In the small opening he'd made, he jumped and aimed his feet above him. It was like falling onto concrete from a second-story building. The landing jarred his bones so hard he could feel it in his teeth.

"The gate is just ahead," she said. "Come on!"

Adhira rolled on the ceiling to avoid an arrow that would have pierced his leg. The sprint to the gate lasted seconds before they were aiming their feet back at the ground. The landing wasn't any softer than the last.

"We're clear! Run!" Neviah yelled.

"*Get on*," Euroclydon said, galloping up on their right.

While running, Adhira tucked away his sword before swinging up into the saddle, holding out his hand for Neviah and pulling her up behind him. He blocked something heavy with his shield while Neviah wrapped her arms around his waist. In a few strides, Euroclydon outpaced their pursuers.

"Where to now?" Neviah asked against the wind assaulting them from the unnatural pace the horse set.

"We came in through the same shadow gate you did," Adhira said.

Neviah groaned. "Not the spiders again."

"*That's the least of our worries*," Euroclydon said. "*The caves will force us to slow, which will allow the fastest Shayatin to close on us. Also, before I killed him, Draven caught me with the edge of his tail, which had a tip like a spear and dripped with poison.*"

"How bad is it?" Adhira asked.

"What?" Neviah asked immediately.

"Euroclydon has been poisoned."

"*I doubt it is enough to kill me,*" the horse said mater-of-fact. "*It is making me feel more sluggish, however. We need to get through the caves before I lose consciousness.*"

"Well?" Neviah asked.

"He'll be okay," Adhira said. "We just need to get through the caves so he can deal with the effects in safety."

"*We are at the entrance,*" the horse said after a few minutes at their breakneck pace.

They quickly dismounted and rushed into the cave. Neviah took point, and Adhira took up the rear. Their pace quickly took them into the depths of the mountain, but Euroclydon's ailment soon hit home as he began to stagger. The first time the horse lost his footing was at a sharp turn, but soon, even moving fast in a straight line proved difficult for the animal.

"We need to slow down," Neviah called back. "Clyde isn't looking so good."

"We can't," Adhira said. "It's only going to get worse, and if he passes out in the tunnels, we will be trapped between Shayatin and who knows what else."

They passed a tunnel on their left, and the unmistakable click of cave spiders could be heard. The clicks resounded through the tunnels like hail striking a tin roof.

"I don't think the spiders are playing around anymore," Neviah said.

After a few more turns, Adhira noticed a considerable change in their pace. The tunnels had narrowed some, and the horse's armor was scraping against one side as if the wall was the only thing holding him up.

"How much further do you think?" Neviah asked. "I don't think I traveled this far in the tunnels last time."

"Please don't tell me we're lost," Adhira said.

"Getting out was easy," Neviah said. "I just had to follow the wind. Now the wind is behind us, so the path isn't so obvious."

Suddenly, a blood-curdling scream echoed through the tunnels. What could make a Shayatin scream like that? They kept moving at their much-reduced pace. Euroclydon no longer spoke, but he didn't stop either. He continued to stumble ahead as they moved blindly through the mountain.

They stopped when they heard fighting up ahead. There was a distinct ring of metal on metal, but it was mixed with a whirring, whistling sound and what appeared to be smashing rocks.

"We need to head back," Neviah said. "There shouldn't be Shayatin in front of us unless we are backtracking."

"Can you see what is going on?" Adhira asked.

"No. I'm only using the faintest glow from the Sword of Re'u. Any more and we would become part of whatever is happening in that cave ahead."

They moved off the way they'd come and took a different turn at the intersection.

Adhira's gift warned him what was coming before the spider landed on him. Instead of being pinned to the ground, he jumped and twisted, aiming his boots at the ceiling to land heavily on the spider's back, pressing it to the ceiling. He deftly severed its head before moving forward and jumping back to the ground. Neviah's bow twanged, and something big thumped the ground right next to him.

"That's my girl," he said, moving forward again.

They moved without event for the better part of an hour before they found reason to pause.

"Describe it to me," Adhira said when Neviah stopped them suddenly.

"There's a large cavern in front of us. At first, I thought the ground was covered in stalagmites, but instead, it's littered with the bodies of freshly slain Shayatin. There has to be nearly a hundred of them, all dead."

"What do you think happened to them?" Adhira asked.

"I don't know, but I don't see a single body that hasn't been ripped apart. It looks like the box of old dolls I used to have, pieces everywhere and piled up on top of each other."

"Then let's go back and find another way," he said.

"I see light coming from the way we came. There are Shayatin coming."

"Would you rather face the Shayatin or something that preys on Shayatin?" he asked.

"When did you start making sense?" she asked, leading them back the way they'd come. It wasn't long before they ran into a very large group of Shayatin traversing another cavern.

"There's too many," Neviah said. "Even for you. This way."

They fled along the side of the cavern and into another passageway. They had to push Euroclydon along as best they could. He kept tripping and stumbling, even falling to the ground sometimes.

"There are some huge stalactites above us," she called back. "Do you think you can drop some on the path behind us to slow them down?"

Adhira was already running up the wall, which seemed unusually tall, considering how narrow the tunnel was. Running along the ceiling, he slashed several of the large stone formations, careful not to drop any on his friends below. The Shayatin were shown no such concern. By the time he was on the path behind Neviah again, the tunnel behind them was clogged with rock and several unfortunate Shayatin.

"A dead spider!" Neviah said excitedly. "I think I killed this one. That smells horrible. We are back on the right path!"

Shouts grew louder behind them, followed by the heavy footfalls of pursuing Shayatin.

"I don't think we are going to make it out of these tunnels before they catch us," Adhira said. "This area is narrow enough that I might be able to hold them off for a while."

"Okay," Neviah said. "I'll get the horse to the ship and come back for you."

The sound of Shayatin continued to grow closer, Adhira waiting for them to catch up. The footfalls ceased for a moment before picking up again, this time moving in the opposite direction. Running, Adhira quickly caught up to the others, who continued at their hobbling pace.

"I think the Shayatin are giving up," he said.

"Maybe they don't know Chemosh is gone. Or maybe they are just ready to be out of the caves. I know I am."

The air pressure quickly changed, telling him they'd finally made it out of the cave. The poisoned waves of water could be heard lapping against the ship.

"This way," Neviah said. She was the first onto the ship, quickly followed by Adhira. "Just a little further," she urged the horse. Adhira heard a dull thud as Euroclydon fell heavily to the ground.

"I am fine," Euroclydon said weakly. "*Nothing should bother me here. But you two should go.*"

"What are you talking about?" Adhira said. "You are coming with us."

"*Only two of us entered,*" the horse said slowly. "*Only two may leave.*"

Adhira leaned heavily on the rail as his head swam. How had he not thought about that? The one thing everyone knew about shadow gates was nothing could come from the Abyss until someone entered from the real world. It was a one-for-one trade.

Euroclydon couldn't come with them.

Chapter 28

"What's going on?" Neviah asked.

"Clyde can't come with us. The shadow gate will only let two of us return."

"But I came through too," she said.

"When you fell into the Abyss, Chemosh escaped."

"Oh no," she said. "Adhira, I didn't know."

"But he knew," Adhira said. "Didn't you? You knew the moment we came to get Neviah, you wouldn't be able to go back."

"*Don't act like I am making some heroic sacrifice,*" Euroclydon said. He talked like someone who was only half awake. "*I expect you to come back for me. Now, go so I can sleep this off.*"

"I will come back for you," Adhira promised as he removed his satchel from the saddlebags. "I don't know how long I'll be gone, so don't become all murder-crazed again before I do."

"Adhira," Neviah said. "I need you to cut us loose, two ropes fore and aft. I'm going to raise the main sail. I spent the better part of a month sewing and patching it. This should be enough of a breeze to get us away from the cliff face."

Adhira numbly moved down the railing and untied the two ropes holding them against the jutting plateau. The ship began to bob more freely with the gentle waves.

"I need your muscles," Neviah called out from the center of the ship. Adhira moved over and helped her haul on a rope. "Okay, it's secure. Now, let's see if I can steer this thing. I need you to turn the sail."

With the two of them running across the deck and making the necessary adjustments, they were able to get the ship moving. It didn't take long before their speed rapidly increased, and he could feel the bow of the ship dip.

"Grab onto something!" he shouted over the roar of the water as they were drenched in ocean spray. The waves pulled at him as they washed over the deck and back into the sea. With a firm hold on the railing, he weathered the worst of it, even as the ship lurched dangerously starboard.

The front of the ship slammed down so hard that Adhira wondered for a moment if they'd struck land. As suddenly as the wild ride had started, it was over. The ship moved forward steadily as the rocking returned to a more natural feel. It felt good to have the sun on his face again.

"Did that look as bad as it felt?" he asked, climbing the stairs to the steering wheel.

"Yes," Neviah said. "I've never fallen up before. We shot out of there like a rocket," she said with a laugh. The sound was musical. Her voice already sounded more like her own again. The Shayatin influence was fading fast.

"Well, hopefully, that was a once-in-a-lifetime experience," he said. "I was thinking we could return as soon as possible with a prisoner to swap for Clyde. We might not have to go back through the gate. I'll try tossing in a bad guy or two and see if Clyde comes out on his own."

"I know you spent a lot of time with him, but Clyde is a Shayatin. Would you really throw someone into the abyss to bring him out?"

"He was changing, Neviah. I know you saw him in full 'I want to murder everyone' mode when you two met last year, but being out of the Abyss has turned him almost friendly." Clyde had been there, encouraging him to let go of the Vapor Blade when its power over him was strongest. The horse had also given him the sword, so Adhira kept that to himself.

"He's still a Shayatin," she said.

"That's just it. I don't think he always was. You yourself nearly became one of them."

"Point taken," she said. "So, is that our next move? Should we head to Tarsis? There, we can meet up with Asa and Victoria. I'm sure there are some murderers there we can bring back and throw into the whirlpool. We can even make them walk the plank."

"Sounds good to me. Get us facing in the right direction, and I'll take the wheel. Maybe you can rustle us up some grub."

"I've eaten all the food on board," she said with a sigh. "I'll toss out a couple of nets. We are going slow enough; maybe we can catch some fish."

While he held the ship on course, he thought about the long and difficult journey that led him to where he stood. Since being blinded, he'd traveled over half the world, started a civil war, and gone into the Abyss and back. And it wasn't over. Somehow, they still had to defeat the Beast, rescue his horse, save Victoria from her nightmare, and keep mankind from being completely wiped out. The months had gone by in a blur of smells and sounds. He found that his mind had put images with the events, though he didn't really know what anything had looked like since Siarl took his sight.

Thinking of the Imprisoned One reminded him he hadn't practiced his sword art in two days. Between riding across the ocean and traversing the Abyss, he hadn't found the time. Where was Siarl? If he was with Chemosh, another confrontation was inevitable. Adhira wasn't ready, not nearly fast enough. Could anyone really be that fast?

The sun had long since set before Neviah came back to where Adhira stood. "I only caught a few fish, and they were dead already. They look weird, too."

"It's Chemosh," Adhira said. "When I spoke with Asa, he said something about the waters near Tarsis being poisoned and the fish dying. It may be spreading."

"Tarsis is weeks from here," Neviah said. "Could the Beast poison the whole ocean?"

"I don't know."

"We need food," she said.

"I'll check," he said, walking away from the steering wheel.

"Good luck. I searched this entire ship while I was in the Abyss. The only thing left is gunpowder."

"If there is food anywhere on this boat, I'll find it." Adhira walked down the stairs to the main deck and slid down the ladder below deck. In reality, he slowly walked among the barrels and crates. With his gift, however, he was lifting lids and prying open boxes to spill their contents. He paused when he heard the faint squeak of a mouse.

"I found a mouse," Adhira said.

Through his helmet, he heard Neviah sigh. "I guess I could eat a mouse. Grab it."

"No," Adhira said. "Well, maybe, but what I mean is if a mouse survived all this time on this ship in the Abyss, then it must have a food source."

"I hope you're right," Neviah said.

Adhira moved toward the squeaks, which stopped when he grew close. Pulling out the Sword of Re'u, he focused on his gift, cutting through the deck and bulkhead. He found nothing, but the mouse scurried upward

The Road to War

in response to his hacking. He moved back up the ladder to the main deck and crossed to what would have once been the captain's quarters.

With wild abandon, he cut away walls, ceiling, and floor, none of it in real time. One of his cuts revealed a hidden compartment in the floor under a few smaller kegs of powder. In real time, he pushed them aside and poked around until he found a hidden latch and opened the trap door on the floor. Reaching into the hole, he found several shards of broken glass along with a dozen jars still intact. With a jar in each hand, he ran all the way back to Neviah.

"Beans!" Neviah said excitedly, snatching the jars from him.

"There are more in the room beneath us," Adhira said, taking the wheel from Neviah.

"I'll have this ready to eat in a jiffy," she said, hurrying away from him.

That night, they feasted on beans and some rice Neviah found in the same hidden compartment. When they were done, Neviah took the wheel, and Adhira moved to the most open section of the deck nearby and pulled out the Sword of Re'u.

As usual, he started off slow but quickly moved his sword art into the more advanced forms, his speed and intensity increasing with each imagined blow. His opponent was always faster and stronger, forcing him to adapt. He parried where a block would not suffice and dodged when he should have set up a counterstrike. Blocking used the least amount of energy, but duels were not won by simply blocking. On the offense, he moved with the speed of a striking snake, but it was never fast enough. He needed to be faster.

The concept of time had all but disappeared with his vision. He didn't know how long he practiced, but as always, he did so until exhaustion prevented him from going further.

When he was done practicing, he toweled off before walking over to Neviah, who still stood at the wheel. She was crying.

"What's wrong?" he asked, putting a hand on her shoulder to turn her toward him.

"I don't like seeing you like this," she said, placing her forehead on his and resting her hands on his shoulders. "You are trying to carry the weight of the world, and I feel helpless. Re'u entrusted this to all four of us, but I feel like I'm not doing my share. More often than not, I don't have a clue what I'm doing. I'm a child pretending to be a grown-up."

"Everyone is just pretending," he said. "I have seen men fighting for a cause they didn't believe in because they were afraid they were the only ones. I had a guard abuse me because he thought that was what others expected of him. And the worst of them all is me."

"You?" she asked softly.

He was suddenly aware of how close she stood, her lips mere inches away from his.

"I pretend to be calloused, but every person who falls to my blade pains me to my core. I joke when I'm too afraid to feel what I'm feeling. And I act fearless when I'm terrified."

"We are all afraid. We face death nearly every day." Her breath was hot on his cheek.

"I don't fear death," he said. "I'm sure I should, but I don't. What I do fear is failing. I fear there are foes that are meant for me, but I'm not ready for them."

She pulled back then and took his face in her hands. "Siarl didn't just take your sight," she said, her voice strained with pent-up emotion. "He took your confidence, too. I thought you seemed less cocky."

"Maybe that was just an act, too," he said.

"Stop that," she said, pushing him away. "Broody does not suit you well. You are cocky, and you have a right to be. You are the best swordsman I know, and you've faced countless foes and saved many lives."

"I *am* kind of a big deal," he said with a smile.

"What have I done?" she said with a laugh. It felt so good to hear her laugh.

"I came over to comfort you," he said.

"Yeah. And you're pretty bad at it. But I'm glad you comforting me made you feel better."

"What are we going to do about navigation?" he asked when she turned back to the steering wheel. "I'm about as useful as a rope, and you need to sleep sometime."

"I figured I'd man the wheel while I'm awake and tie it off when I'm not. We should sleep on deck, though. If we run into anything, hopefully, your gift can give us enough of a heads up."

"If you want," he said. "You can sleep first."

"It feels like all I've done for months is sleep. You go ahead."

The waking dream was waiting for him, but since he was bound to the ship, it was very boring. He tried to conjure up some nightmares to fight but couldn't make it work. The dream was spent practicing his sword art.

★★★

It was the middle of the morning on the third day at sea before anything changed.

"We must be off course," Neviah said. "I don't remember there being an island out this way."

"We traveled much faster with Victoria providing the wind," Adhira pointed out. "And it's not like navigation is an exact science."

"Navigation *is* an exact science."

"If you say so," he said.

"Science says so! You're impossible."

It was nearly an hour later before Neviah spoke again. "Um, you know that island I spotted on the horizon? It's not in the same spot."

"Chemosh," Adhira said before she did.

"If we turn due south, we may be able to go around it," she said.

"No," he said sternly. "We need to head straight for it."

"I'm glad you have your confidence back, but we can't possibly fight that thing without Victoria."

"We have enough black powder on this ship to send it to Colossus," he said.

She didn't respond immediately. "The Beast will be undone by fire," she said slowly. "That's it. We can light a long fuse, aim the ship at the beast, and take one of the rowboats to safety. Asa can come get us on another ship. I admit, it's not ideal, but that thing needs to die."

"There's only one problem with that plan," Adhira said. "We only get one shot. We can't afford to miss."

"We have to stay with the ship," she said suddenly.

"One of us does," he said.

"Oh, no, you don't," she said angrily. "I just got you back. If we do this, we do it together! Don't even try to argue! If you open your mouth again, it had better be to say, 'Yes, ma'am,' and that's it."

He wasn't left much room for arguing. "Yes, ma'am. But you have to make me a promise."

"What?" she asked warily.

"When Siarl shows up, and I mean this in the least male chauvinist way possible, I need you to stay out of the way."

She was quiet for a moment, which for her was akin to someone else yelling. "Maybe we will blow him to pieces with the Beast," she said at length. "He may be afraid to show himself in case Victoria is with us."

"Unless he knows the Nightmare Helm has her trapped in a dream."

"I see Shedim flying high above us!" she said urgently.

Adhira already had his sword out. The sound of wood splintering followed the impact of something heavy crashing onto deck.

"I took your eyes as a mercy," Siarl said in his deep voice. "I will have to take your legs this time. Though, if you surrender, no harm will come to you."

Adhira took a defensive stance, sword ready.

"You were easily defeated when you had sight," Siarl said, confusion in his voice. "What do you hope to accomplish now?" Adhira didn't answer. "At least I have two of you now."

Adhira raised his left-hand palm up, then motioned for the Imprisoned One to come on. And he did.

Chapter 29

In the span of a heartbeat, Siarl closed the distance between them and brought down his sword with such force that, though Adhira parried the blow, he was forced back a step. He quickly C-stepped to get away from the railing, blocking a slash meant for his midsection. The swords rang as they met several more times in quick succession.

Adhira was unable to parry each blow and was forced to block, the impact of which jarred him to the bone. Siarl continued to strike with a flurry of blows, each strike flowing from the last in one continuous movement. Whether with shield or sword, Adhira managed to keep the enemy blade away from his flesh. Without his gift, the fight would have ended after the first stroke.

Their fight took them across the deck as Siarl continually tried to back him against the railing. Adhira refused to be guided, sometimes taking bold chances to change their path. Duels, the ones between two skilled opponents, didn't always go to the better swordsman. A smart fighter used everything at their disposal, including the terrain.

Adhira was doing well at keeping the enemy blade from biting, but he couldn't win by blocking alone. They neared the captain's cabin, which was little more than a wall with a door, all housed under the ship's helm.

Adhira used his shield to block two blows, nearly too late to avoid spilled blood. Then, he blocked the next blow with his sword just in time, which bought him the split second he needed as he jumped into the air and aimed his feet behind him. With the wall of the cabin as the new ground, Adhira landed and immediately sprang off, stabbing out with his sword.

The blow was parried, and he was barely able to avoid the counter strike as he rolled back to his feet, blocking and parrying amidst a flurry of blows. He had risked much for absolutely no gain, but despite the press of the enemy, he smiled. It was the first time he'd taken the offense against Siarl, and it felt good.

With renewed vigor, Siarl punished him for his transgression or maybe for the smile. Either way, it pushed Adhira to his limit. His shoulder ached from the constant blows against his shield, and his elbow throbbed from the strain of parrying and blocking the incessant assault.

Pushing past the pain, he stood his ground and trusted his body to react as it should, freeing his mind to think. He wanted desperately to attack again, but his gift showed him any attack would only end in disaster. Patience. It was what he had the least of but what he needed the most. If he couldn't force an opening, he would have to wait for one. In the meantime, he needed to somehow create an advantage.

Siarl was trying to move him to the left, so Adhira leaned into a strike to force his way right into the tangle of fish nets Neviah had left lying around. When they were both standing on the net, Adhira caught a loop with his foot, pulling it quickly onto the top of his boot before facing his feet at the railing.

The railing became the ground, which pulled the net tight around his opponent as Adhira zoomed away, net in tow. Siarl was pulled off his feet before being dragged along the deck. Before Adhira landed on the railing, he aimed his feet at the ground again. Coming to a sliding halt, he turned and struck down at Siarl. The Imprisoned One parried the blow and rolled out of the net. Adhira followed, striking down with three consecutive strokes aimed at his kneeling opponent. The first two were parried, and the third blocked as Siarl quickly jumped back to his feet and grabbed Adhira's wrist.

The Forest Shield came up between them, forcing Siarl back before he could break the Indian's arm. When he lowered the shield, Siarl sprang at him with a series of strikes that were faster than anything Adhira had ever experienced. It took everything he had to keep his blood in his body, which was where he liked it.

Adhira was still avoiding each blow, but his parries didn't push the enemy blade away as far as he would have liked, and the blocks felt like he was stopping boulders. Back and forth, he was pushed across the deck, no longer able to change their route; he was constantly backed up to the railings, where he had to fight off balance before he could break away again.

He was wondering how long he could keep it up when he heard something that, even with his gift, he couldn't believe. It happened again, and Adhira let himself believe it to be true. Siarl's breaths were coming more forcefully, in great rushes. The Imprisoned One was breathing heavily!

Though his muscles protested and his own breaths were coming in great gulps, he let hope fuel him for the first time in the fight. Whatever type of creature the Imprisoned One was, he didn't have infinite stamina.

"How is this possible?" Siarl grunted, accentuating each word with a strike. He didn't sound concerned. Instead, he seemed confused.

Adhira didn't answer. No quick retort came to him. Instead, he blocked a blow with the Forest Shield and pushed the enemy blade as wide as possible. He stabbed at his opponent's midsection, and though it didn't come close to landing as Siarl stepped back, it marked a turning point in the duel.

Adhira blocked a myriad of blows when Siarl pushed back at him with renewed vigor. Somehow, his strikes seemed angrier, as if they said, "How dare you strike back at me!" Adhira ducked a blow and attempted a shield bash, but Siarl stepped to the side and stabbed at his legs. Adhira was already turning his shield and deflected the blow, which he followed up with a slash aimed at the enemy's shoulder. Siarl rolled backward to escape the Sword of Re'u.

Adhira closed the distance and struck in quick succession, raining blows down on Siarl, who, for the moment, was forced to defend himself over and over. Siarl backed across the deck in a circle to keep away from the railing. Adhira's advantage wasn't enough to guide his opponent. His muscles felt liberated, though, each strike working out the aches and bruises he'd earned in the fight so far.

He became aware of Neviah as she cheered loudly from the upper deck. "You're in for it now! You should have stayed in your prison, you dog-faced freak!" She egged him on with several other colorful expressions while Adhira had the upper hand.

Siarl was eventually able to stall Adhira's push, and they began a series of exchanges, both attacking and blocking equally. The enemy was still far stronger, but his speed had diminished considerably.

Adhira considered using the special move he'd been practicing. It would likely end in his death, but he could take out Siarl with him if it worked. But if it didn't, where would that leave Neviah? He chose to keep fighting.

"How does a human stand before me so?" Siarl asked as he blocked a vertical stroke aimed at his head.

"Mordeth, who you killed, taught me the art," Adhira said, parrying a blow with his sword. "Re'u gave me the ability to rise above human limitations." He stabbed at his opponent, following the strike with an upwards cut that missed flesh. "And you gave me the time I needed to practice." The thought made him smile.

As they exchanged another round of strikes, Adhira began to laugh at the absurdity of what he'd said, but it was true. If he hadn't been blinded, he never would have become so fanatical about his sword art. Without Siarl, he never would have gone south and fought through countless enemies, all the while honing his skill.

After a moment, he realized Siarl was laughing too. Though Adhira's laughter was born of wryness and irony, the Imprisoned One sounded as if his laughter was from joy. Adhira remembered what he'd been taught about Siarl's people. They lived only for battle and dueled themselves into non-existence. The Imprisoned One always asked for the best swordsman to duel at each encounter. Was Siarl just looking for a good fight?

Adhira let the thoughts come and go in a flash. The duel demanded his attention. Back and forth, they fought. They were both tired. It would soon become a game of who slipped up first.

"You got this!" Neviah yelled.

If he died, she would also be killed or worse. Adhira gritted his teeth and pushed through the pain and fatigue. His muscles screamed for a break, but he'd spent months learning to ignore their protests.

Siarl continued to laugh. The sound was beginning to grate on Adhira. Is this why he'd lost his teacher? Because Siarl wanted a good fight? The memory of Mordeth's death, coupled with the incessant laughter, angered Adhira.

The Indian pushed forward with a flurry of strikes, forcing Siarl back again. Faster. He pushed his muscles to their limit, demanding more speed. Faster. Some of the last images he'd seen flashed through his mind. Siarl standing over him while the Finn Folk spit acid in his eyes, blinding him. Faster. He still wasn't fast enough!

Siarl was backing up in a circle, but Adhira forced him to change his intended path over and over. The Imprisoned One was no longer striking back but was instead forced to block and parry without respite.

Adhira thought about how helpless he'd felt when he'd been blinded, when he thought all his friends were dead. He thought about his time traveling south, all the innocent people who were slaughtered because monsters were allowed free reign. That was all Siarl was, another monster who wanted only to kill. There was no end to the list of things that fueled his anger.

Adhira vaguely became aware that he'd spent nearly all the energy he had left, his anger the only thing keeping him going. He needed to be faster!

Adhira put everything he had into the next blow. Then again into the next. Over and over, he pounded against the enemy blade as his own sought a way through.

Siarl struck back once, a stab intended for his opponent's heart. Adhira stepped to the side and raised his shield in time to deflect the blow, but it sliced across his chest as it was knocked away. The cut was shallow and very necessary. Using his gift, Adhira continued down the path he'd just laid out. Siarl had drawn first blood, but Adhira had gained something more: the advantage.

Before Siarl could bring his sword back in, Adhira put his shoulder into his shield and rammed into his opponent. Siarl was knocked back against the railing, where he desperately attempted to block the Sword of Re'u as Adhira rained down blow after blow. The Imprisoned One was trapped, unable to move, unable to plan, and unable to strike back from his off-balance position.

The enemy continued to laugh. If anything, his joy increased at his dire situation. Adhira suddenly felt the soft tug that told him the Sword of Re'u met flesh. Then again and again. Siarl stopped laughing and grunted with each cut.

The Imprisoned One made one last strike at Adhira, a horizontal slash at his midsection. Adhira blocked it with his shield and drove the Sword of Re'u into Siarl's chest. Stepping out of reach of the enemy blade, he moved into a defensive stance. The wound on his chest stung, but thankfully, it was the only one he'd received.

"At last," Siarl said.

After a moment, he heard Siarl tumble to the deck. Adhira used his gift to check for a pulse. Siarl was dead.

Chapter 30

Adhira slumped against the rail, his exhaustion hitting him ten-fold now that his anger and adrenaline had ebbed. Feet hammered across the deck as Neviah ran to him, kneeling down and throwing her arms around his neck.

"You're hurt!" she said, pulling back.

"I've had worse," Adhira said with a weak smile. He felt like he was in a bit of a daze. He'd won, and Siarl was dead, but it didn't feel real.

"Stop being a man, and let me look at it." She quickly pulled his shirt up to look at the cut.

"See," he said, forcing his shirt back down. "It's a scratch."

"It's more than a scratch," she said, her voice strained. "But you'll live."

"What's wrong?" he asked.

"There are so many scars," she said.

"Pretty cool, huh," he said, forcing his most charming smile.

"You're an idiot," she said, but the strength had returned to her voice. The smile had worked. "Now, sit still while I find something to wrap that with," she said before walking away.

While she was gone, he found Siarl's sword, which had become a book. He was done with any sword that didn't come from Re'u. After tossing it overboard, Adhira sat on the ship's rail next to where one of the rowboats was fastened to the side. The rowboats were suspended from a pully system that allowed them to be easily lowered into the water. Sitting on the rail and leaning back against the pully's post, he was glad for a chance to catch his breath.

"All right," Neviah said, walking back up. "Now, get your shirt off. And wipe that smirk off your face!"

"I can't blame you for wanting to see my manly muscles," he said as he gingerly removed his shirt.

"Manly? Real men have hair on their chest," she said as she began to wrap a bandage around his chest and back.

"That's not fair," he said with a smile. "I'm half Indian and half Indian. Neither race is particularly hairy."

They both fell quiet for a moment while Neviah finished wrapping his bandage, her cheek pressing against his whenever she reached around his back with the bandage. When she was done, he put his shirt back on and stood. Neviah didn't move, which meant they were standing face-to-face for a moment.

She moved to stand beside him. "He was a strange one," Neviah said solemnly.

"What do you mean?" Adhira asked.

"Siarl fought on the side of evil, but he also fought with honor. When you stabbed him and stepped back, Siarl actually bowed to you before he died."

"Too bad he was allied with evil," Adhira said. "How close are we now?"

She knew what he meant. "We closed about half the distance," she said. "I've aimed us at the Beast and tied off the wheel. It doesn't matter much anyway since it is obviously coming for us now. I found the flint and fuses and put them in the captain's cabin. I don't know how to time it."

"It doesn't matter," he said.

"Are you sure you don't want to light a longer fuse and jump ship?" she asked.

"We have one shot at this," he reminded her. "The timing has to be perfect. We can't let Chemosh make landfall. It'll destroy everything."

"We are really doing this, then," she said in wonder. "When I woke up this morning, I didn't realize it would be the last. It's kind of surreal, isn't it?"

He put an arm around her shoulder. She put her head on his shoulder, nuzzling her forehead against his cheek. After a moment, she turned her face up at him. He could feel her cheek against his. Grabbing her chin gently, he tilted her head up and kissed her.

And his cheek exploded with pain when she slapped him across the face. He knew it was coming, but the price was worth it. That kiss had been a long time coming, even if she didn't feel the same way he did.

"I'm sorry," he said, pulling away. She didn't respond but wrapped her arms around him, holding him in place. "I'm getting mixed signals here," he said. Then he saw what was coming.

She pulled his head down and kissed him. Where his kiss had been gentle, hers was rough, almost frantic. When she pulled away, they were both gulping for air.

"What took you so long, you idiot?" she shouted.

"What do you mean? Anytime I thought about kissing you, I would see you were going to slap me in the face!"

"I decided a long time ago that if you ever kissed me, I would slap you."

"Why in the world would you want to do that?"

"I wanted it to be real," she said. "I didn't want you using your gift to find the perfect time to lay one on me. If you ever kissed me, it needed to be worth the consequences."

"Of all the women in the world, in all the worlds, I had to fall for the craziest, most stubborn one of all!"

She pulled his head down for another breath-stealing kiss, pressing into him so he had to hold her up. He wrapped his arms around her tight, pulling her lips more firmly against his as he easily lifted her.

"I love you," she breathed when he sat her down again. "If we have to die today, at least we are together."

"I've loved you since before we ever came to this world," Adhira said slowly, deliberately, savoring the moment. "And I want nothing more than to be with you." He paused to take a steadying breath, filling his senses with the smell that was wholly her one last time. "But we both know this isn't how you die."

"Wha—" she started to say, but on his last word, he pushed her into the rowboat hanging over the side of the ship and, in one deft motion, pulled out the Sword of Re'u and sliced the rope, sending the boat to the waves below.

Neviah was yelling furiously from below, though the speed of his ship was rapidly carrying him away. Adhira wasted no time. Running to the starboard side of the ship, he cut loose one of the water barrels; he made sure it had a cork in it before shoving it over the side. After quickly locating the sealed jars of beans, he tossed them over the side, too.

He put on his helmet to inform Asa of Neviah's predicament, but Neviah was immediately yelling into his ear.

"...right to do that! Men think they are the only ones who can be brave! Now turn that ship around and pick me up right now!"

After removing the helmet again, he went in search of the fuses and flint. Neviah would be able to contact Asa herself. As he moved across the deck, he became aware of the extra lift as the ship crested waves that were growing increasingly choppy. After lighting a fuse, using only his gift, he quickly cut a fifteen-second length.

He found a stack of barrels at the back and attached the fuse to it so it was barely sticking out of the crack of the lid.

He lit the fuse, and after a few seconds, there was a flash, and everything went black.

At least the barrels exploded like they were supposed to. The rushing water crashed around the ship, and suddenly, the warmth of the sun was gone. There was a groaning sound all around him.

This was it. With a lit fire stick, he stood beside the barrel with the fuse, waiting for the right moment. The ship listed as its hull scraped against something. There was no doubt in his mind he was entering Chemosh's mouth. Still, he waited. The further he made it inside, the better chance he had of killing it.

He wondered if he should be considering the meaning of life or some such, but he was so happy his friends were still alive and he was doing something that would save thousands that he simply felt peace. Peace in his head. His heart felt as if it was going to pound out of his chest. Still, he waited, focusing entirely on the part of his gift fifteen seconds out.

The hull of the ship groaned louder, nearly tossing him to the deck as the ship listed more heavily toward the port side. He held onto his barrel, still waiting.

There was a splintering crack of what could only be the ship's mast. Surely, he was as deep inside the Beast's maw as he would get without being crushed. He lit the fuse.

There were fifteen seconds before a flash that was followed by the blackness he recognized as his death. His death was something he'd faced countless times. Always, there was blackness, but always, he'd avoided actually dying. What would it be like to die for real?

The blackness was only thirteen seconds away. He focused on the part of his gift that was fifteen seconds out, hoping to see what came next. There had to be something after the blackness. His mind began to race as fast as his heart, the fight or flight response coming over him in full force.

Twelve seconds became eleven, and still only darkness. There had to be something. His mind raced, but there was nothing left for him to do but wait. If nothing came next, did anything really matter? Was blackness all that waited for any of them? His brain was still bouncing between finding a way out of his situation and finding meaning in life when he finally saw what was coming. And he smiled.

The Armor of Light

The night is far spent; the day is at hand: let us, therefore, cast off the works of darkness, and let us put on the Armor of Light.

Other Works

The Armor of Light Series

The Sword of Re'u

The House of The Forest

The Road to War

The Tower of Leethaar

For more information, visit thearmoroflight.net.